BEST OF ALL WORLDS

BEST OF ALL WORLDS

KENNETH OPPEL

Scholastic Press / New York

Copyright © 2025 by Firewing Productions Inc.

All rights reserved. Published by Scholastic Press, an imprint of Scholastic Inc., *Publishers since 1920*. SCHOLASTIC, SCHOLASTIC PRESS, and associated logos are trademarks and/or registered trademarks of Scholastic Inc.

The publisher does not have any control over and does not assume any responsibility for author or third-party websites or their content.

No part of this publication may be reproduced, stored in a retrieval system, or transmitted in any form or by any means, electronic, mechanical, photocopying, recording, or otherwise, or used to train any artificial intelligence technologies, without written permission of the publisher. For information regarding permission, write to Scholastic Inc., Attention: Permissions Department, 557 Broadway, New York, NY 10012.

This book is a work of fiction. Names, characters, places, and incidents are either the product of the author's imagination or are used fictitiously, and any resemblance to actual persons, living or dead, business establishments, events, or locales is entirely coincidental.

Library of Congress Cataloging-in-Publication Data available

ISBN 978-1-5461-5820-2

10 9 8 7 6 5 4 3 2 1   25 26 27 28 29

Printed in Italy   183

First edition, June 2025

Book design by Stephanie Yang

FOR MY FAMILY

We made a grave marker, even though there was no body to bury.

We'd waited a long time before doing it. Despite what I'd seen, what I'd told everyone, it was hard for some people to stop hoping. They said, *Maybe you were mistaken; maybe it was just an illusion.* They said, *Maybe he's still alive, figuring out how to get back to us.*

But eventually, after a couple months, everyone agreed there was no point putting it off. When we finally placed the marker, I wasn't sure anyone had changed their mind about anything, but you could tell people felt it was necessary. It was an acknowledgment that things had changed.

Everyone said goodbye in their own way. There was crying, halting farewells, prayers. Any words I had stayed in my head. They'd told me over and over that it wasn't my fault, and I'd nodded and said, *Yeah, I know,* but I didn't believe it. I'd been there when it happened. I kept imagining how I might've done things differently that day. Bolder action, more persuasive words. Anything to stop him from dying.

And as I stood there at the grave, I thought of other people who were lost to me. My mother. Sam. My mind tumbled backward down the endless road of if-onlys. You could waste a lot of time wishing things had been otherwise. Maybe that had been part of the problem from the outset. Striving for things that were impossible.

But down that terrible potholed road I hurtled. All the way back to those very first days, when we arrived over three years ago.

1

I snatched up my phone as soon as I woke, suddenly knowing how to get inside the castle. We'd been wasting our time trying to cross the moat, hopping on alligators' backs or crawling underwater with breathing tubes. We'd been bitten, pierced with arrows, and doused with boiling oil. Throcknor actually drowned because his plate armor (he was so proud of it) was incredibly heavy, and we had to use up a resurrection spell to bring him back.

What we needed to do was slog back to the village, break the Grygax out of its cage, feed it a goat so it liked us, and then I would straddle its mangy back and get it to *fly* me over the castle wall. Once inside, I'd open the gate, drop the bridge for the others, and we'd storm the keep. This would work.

I needed to run this by the other players. Really it was Serena's opinion I wanted. Our D&D camp was opposed to dungeoneer groups having "leaders" because that was too hierarchical. But Serena was a natural leader, and was very good at getting the other players to make decisions that were usually her decisions.

Right away Serena and I had seen eye to eye. Less debating, more playing. We also agreed that the camp's athletic activities were cruel and unusual punishment. The counselors made us play capture the flag, do things with Hula-Hoops, and sometimes even run laps. Serena and I would fall behind and talk. She liked e-gaming but, just like me, she loved the old-school RPGs best: just you and the graph paper and your imagined character, burning with purpose.

I was glad she didn't go to my school and know how deeply uncool I was. All she knew about me when we first met was that I usually played a seventh-level thief with an invisibility cloak.

I was pretty sure Serena would be all over my Grygax idea, but when I tried to open our dungeoneer group chat, my phone said there was no connection.

"Oh, come on . . ."

I wondered if Nia had switched off the router after we'd arrived last night. She and Dad had left their laptops in the city, and she'd been talking about how wonderful it would be if we didn't have *any* Wi-Fi because it was so important to "decompress." We would do this, she said, by swimming and canoeing and reading and talking together the whole weekend. Which was absurd, especially when I had a castle to plunder. Why did Dad's new wife even get a say about the internet?

I slipped out of bed to go check the router. I glanced at the top bunk where Sam usually slept. He'd stayed behind in the city for a soccer match. Cottage weekends were never as much fun without him. I really hadn't wanted to come. It was the second heat dome of the summer, and yesterday it had been ninety degrees. The cottage didn't have AC. When we'd walked in last night, it was like a sauna. We'd opened all the windows and set the fans going.

Nia was against us getting AC because we'd just be making the climate emergency worse. We'd have to learn to live with the extreme weather that all us greedy humans had created. She'd eaten a banana, taken a cool shower, and gone to bed with a fan blasting right on her. I'd done the same (without eating a banana) and it actually worked really well. I had to hand it to Nia—she ran a great apocalypse.

When I went out into the hall, it was so much cooler than last night, but it smelled weird. The cottage was often musty when you first opened it up, but this morning it had a faint chemical smell, like new carpet. I hadn't noticed any new carpet.

Dad and Nia's door was still closed. I was usually the first one up on weekends, especially lately. Nia had been having trouble sleeping because her stomach was so big with the baby. She usually slept in. Dad, too.

The router was way at the back of the weird little closet beside the bathroom. Its lights were flickering, which was good, but one was red, which was bad. I unplugged it, counted to ten, then plugged it back in.

In the family room, I dropped into my favorite green chair and checked my music while waiting for the router to reboot. Smiling, I scrolled through the new songs Sam had dumped onto my phone yesterday. He was my music guru. He didn't know just the latest music but also cool bands I'd never heard of, going as far back as the '80s. He knew all the side projects and solo efforts, the best producers and session drummers. We'd listen to songs together and he'd peel back the layers and identify every single instrument in the mix. Yesterday, when assessing my playlist, he'd shaken his head sadly and said, "Little bro, you badly need some new sounds." I now had an album called *Brotherhood* and another called *Is This It* and a bunch of assorted songs to help get me through the weekend.

A goat bleated, and it took me a few seconds to realize this was not a normal cottage sound. For the first time that morning, I looked out the window, and the lake was ... gone. Instead of a lawn sloping gently to the dock, there was a red barn and a fenced pasture. Inside the pasture was a shelter with an open front, and beside it stood a brown-and-white goat.

I stood. To the right of the pasture were rows of green plants. Farther off was a cornfield. My brain was already telling me a story, reasonably explaining how this must have been done overnight: building the barn, planting the crops, draining an entire lake. Or maybe it had dried up overnight from the heat dome. Wasn't stuff like that happening all over the world now? I stopped myself. No. It wasn't just a change. It was *completely* different.

I usually avoided going into Dad's bedroom now that it was also Nia's bedroom, but this was important. The two of them were still asleep. Dad had on one of his weird nose strips that Nia made him wear because he snored.

"Dad. Dad!"

He lifted his head from the pillow. "What's wrong?"

"Outside is all different. The cottage—it's moved."

His head dropped back onto the pillow. "Xavier."

"I'm not joking. We're on a farm. There's a *goat*."

Helpfully, the sound of bleating came through their curtained window.

"That's definitely a goat," Nia said, stirring.

"Just come look!"

Nia raised herself onto her elbows and affectionately rubbed her humped belly. With a grunt, Dad levered himself into sitting and followed me down the hall in his boxers and a McGill T-shirt.

"Must've gotten loose," Dad said, yawning. "Didn't the people down the road get a..."

At the window he stopped talking. There were now two goats in the pasture. From Dad's lips slid a word that sounded like "faaaaawk." He walked to the kitchen, whose windows looked out front. Our car wasn't in the driveway. There was no driveway at all, no road connecting us to the other houses built around the lake. Instead there were more fields of crops, a small orchard, and a big blue sky over all of it.

Nia was laughing in the family room, and I felt hopeful. It was all a joke, and now they'd explain it to me. When Dad and I joined her by the big windows, the view was unchanged.

"Why're you laughing?" Dad asked her.

"I just can't take it seriously." She stood there in her mauve maternity yoga gear, shaking her head as she took in the view. "Everything I can think of is insane. Unless I'm still asleep."

"We're not asleep," Dad assured her.

"Maybe it's just video screens," I said. "Pushed up against all the windows?"

Dad looked at me, bewildered. "Why would anyone do that?"

"I don't know! Why would anyone move our lake?"

"You can't just move a lake," said Nia.

"Can't just move a house either," Dad said.

"You can," I told him. "There's this video where people moved a three-story house on a flatbed trailer."

"Not with people sleeping inside. It'd be a huge job—and noisy, especially in the middle of the night. Ripping a cottage off its foundations?" Something occurred to him and he returned to the kitchen and turned on the tap. Water gushed out. "And we wouldn't have plumbing. Or electricity." He flipped a switch and the lights came on. He looked out where the driveway used to be. "How would you get a flatbed trailer in here without a road? I'm not even seeing tire tracks."

"Does it smell weird to you?" I asked.

"I'm getting my phone," Nia said impatiently, marching to the bedroom.

"How do we even have electricity?" I asked Dad, pointing out the window. It wasn't just the road that was gone; there wasn't a power pole in sight.

When Nia returned, she was holding her phone as well as Dad's, and shaking her head. "No service."

Outside in the pasture, both goats were still bleating.

"Where the hell are we?" said Nia angrily, like Dad or I was responsible.

I opened the map app on my phone. Instead of the familiar outlines of the township, it was just a blank grid. That wasn't so unusual when you didn't have data. What *was* unusual was that there was no blue GPS dot.

"We're not anywhere," I said, showing the phone to Dad.

I'd grown up with blue dots: *You are here. Behold, the blue dot travels with you wherever you go. You will never be lost or alone.* My chest felt smaller suddenly. I forced in a breath.

Nia checked on her own phone. "This is unbelievable."

She reached for the latch on the sliding door, but my father caught her hand.

"Wait."

I felt it now, too: a first jab of fear. Whatever was out there—a farm or a bunch of video screens—was unquestionably weird.

"Let's just take a moment." Dad sat down on the beige sofa that Nia had bought last summer. She'd said the old red one was threadbare and smelled bad, and she was right, but I'd still resented her changing the furniture.

My father stared out the window. Last year my class had visited St. Claire Farm and there'd been old machinery rusting all over the place, busted fences and snarled wire. This barn looked like it had just been painted a cheery red. One side of it was covered with a flowering vine. It looked like a picture book illustration.

"I'm not sure charging out there is the best idea," Dad said.

"It doesn't look dangerous," I ventured.

I was freaked out, too, but I wanted to find out what was going on, and where we were.

"You just want to stay in here?" Nia asked him.

"Someone might come," he said vaguely. "And explain."

I said, "Like knock on our door and say it's all been a big mistake and they'll give us back our lake next week?"

Dad chuckled. "Something like that."

I pictured a rumpled man in a suit, holding a briefcase. *Mr. Oak? I'm frightfully sorry*, he'd say in an English accent. (He would definitely have an English accent.) *This is all a terrible misunderstanding. Complete cock-up at HQ.* It made me smile. I needed a smile right now.

"Why wait?" Nia said. "There might be someone outside who can help us."

Dad stood. "Okay. Let me get my jeans on." Whatever was going to happen next, he figured it would be better with pants. I went to my room and pulled on yesterday's clothes. Then I texted Sam.

i think we've been kidnapped??

When I hit send, it said *Not delivered*.

we're on a farm somewhere

(Not delivered.)

our whole cottage has been moved to a farm

(Not delivered.)

Back in the family room, Dad was dressed and holding the just-in-case crowbar. I'd known he kept it under the bed, but I'd never seen him actually hold it. My father was not a crowbar kind of guy, although Mom always said he was very persuasive in a boardroom.

"We ready?" Dad said, reaching for the latch.

The serious way he said it made me wonder, *Am I sure?* I was a little scared, but more than that, I was shot through with the feeling that once that door opened and we passed through it, things would never be the same.

"Ready," I said.

2

Dad slid the door open a little bit and gave the air a poke with his crowbar. "No video screen," he said.

We followed him out onto the deck. Gone was the blistering heat of yesterday, and gone was the haze from the wildfires raging up north. It smelled like it had rained not long ago. In the slant morning light, dew glittered on the rows of plants. The goats moved right up to the fence and bleated at us expectantly. From somewhere else came the faint sound of clucking.

I turned back to our cottage. It certainly didn't look like it had been dumped off a truck. It looked like it had always been right here. When Nia shouted out a hello, the returning silence made my skin crawl. Even the goats stopped their noise for a couple seconds.

"Let's check the barn first," I said. "Maybe there's someone working."

As we walked, the goats kept pace with us on the other side of the fence. Their eyes had narrow horizontal pupils.

"Why're they following us?" I asked.

"They're hungry," Nia said. "And they need to be milked."

"How can you tell?"

"Swollen udders."

"Not our problem," said Dad.

Maybe it was the crowbar, but he sounded tougher than usual. The clucking

I'd heard was coming from a coop at the very back of the pasture. It had to be the nicest chicken coop I'd ever seen. It was a miniature house with flower boxes under its windows.

"Someone's got to live around here," Nia said. "To milk the goats, collect the eggs."

"Where?" Dad asked, turning in a slow circle. "Far as I can see, our cottage is the only place around."

"The farmer's going to be pretty pissed we built a house on his land," I said, but no one laughed.

"Hello!" Nia called out again as we entered the barn.

The last barn I'd been inside was dingy and stank of manure. This one smelled like warm wood and fresh straw. The floor looked like it had just been swept. There were six stalls, empty except for one filled high with bales of hay. At one end of the barn was a bunch of farm equipment, including a plow with two long handles and a triangular blade rigged between a pair of metal wheels.

"Not a single power tool," Nia remarked. "Very old-school."

There were a couple worktables with things like saws and hammers and spools of twine. Hanging between nails on the wall were shovels, hoes, rakes, and a staggering number of pitchforks, some with two prongs, some with three. There were several longer saws and a couple axes. I felt like a contestant on one of those survival shows—except no one had asked my permission. I considered saying this aloud, but I didn't think anyone was in the mood, especially Nia, who never really got my sense of humor anyway.

I thought about taking one of the axes. In D&D I'd had an axe for a while, but it slowed me down in combat. Right now, the idea of swinging an axe into someone made me wince. I grabbed a shovel instead. I'd have no problem whacking someone with a shovel. Dad gave me a little nod. My just-in-case shovel.

Nia said to my father, "That jury you were on in February. What if this is some kind of relocation?"

"They only do that for witnesses, not jurors. And only if the criminal is really dangerous."

"Wasn't he?"

"I never heard about this!" I said.

"And they'd *tell* you first," Dad said. "Before just moving you somewhere."

"Witness relocation?" I said. "Was he a serial killer or something?"

"No, Zay."

"So there's no one who wants revenge on you?"

"No. We have not been relocated."

Nia rubbed her face. "Sorry. I'm just trying to make sense of this."

We climbed the steps to the loft. Like the main floor, it was clean and well organized. There were more bales of hay, and lots of big metal and plastic barrels. Nia unclasped one and lifted the lid.

"Cornmeal."

Another was filled with lentils. On shelves were rows of glass canning jars, waiting to be filled. Empty baskets were stacked under the sloped ceiling. At the back of the loft was a big door. Dad swung both sides open. We looked out over the pastures, our little cottage, the neat rows of crops, the orchard. Beyond that, nothing.

Not *nothing*. There were fields of wild grass and, after that, forest. Not too far away was a hill. It was totally unlike the countryside that should have surrounded our cottage. On a different day, I might've said it was a pretty view. Right now, all I wanted to see were other buildings, roads, even a power line.

"Is anyone here?" Nia shouted.

The silence felt huge. The goats resumed bleating. I tapped my shovel blade against the floor.

"Still no signal," Dad said, checking his phone.

"This is going to sound weird," Nia said, "but have we died?"

Astonished, my father looked at her. "You believe in heaven all of a sudden?"

"I didn't say heaven. Just, you know, somewhere else."

"I don't feel dead," I said. And no way did my idea of heaven include a farm—or Nia.

We left the loft. The goats were bleating louder than ever.

"I'm going to milk them," Nia said.

I wasn't sure what surprised me more: that she knew *how* to milk a goat, or that she wanted to do it *right now*.

"They aren't even ours," Dad said.

"It's painful for them, Caleb. It'll just take a few minutes."

"How do you even know this stuff?" I asked.

"I spent four months homesteading after university."

I wouldn't have said milking goats was our number-one priority, but Nia had made up her mind. She opened the gate to the pasture, and the goats pushed past her and scampered inside the barn. One of them hopped right up onto a low wooden platform and poked its head through the rails at one end.

"Well trained," Nia remarked. "That's the milking stand."

She adjusted the slats so they gently closed around the goat's neck to keep her still. There were two metal pails nearby, and Nia put one underneath the udders.

"Let's see if I remember how to do this."

She closed her hand around one of the long teats and made several tugs. Nothing came out. Next time she squeezed with just her thumb and index finger, then quickly closed her other fingers one after another, down to her pinkie. After a couple tries, a thin line of milk rang against the bottom of the pail.

"That's it!" she said happily.

In a horror movie this would've been the moment an unhinged farmer with his pitchfork appeared silhouetted in the doorway and said, "Y'all get back in your stalls now."

When Nia finished with both goats, we had about a half pail of milk. Nia got the goats back into the pasture and told me and Dad to bring some hay. I felt like

I was on the weirdest field trip ever. We filled up a wheelbarrow and dumped it out for the goats, who went at it eagerly.

"We should probably check on the chickens," Nia said, looking toward the coop.

I wondered if she was having a nervous breakdown, or if this was just her way of coping. What was my way of coping? Keep looking. Figure things out. Make a plan. Don't stop to pet the animals.

As we got closer to the coop she called out a hello, in case there was some weirdo lurking inside who needed time to get ready for us. When I peeped through a window, I was relieved to see only chickens.

Built low against the coop's outside wall was a long wooden box with a hinged lid. When Nia lifted it, a warm, pungent smell wafted out, along with flustered clucking. The box was divided into five compartments, each filled with straw. All but one contained an egg or two.

"No one's collected yet," she said, closing the lid. "We should let them out."

"Are you serious?" I said.

"They need to forage."

Near the bottom of the wall was a small square door. When she opened it, chickens strutted out, looking slightly indignant. I counted fifteen. They began pecking at the ground. Hanging from a hook on the wall was a pail of dried corn. Nia grabbed a couple fistfuls and scattered it.

"Maybe we can find you a piglet to raise," I said.

Nia frowned into the distance. "There's got to be a road. To bring in supplies, just to *build* this place. You don't hike all this stuff through the woods."

That was more like it. Nia worked for an NGO that got food to some of the poorest and most disaster-stricken areas of the world, and she knew about logistics. Good strategy was one of the few things we had in common.

"Let's find that road," I said.

We decided to walk all the way around the farm. Nia pointed out rows of lentils, beets, and potatoes. We reached a small orchard of apple and pear trees. Nearby were three big boxes that Nia said were beehives. We skirted a field of waist-high grass.

"Pretty sure this is alfalfa," Nia said. "Great feeding hay."

The whole way round, there was no sign of a road or even a rutted path. It was as if the farm had been set down in the middle of nowhere.

"How's he doing?" Dad asked Nia, who was giving her tummy a rub.

"Just gave a little kick."

Dad put a hand on her stomach and smiled. "There he is."

"I don't want to give birth out here."

"Well, you did want a home birth," Dad joked.

"Not funny."

"It'll be fine."

With a sigh, Nia suddenly leaned against my father. "Caleb, I really need to eat something."

"Right. Sorry, darling." I couldn't remember ever hearing him call Mom darling, and it made me feel sad.

Back inside the cottage, Dad made sure the patio door was locked, then told Nia to sit down. He brought her a glass of water, which luckily was still flowing from the tap. He asked her what she wanted to eat. Last night we'd picked up a few things on the drive up. While Dad started the omelet, I made a salad with cherry tomatoes, baby carrots, and nuts. Dad said we should add some feta because Nia needed extra protein. He made a dressing and I cut some thick slices of the granary loaf.

The three of us sat around the table and ate. It was a comforting, familiar thing. A normal thing to do. But whenever my eyes strayed to the windows, I was reminded there was nothing normal or familiar about what was going on.

I could have been back home with Mom and Sam. I was supposed to go over to Serena's later. She'd invited me to her house to watch *Metropolis*, a movie I'd never seen that she said I *had* to see. A girl had never invited me, just *me*, over to her house (not since I was five anyway) and I'd been nervous but also excited because I really liked Serena, and the freckle near her mouth made me think about what it would be like to kiss her.

"Better?" Dad asked Nia when she'd finished her meal.

She nodded. "You guys ready to take another look around?"

Dad said, "I'm still trying to process how we got here."

I'd been chasing that question in circles the whole meal. "There are only two possibilities, right? One: Our entire cottage was moved. Two: This place is a perfect replica."

I looked around the room where I'd spent parts of every summer since I was born. If this was a replica, they'd done the purple stain from the Popsicle I'd let melt on the carpet when I was six, the gouges in the hardwood from Sam's snowshoes, and the three dents in the ceiling from when we'd fired marbles with our homemade slingshots.

"If this was a replica," my father said, "that would mean they'd already built it, way out here, wherever this is."

Which meant this had been planned far in advance, which was terrifying. It meant people would have studied our cottage, inside and out.

"And then, last night," Nia continued, "they would've had to move everything out of the real cottage. Someone would've heard all *that*. Our furniture, appliances, all our things loaded into a moving van, then brought out here and put back in *exactly* the same places? My clothes, my phone, the extra pillow I tossed onto the chair? No one could be that precise."

"They might be very good at this," Dad said.

I went to the kitchen and opened the fridge. "The pickle is still here!" I said triumphantly. In the back right corner of the bottom shelf was an ancient jar with a single warty pickle bobbing in brine. It had been there for years, and everyone was too terrified to eat it, but for some reason no one had thrown it out.

I opened the garbage under the sink. The crumpled wrapper from the sub I'd eaten on the way here last night was in exactly the same position—I remembered that big splotch of mayonnaise on the logo. "Even the garbage's the same. No one's that good, right?"

"They would've had to move one other thing," Nia said. "Us. We must've been *very* fast asleep."

Reluctantly, Dad said, "Or drugged."

I wasn't sure which was more horrifying: being drugged or being *handled* while we were unconscious and helpless.

"How?" The only time I'd been drugged was when I'd had my appendix out. The doctor had injected anesthetic into my hand and told me to count backward from ten. I got to seven, then oblivion.

"Did anyone feel woozy when they woke up?" Dad asked.

Not me. I'd woken up with a great D&D idea.

Nia shook her head, but she was holding her belly with both hands. "What if it hurt the baby?"

Dad put his arm around her. I could tell from his face he already regretted bringing it up. "He moved earlier, remember? We both felt it."

Her breath came fast and shallow. "What if it was something really heavy duty? Anesthetic goes right to the baby."

Nia had been very dedicated about her pregnancy. She did yoga and stayed fit and ate only the healthiest foods. This was her first baby and she'd read a ton of books about being a mother.

"He's fine," Dad said. "That was a strong kick he gave."

Anxiously, Nia inspected her arms. "Do you see any needle marks? In my elbows or hands?"

"I don't think so. No, I don't see anything."

"I want you to check. Everywhere."

She hurried to the bathroom. Dad gave me a grim nod and followed her. It was quiet for a bit, then I heard Nia crying and Dad murmuring something I couldn't make out. In a strangled voice, Nia said, "What about you? Let me see."

"Are you guys okay?" I asked through the door, starting to freak out.

"We're okay, Zay," Dad said.

I paced. A minute later, Nia opened the door, looking ashen, and walked past me into their bedroom.

"You okay?" I asked her, but she just closed the door.

"Hey, Zay," Dad said, "come in for a second."

My stomach felt sick. "What's going on?"

"Just turn around. I want to check your lower back."

He lifted my T-shirt a bit and I sensed his face close to my skin.

"Okay." Dad let my shirt drop.

I turned to him. "What did you see?"

"We all have the same marks."

My head felt swimmy. I touched the counter for balance. "Show me."

He lifted his own shirt and with a finger circled an area along his backbone. Arranged in a triangle were three red dots. One was bigger than the others. I thought of needles sinking deep, tubes snaking through my veins and guts. My stomach folded over, and I leaned over the sink and retched up a few strings of saliva. Dad rubbed my back.

Before, it had been possible to imagine that this thing just *happened* to us. *We woke up on a farm, can you believe it?* But now the fact was unavoidable: Someone had intentionally done this to us.

I was suddenly furious. "I could be back home! With Mom and Sam! Where I actually wanted to be, instead of here with you two and your stupid baby!"

"Zay."

He didn't look angry, just sorrowful. He tried to hug me, but I shrugged him off. I wanted to burst free of my body and fly.

"And now look what's happened! Some weirdos got into the cottage. They came inside and did all sorts of weird shit to us and dumped us out here like some psycho game!"

My father looked at me. "If it's a game, you'll win it."

Usually all he said about my gaming was that I spent too much time doing it. That I needed to develop some other skills. Like learning German or playing the trumpet.

"I know how complicated those games are," he said.

"No, you don't."

He'd never played D&D. Only once had he offered to play a video game with me. It was an easy shooter and he'd only lasted three rounds. Each time, I killed him in a couple minutes, while he stared gormlessly up at the sky or down at his feet, trying to figure out how to move his body.

"I've watched you play WarpWorld; I've seen you planning for D&D. I can tell how much strategy goes into those campaigns." I could tell he was pleased with himself for using the word *campaigns*. "We're going to need that strategic mind of yours."

"Yeah," I said, feeling calmer. "Okay."

"So if this were a game, what's the first thing you'd do?"

"Figure out the rules," I said.

3

In a game, you always have an objective. There are forces or villains acting against you, so it's good if you can predict their actions. That way, you aren't just reacting. You can plan ahead, go on the offensive.

I knew our objective: *escape*.

The problem was, I didn't know their objective yet.

But in all games, if you waited around, you never learned anything—your enemies found you, and you got killed.

"We should head up the hill," I said to Dad. "We'll get a pretty good view."

"Let's do it," said Nia, coming out of the bedroom, looking very determined.

"You up for it?" Dad asked her.

"As long as it's not too steep."

Last night on the drive, I'd heard her telling Dad she sometimes felt a little breathless because the baby was so big now. *Just three more weeks*, he'd replied.

We packed water bottles, nuts, sunscreen. We put on our hats, and my father patted his back pocket to make sure he had his wallet, which I found weirdly reassuring. Like maybe we'd need to buy a slushee somewhere. Or bribe someone for a ride out of here. I grabbed my shovel and Dad brought his crowbar, and we headed out like a bunch of doomed D&D newbies.

"Hang on," I said on the deck. "We should be making a map."

"Seriously?" Dad said.

"Zay's right," Nia said.

I checked the compass app on my phone.

"Yes!"

"How, if the map app didn't work?" Dad asked, looking over my shoulder.

"The compass uses magnets, not GPS."

Even if we didn't have a blue dot, at least we still had north, south, east, and west. I suddenly felt way more optimistic.

"Nia, your phone has a pedometer, right?" I knew she had a health app because she was very up on how many steps she got in each day.

"Yeah," she said, tapping her phone, "and that gives us distances. All the ingredients we need to make a map."

We looked at each other in a rare moment of mutual admiration.

"Well, you two are very impressive," Dad said.

I went back inside to get paper and a pencil. Then I set our bearing for the hill, Nia reset her pedometer, and we started off. On the outskirts of the farm, we trampled a path through a field of waist-high grass. Even in the full sun it wasn't unpleasantly hot. Wherever we were, it had a nicer climate.

"Have you seen any planes?" I was looking up at the clear sky and couldn't see a single jet trail.

"Haven't been checking," Dad said, though I knew he would have noticed.

Before we got to the woods, I turned back the way we'd come. It was surreal to see our cottage plonked down in the middle of a strange farm. Still, it was the closest thing we had to normal, and it made me nervous walking away from it.

The forest was mostly pines, which was what I called any tree that didn't have big leafy leaves. The ground, carpeted with soft brown needles, began to rise gently, but there wasn't much undergrowth and it was easy going. After a while we paused to have some water. Nia chewed some nuts.

She said, "It's so quiet."

As a general rule, I avoided forests, so didn't know if this was unusual. But she was right: I hadn't heard birds singing, or anything scrambling in the bushes. I *had* noticed that I hadn't been bitten by a single mosquito yet, and they usually loved me.

We kept going.

"Who would do this?" she wondered.

"A conventional kidnapping doesn't make much sense," Dad said. "We're not rich. Which means there isn't much of a payoff for the kidnappers."

"Especially after all the money they blew, moving our cottage or building a replica," I added.

We disqualified witness relocation, reality TV show, and being dead.

That left the real doozies.

A sinister government experiment in which our unconscious bodies floated in goo while our hijacked minds experienced this virtual reality.

"Alien abduction," I finally said, because I could tell no one else was going to. "It ticks some boxes. Our cottage being moved or duplicated. Waking up somewhere strange with weird marks on our bodies."

"These all sound like movie plots," Nia muttered.

As we walked, I pulled out my phone and texted Sam.

send cops to cottage

(Not delivered.)

is it still there? maybe there's clues

(Not delivered.)

wish I were back home

(Not delivered.)

Up ahead the trees began to thin, and I saw a meadow, bright in the sunlight.

As we left the forest behind, Nia checked her phone for a signal. "Nothing."

I turned to take in the view. It was a good one, even though we hadn't reached the top of the hill yet. But the only human things I could see, spread out before us, were our cottage and the barn. Surrounding the farm was forest and wild fields. No other buildings, no roads, no cell phone towers.

"How far have we come?" I asked.

Nia checked her pedometer. "Four point three seven kilometers."

I updated the map. "Maybe we'll see something at the top."

We were back among trees. Mid-stride, my foot struck something, and then something hit me in the chest and face. I stumbled back with a grunt, more angry than hurt. There was nothing in front of me except the view. I turned to warn Dad and Nia just as they collided with the air. Dad swore and checked his nose for blood. Nia had been bounced back by her tummy, and now placed both hands protectively around it.

"You okay?" Dad asked her.

"What the hell was that?"

Cautiously, I reached out. My fingers touched something that felt like a gym mat, dense but with a bit of give. Whatever I was touching, I couldn't see it. I followed it all the way down to the ground, then as high as I could reach. I walked to the left, running my fingertips along it.

"I think it's a wall."

"Keeps going this way, too," Dad said, taking some steps to the right. We looked at each other. In D&D there were invisible walls; in the real world, no. Nia was whipping rocks at it, aiming as high up as she could. They all bounced off. The wall must have been at least thirty feet tall.

"Is it to keep us out or keep us in?" she said.

On the other side, the forest continued to rise gently toward the summit. Was there something dangerous or top secret up there?

"How far have we come?" I asked Nia.

"Four point eight two kilometers."

I marked the wall on our map.

"Should we see how far it goes?" Dad asked.

I made a note of our new bearing, and we followed the wall across the slope, pausing every so often to throw more rocks at it. We couldn't get one over the top. After a couple minutes I heard burbling water. Before long we saw the creek, flowing downhill. We followed the wall right to the bank. When Dad stretched his arm as far as he could over the creek, he said the wall kept going.

"There must be a gap to let the water through," I said.

The creek wasn't more than twenty feet across, with a pebbly bottom that didn't look too deep. Dad removed his backpack and stripped down to his boxers. He handed his crowbar to Nia and waded in.

"Be careful, Caleb."

Dad slowly patted his way along the invisible wall, his hands at water level.

"No gap yet."

It didn't make sense. The creek seemed to flow seamlessly through the invisible wall, bank to bank.

"Maybe the opening's deeper down," I said.

He was halfway across now, up to his chest.

"I'll check." He reached lower, his cheek grazing the water. He shook his head. "Still feeling the wall. I'm just going to go under so I can reach all the way to the bottom."

"Caleb, don't," Nia said, suddenly sounding so anxious that it scared me.

"It's fine." Dad took a breath and dipped down. I saw tiny air bubbles trapped in his curly hair. My fear coagulated into panic. I didn't want him underwater. His crouched shape shuffled across the bottom. I counted seconds and was so relieved when he came up, wiping his eyes.

"I don't think this water's coming from up there," he said, pointing at the creek on the other side of the wall.

"Where, then?" Nia asked.

"Underground. There's a long vent along the bottom, right against the wall. Pretty sure I felt water pumping up."

"Come back," Nia said.

I gave him the towel I'd rolled up in my backpack, and he gratefully patted himself dry.

"So is that even real?" I asked, waving at the view beyond the wall. I'd assumed the wall was transparent, because both sides meshed so perfectly, but now I wasn't at all sure.

"Let's see."

Dad, who was now very much a crowbar guy, hefted it behind his shoulder like a baseball bat. The ruthless expression on his face wasn't one I'd seen before. He swung. The first couple of times, the crowbar bounced off. The third time, with a moist smack, the hooked end bit into the wall. When he wrenched it loose, it left a flickering orange gash in the air. Dad swung again and a shard of what looked like slimy orange Styrofoam landed near my feet.

"What is that?" Nia asked.

"Keep going!" I said.

Dad swung again and this time didn't stop. Orange chunks flew to the ground. He was grunting and huffing, his face clenched with effort. He'd just managed to hack out a shallow crater the size of a plum when a spark snapped from the wall to his crowbar. With a cry he dropped it.

"Dad!"

"I'm okay." He clenched and unclenched his hands.

"It's electrified," Nia said.

"Wasn't at first," he murmured.

"It burned you," Nia said, taking his hands. Across each palm was a red band of skin.

The crater in the wall flinched and began to shrink. With a wet clicking sound, the wound healed itself and became transparent again. Once more we saw an unblemished view of the creek and hillside.

4

Dad and I wanted to keep following the wall, to see how far it went, but Nia said she was tired, and my father needed his hands bandaged. We headed back, retracing our steps.

"Did you know there were walls like that?" Nia asked us, sounding almost angry.

"No," said my father.

"Zay, you're into all the latest stuff. You heard of a wall that can do that?"

"Only in D&D and WarpWorld."

As we trudged down through the trees, I kept hoping that we'd find our cottage back in its usual place on the lake. Our car would be in the driveway that connected to a road that would take us back to the city. I wouldn't have asked too many questions. But when we emerged from the forest, I could still see the farm in the distance.

Back inside the cottage, Dad changed out of his wet clothes and we sat together in the family room. Nia put some antibiotic ointment on his burns and covered them with gauze. For what seemed a long time, we were silent. I could tell by the measured rise and fall of Nia's belly she was doing breath work to stay calm. Outside, we'd all stayed pretty cool about the invisible wall, or maybe we were just too frightened of what it might mean.

"We need to make a plan," I said.

We transferred my map to a bigger piece of paper, trying to draw it to scale.

We marked the farm, the field of tall grass beyond the orchard, the hill, the wall, and the creek. Everything felt more urgent now. More dangerous.

At overnight camp in the Laurentians, the guides had told us that if you ever got lost in the woods, the best thing to do was to stay put and wait until someone rescued you. We weren't lost in any normal sense, and I was pretty sure that even when my mom inevitably freaked out and came looking for us, there wouldn't be anything to find. No one was coming for us—except maybe the people who'd drugged us and moved us here.

"How about we follow the creek downstream?" I said. A last resort, the camp guides had told us. "Might lead to a road or trail."

"We should go the opposite direction we just tried," Nia said. "We can't be that far from something. It's not like we're in the far north. This isn't boreal forest. There's got to be other farms."

"How far are we willing to go?" Dad asked.

"As far as it takes," Nia said.

But I realized what Dad was getting at. Unless we were planning on carrying heavy packs with food and overnight camping gear (which we didn't have), we'd always need to factor in the return trip to the cottage, especially now that Nia got tired faster.

"If we stay out too long, our phones will die," I pointed out. "And there goes our compass and pedometer."

"It's almost five o'clock," Dad said. "We're not going anywhere today. Tomorrow morning, we'll try the opposite direction."

Nia put a frozen margherita pizza into the oven. We went around collecting things that might be useful. Like all cottages, ours had been accumulating things for decades. I thought of Sam as I rummaged through our drawers and shelves. I collected stray batteries, found a couple flashlights, a jittery plastic compass that I didn't trust, and a pair of cheap walkie-talkies.

On the dining room table, Dad and Nia had assembled things from the medicine cabinet: hydrogen peroxide, bandages, painkillers, tweezers, nail scissors. They'd gathered candles and a couple boxes of matches. A Swiss Army knife. There was a boat safety kit with a coil of thin yellow rope, a whistle, a bailer, and a couple of glow sticks. I wished we had a flare. I recognized Mom's binoculars, the ones she'd used for birding.

Nia was making a list of the cans and dried goods in the cupboard. I noticed they'd lined up all the knives on the counter, maybe trying to figure out which ones were the sharpest.

"The food we've got here," said Nia, "I'd say is maybe three, four days."

We made a small salad and ate it with the pizza. Afterward, as I helped clear up, I said, "We've been abducted and I'm loading a dishwasher."

"I'm just grateful we have electricity," Dad said.

"We should juice up our phones," I said. "It might not last."

Dad's phone pinged and we all jumped.

"Have you got a signal?" Nia gasped as we all scrambled for our own phones.

Dad stared sadly at his screen. "Sorry, guys. It's just a reminder I set yesterday. *Buy firewood.*"

For the firepit. So we could roast marshmallows and have campfire fun by the lake that was no longer there.

From the pasture came an insistent bleating.

"They need milking again?" I asked.

"Twice a day."

We all went together, me with my shovel, Dad with his crowbar. The sky was streaked with clouds. Still no jet trails. I wondered how far we were from the nearest airport.

While Nia milked the goat, she rested her cheek against its flank and closed her eyes for a second. When it was the second goat's turn, I helped encourage it onto the stand. I could see why Nia liked touching it; the warmth and simple *aliveness* of it was comforting.

"You should pick a weapon," Dad told her, nodding at the wall of tools. She chose a pitchfork, which I had to admit was kind of badass, though unwieldy, and I wouldn't have recommended it for close-quarters combat. Then again, I had a shovel. Dad upgraded himself to an axe.

"Zay, you want to get a basket from the loft?" Nia asked.

"What for?"

"The eggs. If we leave them, the hens'll stop laying."

The worry in her face said everything: We might need that food.

"We're not going to be here that long," Dad promised.

I went up to the loft and grabbed one of the baskets. The sun was low in the west and shone directly through the open doors. It felt good on my face, like hope. But I also realized it would be dark soon.

We collected the eggs, and Nia said we should get the chickens back inside in case there were predators. Like the goats, the hens knew their routine and strutted through the low hatch into the coop. I secured the little door. Keeping them safe from a fox seemed manageable, compared to what might be waiting out there for us.

On the way back to the cottage, Nia detoured through the vegetables. She plucked some tomatoes from their vines, dug up a few beets and potatoes. At the herb garden she added some basil and oregano to our basket.

Inside, I latched the sliding door and put the security bar across the bottom. I made sure the front door was locked and chained. I went room to room to close all the windows. Last night, we'd made it easy for them to come inside. Not tonight.

In the family room, I looked out at the darkening sky and felt it like a growing presence inside me, squeezing my lungs. I drew the curtains against my nervous reflection.

"We should go back to the hayloft," I said. "We shouldn't sleep here."

I saw the resistance in Nia's face; Dad's, too.

"I think this is the safest place we've got, Zay," he said gently.

"Not if they come back tonight."

Nia said, "At least we've got doors with locks."

"They could have some drug they just spray inside to knock us out. Who knows what they'll do to us next?"

Nia's hand moved to her belly. She looked at my father.

"In the hayloft," I said, "we'll see them coming if they try to get inside the cottage."

"The barn's probably the next place they'd look," Dad said.

"But we'd be ready for them."

Nia was nodding now. "And we'd see who they were."

Wearily, Dad scratched his stubbled cheek. "We'd have a good vantage point," he agreed. "And if there's anything out there that's lit up, a house, a car on a road, we'd see it way easier in the dark. Okay."

We got our things ready, including some blankets and pillows. We left all the lights on, including the ones outside. We wanted a nice glow around the cottage, so we'd be able to see if anyone came creeping around.

Up in the loft, we arranged our bedding to either side of the open doors, so we still had a good view but were out of sight from the ground. Dad and I shifted a couple full barrels to the top of the stairs. If anyone started coming up, we'd send those barrels hurtling down.

We watched the sky lose its color and become star-speckled. The three-quarter moon supplied quite a bit of light. I liked being up high. It felt safer. I thought of the times Sam and I would lie on our backs on the deck with Mom and Dad, when we were still a family, and watch the Perseid meteor showers. I wished Sam and Mom were here now, even though I knew that was selfish. I worried I'd start to cry, so I picked out Orion and the Big Dipper, and willed my body to unclench.

The three of us took turns with the binoculars, but I felt like I could watch better without them. You could let your gaze go wide, and even if it was out of focus, you'd still catch movement or a little speck of light.

I wasn't seeing anything, or hearing anything either. Not crickets or grasshoppers or whatever bugs you heard on a summer night. Not the low rumble of a high-up jet taking families on holidays, or bringing them back home. Home. Mom always sent me good-night texts when I was away, and she worried when I didn't answer them. She might let it go for a night or two, assuming I was busy or tired or just forgetful. But after that, she'd raise the alarm. She'd call Dad and when he didn't answer she'd call some friends on the lake and ask them to swing by. And then she'd raise hell. It made me feel better, knowing that Mom and Sam would do everything they could to find us.

From the barn loft, we watched for someone to come skulking around the cottage. Would it be just one person or ten? Would they be dressed like Special Ops soldiers or lab-coated scientists? Or would they be something not of this world?

Those three red marks on our backs. An invisible wall that regenerated.

Dad said he wasn't sleepy yet and we should get some rest. It didn't make sense for all of us to stay up. We could take shifts.

Nia said, "You see anything, you hear anything, I mean *anything*, a squeak, you wake us all up."

I settled down on a blanket. Nia grumbled as she shifted to get comfortable. She was the one who was always talking about being unplugged. Well, we were unplugged now. Except that we had power. The miraculous electrified cottage in the middle of nowhere.

Dad reached over and gave my shoulder a squeeze. I patted him back, then rested a hand on my shovel.

Nothing happened during the night, and early next morning, we walked south. We went through fields and woods without seeing a road, farm, or anything you could call a trail. We stopped to rest and update the map, check our distance and bearing. A creek cut in from the east, maybe the same one we'd seen at the top of the hill. It was easy to cross. Later, we passed a big pond fringed with bulrushes. I was happy to see ducks—the first animals we'd encountered apart from our goats and chickens.

After another hour we hit the invisible wall.

We tried to find the top by throwing rocks; they all bounced back.

I'm pretty sure we were all trying to hide how scared we were.

"What do you think?" Dad said. "Follow the wall or try a completely different direction?"

Nia's face was grim. "Follow it."

I updated our map. We reset the pedometer, took a new bearing, and started out, trailing our fingers against the wall. Every minute or so, my compass heading shifted one degree. It felt like we were walking in a straight line, but it was undeniable: The wall was very slowly curving inward. We all had to be thinking the same thought, but we said nothing.

In seven hours, taking rest breaks, we'd walked almost thirty-three kilometers and gone full circle.

When we dragged ourselves back to the cottage, mute with disappointment and fear, there was a crib waiting for us on the deck.

When Nia saw that crib, she lost it.

I'd never seen her cry. In fact, I'd never seen *anyone* cry like that. That crib said a lot.

It said, *You're going to have that baby right here.*

It said, *You're not going anywhere.*

5

The next day, we carried three shovels out to the wall and tried to dig under.

We tried two different locations. Foot after foot, the wall just kept going deeper.

The day after that, we tried going *over*. We picked a tall tree that grew right against the wall. Carrying the coil of lightweight yellow rope, I climbed up. I was good at climbing trees. Around the cottage, Sam and I had scaled all the ones that were scalable. He'd usually been the one to go highest because I chickened out. But this time I went so high that Dad told me to stop. He thought I was maybe forty feet up. We'd weighted one end of the line. I made sure I had a clear shot and hurled it high. It bounced off. After four tries, Dad told me to come back down.

Next, we tried going *through*.

Drilling had been my idea. I'd looked at all the tools in the barn, all the materials we had, and used my best gaming instincts to draft one strategy after another until Dad and Nia agreed on the plan.

Now, with every turn of the drill, Dad and I bored deeper into the wall. The drill was old-fashioned, and its shaft and T-handle were wood, which I hoped would stop us from getting shocked. So far so good. We worked fast, the eerie orange goo churning from the narrow hole we made.

"Are we through?" I asked. The bit was two feet long, and we'd sunk it as far as it would go; the handle was almost grazing the wall. But I hadn't felt that sudden give when you punch through.

"Let's find out," said Dad. "Ready?"

We'd seen how fast the wall could heal itself. Quickly we pulled out the bit. Nia handed us a long wooden dowel, and we shoved it in until we hit something.

"We're not through," Dad said, grabbing the mallet.

We'd made sure to sharpen the end of the dowel. With each blow, it went a little deeper, then suddenly a *lot* deeper.

"I think it went through!"

We looked at each other, trying not to get too excited. But I was overjoyed. It was just a wall, a very strange one that could shock us, but it was still a wall that we could *drill through*. And we'd just made a tiny tunnel. It was the first time in days Nia had smiled.

"Let's start the next hole," I said.

We drilled it right beside the first, hammered in another dowel until it punched through, and did it again. The plan was to drill enough holes close together to make one bigger hole. Big enough for us to crawl through.

The more holes we drilled, the more I worried that something would go wrong. The wall would zap us or crush the wooden dowels, and our chance to escape would be snatched from us.

We didn't take any breaks. If someone needed to rest their aching wrists, the third person filled in. After an hour we'd sunk enough dowels to make a hole that we reckoned we could each fit through—even Nia, who needed the most room right now. The bottom of the hole was at waist level. All we'd have to do was scramble through, maybe three feet to the other side. Easy.

"Good to go?" Dad said.

Fear flitted through my guts. We had no idea what was on the other side. The tightly wedged dowels were blocking our view. Would it be the forest that we saw through the transparent wall? Or somewhere totally different? A room?

A prison? And would there be anyone on the other side waiting for us?

We'd talked and argued about the order we should go through the hole. I said it made sense for Nia to go first, since she was the biggest, and the hole would only get smaller as it healed itself. Dad said it wouldn't grow *that* fast, and no way was he letting Nia go first. He would make sure no one got electrocuted, then I would go, and Nia would bring up the rear. Dad and I would help her through.

"Let's do it," I said.

Getting out the first dowel was the hardest. We should've greased them ahead of time. Twisting and pulling and swearing, we finally got it out. After that, all three of us were yanking them as fast as we could.

Nia grabbed her yoga mat and unrolled it into the hole—her idea. The rubber might insulate us from any electrical current. I shone my light inside and we all bent to look. It was like peering into some terrible, slick wound. But there was no opening at the end. No light at the end of the tunnel. No blue sky. Nothing except a circle of gooey orange material.

"But we punched through!" I shouted.

"Must've already healed over," said Nia.

"Can't be very thick yet," Dad said.

He grabbed a wood-handled trowel and leaned inside. The walls were making a sound like a tongue clacking around in a dry mouth.

"Caleb," said Nia nervously.

Seeing Dad's head and torso disappear into the hole made my heart kick. Nia and I kept lights shining inside.

"Maybe just a thin skin," he said, stabbing the trowel into the back of the tunnel. His body was mostly blocking my view, but I could hear the wet sound of the blade biting.

"You through?" I asked.

"Not yet. Thicker than I thought."

I looked at the walls, already excreting new tissue.

"Caleb, it's growing back pretty fast," Nia warned.

"I think I'm almost through . . ."

Like a layer of orange frost, the wall had already grown over the yoga mat and was creeping toward Dad's hips and torso.

"Dad, come out!"

"Almost there."

"Caleb, it's already too narrow. I won't fit!"

"Dad! Now!"

I looked helplessly at Nia, and simultaneously we grabbed his belt and waistband and hauled. We shifted him no more than a couple inches before he stuck.

"It's got my left arm!" he yelled. "It's grown over my left arm. I'm just trying to—"

Nia and I pulled harder. With a horrific burst of speed, the walls contracted against my father's torso.

"I can't get myself—" I heard Dad say, and then it sounded like something had filled up his mouth.

His legs started kicking. The wall gulped him in up to his feet.

"It's gonna crush him!" I screamed.

I grabbed one of the big shovels, but the moment the blade touched the wall, it sparked and the shaft splintered in my hands. Dad's feet gave a final weak kick and disappeared.

The wall shuddered and the section in front of me suddenly became translucent, so I could see the shadowy form of my father, his limbs struggling like he was caught in some terrible viscous Jell-O.

I ran at the wall, ready to gouge at it with my fists, but Nia caught me and held me back. She was strong. She told me I'd be electrocuted, and I kept saying, "It's Dad, help me, fucking let me go!"

The wall puckered and Dad slid out, slick with orange goo. We rushed over to him as he lay gasping on the ground.

"Dad!"

"I'm okay," he coughed. "I'm okay."

Nia was wiping off the goo and checking him for wounds. "What happened?"

He said it was like being swallowed. It was all muscle. It went into his mouth and up his nostrils. He could still breathe, but he was powerless. He was being pushed, he had no idea which way, then out he came.

"It could've crushed me," he said. "Or suffocated me. It was so strong."

"Did you see anything?" I asked. "Could you see through to the other side?"

"For a second, I thought it was getting thinner, but then . . ." He shook his head. "I think it can make itself thicker wherever it wants."

"You didn't get shocked?" Nia asked

"Not even a little," he said.

The wall might have spared his life, but it had also given us an unmistakable warning.

Don't try this again.

6

"That wall's not human," I said when we got back to the cottage.

"We don't know that," Nia said, furiously chopping tomatoes for the frittata.

I couldn't believe I had to say it. The entire walk home, no one had even brought it up. "Guys, come on. It's an invisible wall that—"

"Transparent," Nia said firmly, adding the tomatoes to the other vegetables sautéing in the pan. "*Invisible* makes it sound like magic."

"I didn't say magic, Nia. I said *not human*. It heals itself. It electrocutes people. It *eats* people."

I looked over at Dad, who was whisking the eggs, and he gave a little headshake that said, *Not now.*

Maybe he was trying to protect Nia, but what about me? I was freaking out, too, and I needed to talk.

"What if we've been abducted by aliens?"

Nia grunted and gripped her belly. "Ohhhhhhh," she said, wincing.

"Contraction?" Dad asked, instantly at her side.

"It's not time," she said worriedly.

"If it's now," Dad said calmly, "it's exactly the right time."

"He's too early!"

"Not for this baby. For this baby, he's right on schedule."

"Caleb."

"It's going to be fine. You're ready for this. We went to all the sessions. You have a birth plan and I am your midwife."

"I'm scared," she said, and grunted again in pain.

"People have been doing this for millions of years. Let's get you comfy on the bed."

Dad turned off the oven and asked me to get a stack of fresh towels and a new pair of rubber gloves from under the sink. He told me to clean out the bucket in the closet really, really well, and fill it with warm soapy water. He was super calm, and having jobs to do helped me stay calm, too.

"We're all set here, Zay," he said when I brought the things to the bedroom.

Nia gave me a little smile, like she was trying to reassure me. I couldn't even imagine how she must be feeling, but I thought she was really brave.

"Just stand by in case we need something, okay?" Dad said.

I closed the door behind me, dragged my green chair into the hallway, and sat down right outside the room. I pulled out my phone. Just holding it made me feel a little better, which was pathetic because there wasn't even a signal. It didn't stop me from texting Mom.

please don't think we drowned in the lake or anything

(Not delivered.)

I just wanted her to hug me right now.

we tried everything to get through the wall

(Not delivered.)

I really needed her to tell me everything was going to be okay. She was the only person who could say that so that I truly believed it.

Nia's having her baby right now

(Not delivered.)

My hands were shaking.

i'm worried we've been abducted by aliens.

I erased it. If it was true, there was absolutely nothing she could do about it, and I didn't want to freak her out any more than she already was.

please keep looking for us.

(Not delivered.)

I heard Dad telling Nia, "Remember, don't push until you absolutely have to. You're doing great."

I heard Nia straining and gasping. Then she went quiet. Then, gasping again.

"Is he coming?" Nia asked. "Can you see him? Is he tangled up? Check, can you check? Caleb, I can't feel him moving."

"He's just a little stuck."

I wondered what "a little stuck" meant. You were either stuck or you weren't.

Dad told her she was doing fantastic, everything was great. But his voice had changed, and Nia kept asking if he was coming and why he wasn't coming. I couldn't sit still. I paced the hallway. Dad told her she was almost there, just a little more, and that he was going to shift the baby a bit. There was another grunting cry, and then silence.

Nia's voice sounded weak. "Is there a heartbeat? Caleb?"

Terror jolted through my body. I wanted to go inside the room but was also afraid of what I'd see, so I sat down on the floor and covered my ears and tried not to hear anything else. But I still heard my father saying, "I can't tell," and then, "I'm not sure," and then, "I don't think he's breathing," and then Nia was sobbing and I clamped my hands harder over my ears and shut my eyes.

All I heard now was the quick rasp of my breath, and the deep hum inside my skull, and—

I was sprawled in the hallway, no idea how I got there. My cheek hurt against the floor. It was quiet. I sat up. I had no memory of falling asleep, of what had happened beforehand. Then my head lit up with memory. My eyes shot to the closed door.

When I burst inside, Dad was leaning unsteadily against the bed, like he'd just woken up himself. We looked at each other in bewilderment.

Nia was sleeping peacefully on clean sheets. Nestled in her arms, nursing, was a baby.

THREE YEARS LATER

7

The goats always made the biggest racket in the morning, so I took care of them first. We had seven now. After feeding them and doing the milking, I went to the coop to collect the eggs and let the chickens out. Over in the west pasture, Herk was bleating and snorting and peeing on himself because the females were in heat and he was tired of being fenced off from them. *Just gotta wait two more months, Herk.* We didn't let the goats mate till October, so the kids would come in spring when it was warmer. *Hey, Herk, at least you're gonna get sex eventually. Me, not ever.* I scattered some grain and garden waste for the hens, topped up their water, then returned the hose to the barn.

"Zay! Look!"

I turned to see Noah standing in the doorway, holding something that I hadn't seen in a very long time. Nestled against his chest was a golden-haired puppy, a retriever maybe.

"Where'd you find it?"

"In the orchard. I heard him whimpering!"

There were no dogs here. Which meant *they* must have brought it. I glanced in the direction of the orchard. As if I'd ever catch sight of them. It still unsettled me when they left things. Usually it was at night when we were asleep. We'd wake up and find something just outside the cottage. There was nothing stopping them from entering, standing at the foot of our beds. Doing whatever they wanted to us. But they hadn't. Not so far.

Noah beamed. There was a narrow gap between his front teeth that always made his smile even happier. He had his mother's abundant black hair, full mouth, light brown skin, and tapered face. She was always saying that we definitely looked like brothers, but I wasn't so sure. Maybe we shared something around the eyes and forehead? I think Nia was just trying to make sure we bonded, to encourage me to be good to him, which I was anyway. I had no problem with Noah. He just wasn't Sam.

"Is it a dog?" he asked.

He'd seen pictures, but never the real thing. Hadn't stopped him from picking it up. But any little kid would've done the same. None of the animals he'd grown up with here were dangerous. The chickens might peck and the billy goats might butt if they were in rut or feeling ornery. But this puppy looked absolutely harmless. Its tail whacked against Noah's small chest as I approached.

"Yep, it's just a baby."

As much as I wanted to pat its silky hair, I held back. Just hours ago, *they* had held it.

"Ah, so this is where you've gone," Dad called out, pushing a wheelbarrow toward the barn. "My missing helper. You were supposed to scatter seeds with me."

It was early August, and Dad had been planting winter crops. Kale, carrots, spinach, beets, turnips. His shirtsleeves were rolled back, and he was tanned, muscled, and sweaty. His hands were mapped with dirt. He'd shed weight since we'd arrived. Not that he'd been overweight before, but everything on his frame now was necessary. He'd grown a beard, mainly because we'd run out of razors long ago. He was kind of like Pa in those *Little House on the Prairie* books, except he wasn't crazy and moving on all the time. Dad knew how to plow and build a fence. He talked about crop yields, the best way to store pulses.

I guess I did, too.

You, Xavier Oak, have become a farmer.

When I checked myself in the mirror after a shower, I liked how I could see the ridges of my arms and stomach. I never thought I'd have a body like this, but I had no one to show it to. No one who'd admire it, anyway.

Noah still had a softness to him because he was only three, but even he was expected to help out around the farm. He dug up onions and washed off beets, but sometimes he got bored and wandered off to visit the chickens or the goats. He'd spent so much time with Surly, one of the spring kids, that the goats thought he was part of the herd and bleated for him when he wasn't there.

"Daddy, look!" Noah said, turning so our father could see the puppy properly.

"Wow! Look at that."

My father's first question was the same as mine. We exchanged a knowing look. Unseen, *they'd* come and gone through some door we'd never been able to find.

Almost all the things they'd left had been for Noah. Only days after his birth, a pile of baby clothes and a mobile for his crib had appeared. Later: rattles, things he could chew when he started teething, cloth books, then plush toys. A year ago there was a large plastic barn that opened to reveal stalls filled with horses, pigs, sheep, and what I called the "mistake animal"—a melty concoction that maybe was meant to be a farmer or a cow, but had gone terribly wrong. Perversely, it had become Noah's favorite. He even had a name for it: Rumpety.

"Doesn't it creep you out," I'd asked Dad and Nia a while back, "how they keep giving him stuff?"

Nia shrugged. "How else would he get toys?"

There were still plenty of toys kicking around the cottage from Sam and me.

"They certainly take a special interest in him," Dad admitted.

"First born in captivity," I'd muttered.

Nia said, "Don't talk about him like that."

"Like what?"

"Like he's a zoo animal."

"Aren't we all?" I said.

The puppy squirmed in Noah's arms and gave a few yips.

"Is it a boy or a girl?" he asked.

Dad checked. "Boy."

"He's for my birthday!" Noah said, putting his cheek against the puppy's head.

It was, in fact, Noah's birthday today.

Dad chuckled. "Quite a birthday present."

When I was little, before all this, when my parents were still together, I used to ask Dad for a dog and the answer was always no: too much work, he'd end up looking after it himself, it would tie us down. I guess we couldn't be any more tied down than we were now. Still, it was a bit nauseating how easily Noah had scored himself a dog.

"Might be a good idea, having a dog around," Dad said. "Watch over the chickens."

I raised my eyebrows sardonically. The chickens didn't need watching. There were no coyotes or foxes here, no predators at all, not even for the crops. We'd never seen beetles, weevils, or locusts. The only insects were the bees, who did all the pollinating and gave us honey as a bonus. We barely needed to weed. It was the perfect farm for idiot city people. It always rained just enough, usually overnight. The winters were mild. The soil seemed to replenish itself naturally and needed no fertilizer. Having enough food had never been a problem, though it changed how we ate. We were basically vegetarians, except for meat on special occasions, like tonight, when Noah had asked for duck.

"This dog's the only thing that might hurt the chickens," I sniffed.

"Nah," Dad said, patting the puppy. "We'll introduce him early."

"Is he from Erf?" Noah asked.

It had been impossible to keep Earth a secret from him. For a while, Nia had wanted us to pretend that we'd always lived here. She felt he'd be happier if he thought this was all there was. That this was *completely normal*. But he was a smart kid, and we'd all slipped up enough times that he'd figured out there was an "Up Here" and an "On Erf."

Up Here hadn't been easy for the rest of us to accept. But after three years, after all that had happened, it was the only explanation that made any sense to us.

We'd been abducted by aliens.

It sounded ridiculous when you said it like that. Maybe: We had been "acquired by beings with vastly superior intelligence and technology" who had taken us off planet. Where exactly? Who knew? We had been placed in a biodome with a diameter of about ten kilometers, and a circumference of thirty-two. You could walk all the way around in six or seven hours. Why had we been put here? No idea, though of course we had theories.

They seemed kindly, as far as kidnappers or prison wardens went. When we'd tried to tunnel through their wall, they could have electrocuted us, or crushed Dad, but they hadn't. They just burped him back out. When Nia gave birth, they could have let Noah die. But they'd saved him and given him presents.

"I don't think the puppy's from Erf," I told Noah. As much as they liked Noah, I doubted they'd travel across the universe just to grab him a puppy. "There are other animals Up Here."

This was what we assumed anyway, after our billy goat Herk had appeared in the pasture one morning during our first autumn. When Nia had seen him, she'd said:

"Right on schedule. Thank goodness."

"Why?" I'd asked.

"The females don't keep making milk forever, Zay. They need to get pregnant and have kids."

"Oh. Right." And I'd blushed. I'd never actually thought about it, even with Nia nursing Noah.

Since then, I'd done my fair share taking care of baby goats. I could even help deliver kids, which was not something I'd ever imagined putting on my résumé.

I looked at the adorable puppy in Noah's arms.

"You're taking care of him," I told him.

"I know!"

"Let's see how long that lasts," I muttered to Dad.

Truthfully, I was pretty excited about having a puppy around. I still hadn't patted him yet, and couldn't resist anymore. I touched the warm hair below his throat. It was like remembering something from long ago. My eyes prickled with tears. *Erf.* The puppy licked me, then bit me. It was a harmless puppy's bite with its milk teeth, but it was just sharp enough to make a point. Noah's dog.

"He likes you, Zay!" Noah said.

When Noah was being born he got stuck and came out the wrong way, tangled up in the umbilical cord. He wasn't breathing; he didn't have a heartbeat.

They must have been watching, because they put us all to sleep instantly, entered the cottage, and saved Noah's life. Whether they did it right there in the room or took Noah away somewhere, we didn't know. Nor did we know how long we'd all been knocked out. They'd taken the time to change the bloody sheets, which was very considerate. None of us had seen them, none of us knew how they'd brought Noah back to life, and we didn't care. All Dad and I remembered was waking up dazed and seeing the baby alive and healthy. Then Nia had stirred and opened her eyes and we'd all cried with relief, hugged one another, and kissed the baby's good-smelling head.

In the kitchen, Nia was preparing a lunch for us to take to the pond. Noah got to pick what we did on his birthday, and he'd chosen a picnic and a swim.

"What on earth!" Nia said when she saw the puppy in Noah's arms.

"A mystery gift," Dad explained.

"Ah." She brushed back a strand of dark hair that had escaped her ponytail. It was much curlier now, she'd said, because she'd forgotten her straightener that long-ago weekend. "Well, he's adorable."

Noah put the puppy down, and he skittered around everyone's feet and was so excited he peed on the floor.

"He's not potty trained yet!" Noah said.

"I can see that," said Nia. "Which means you, sir, have a new job." She told him to get a rag to clean up.

"Fair's fair," Noah said cheerfully as he mopped up after his new pet.

By the sink were the two ducks Nia had snared a few days ago and aged in the fridge. They were plucked but still had their heads on. We never killed the chickens because we needed their eggs, and also got pretty attached to them. They all had names. Same with the goats, but we did eat them from time to time. After two breeding seasons, we had too many to look after, and more than enough milk.

At first, none of us had known how to butcher them. We had no internet to rely on, so we'd gone through the cottage top to bottom, searching for anything useful. Luckily, like most cottages, ours had acquired its fair share of weird books. Under a stack of ancient *National Geographic*s we found the 1982 *Old Farmer's Almanac* and, the real prize, a book called *How to Live on Almost Nothing and Have Plenty*. Maybe it had always been there, even before Mom and Dad bought the cottage. On Erf, it was the kind of book I wouldn't have read in a million years.

Up Here, we'd all read it, cover to cover.

It told you how to do things like save enough seeds for next season and humanely kill and prepare livestock. There was a section about goats and how, if you planned to eat the males, you needed to castrate them first, or their meat tasted awful. Castrating them wasn't as hard as I thought. You needed to put really tight rubber bands around their testicles, and eventually they just fell off. The goats didn't seem too bothered about it, honestly.

Nia had turned out to be the best at butchering—no surprise with that homesteading experience of hers. She would take a goat out behind the barn, out of sight of the other goats. With the blunt end of a hatchet, she'd knock it out, hang it up by its hind legs, and slit its throat. She'd figured out how to skin it, like peeling off a wet rubber glove. The first time I'd seen her do it, I threw up. But later I gratefully ate the meat.

"Take this," Nia said, handing Noah the egg timer. "Turn it to one hour, and when it dings, you take the puppy outside to go to the bathroom."

"Where?"

"He'll pick a place. Just make sure you take him to the same place each time."

"Okay!"

"I think we need to make a leash," Dad said.

"Good idea," said Nia. "Now, please keep him out of here while I prepare these ducks. And then we can go swimming."

There were some things that were surprisingly easy to get used to:

No sugar.

We just added honey to things now.

No toilet paper.

It ran out within a week. Luckily, the 1982 *Farmer's Almanac* had an article about pioneer life, and mentioned corn husks. So we always had a big store of corn husks in the bathroom. We cut them into small pieces to make them last longer. We became very frugal wipers.

No hamburgers.

Not that we ate much beef in the old days, but sometimes I still had a craving for a burger smothered with pickles and mustard and grilled mushrooms and cheddar and ketchup. But going without wasn't too bad.

And then there were some things that were a bit harder to get used to:

Goat's milk.

When I first drank it, I couldn't really find the words to describe it. *Goaty* kept coming to mind, which wasn't very helpful. It was fine once we learned how to make it into cheese, or used it as an ingredient in something. It took some time, though, before I could drink it fresh without wincing. Noah had never known plant-based or cow's milk, so for him it was wonderful.

No school.

I'd never been Mr. Popularity, but I'd liked school. I was good at my classes and I missed the ragtag group of urban Hobbits I called my friends.

And then there were things that I *still* hadn't gotten used to:

No internet.

This meant no email, no messaging, no finding things out, no solving arguments at the dinner table, and no cheating at Scrabble. The hardest part was feeling cut off from everyone I knew, from a bigger world, from Erf. Wherever it was.

No sex.

True, I had never had sex, but it didn't stop me thinking about it every day. I'd imagined an alternate history in which I'd gone over to Serena's house to watch *Metropolis* and halfway through we'd started making out like maniacs. The reality was I hadn't ever been kissed and never would be. I'd go through my life without anyone falling in love with me, and I'd get old and die.

No gaming.

After no sex, this might seem trivial. But gaming was a huge part of my life. My imaginary life anyway—and when you thought about it, wasn't your imaginary life still part of your *real* life? You could have all the same emotions and thoughts in your imaginary life as your so-called real life. I'd written a small new D&D campaign—I'd brought my *Player's Handbook* and *Monster Manual* with me—and Dad and Nia said they'd give it a try, but I could tell they were just humoring me and their hearts weren't in it. No one would ever play with me the same way my friends did, and without other devoted players, what was the point?

Sometimes, as I did my chores, I'd think, *We've accumulated lots of experience points. We've learned how to farm and raise goats and chickens, we know how to can fruits and vegetables. We take care of bees and make wine. We should have leveled up by now.* But one thing we'd absolutely failed to do was find a way out of here.

And there were two things I'd *never* get used to:

No Mom.

She was brave when Dad had left. She held it all together. She always thought about me and Sam first. She never trash-talked Dad, and told us we needed to spend alternate weeks with him at his new condo, even when we'd rather have stayed with her. She spent a ton of time listening to us talk about ourselves. Thinking back on it, I probably never asked much about her. Every night she'd set the table nicely and light candles. She always made a big fuss on our birthdays. Every special day she went all out: Thanksgiving, Christmas—even Pancake Tuesday; she'd get out Mardi Gras masks and bead necklaces and flip a pancake in the air. Even though Sam and I thought it was kind of corny, we would've missed it. She baked huge batches of chocolate chip cookies and froze them so we never ran out.

When I couldn't sleep, I often wondered where she thought I was right now. Did she think I'd abandoned her for Dad? Just taken off forever? It made me twist inside to think how devastated she'd feel. Or maybe she thought we were dead. Which was also terrible. At least she still had Sam.

Which was the last thing I'd never get used to:

No Sam.

I had other friends, but Sam was my best. I'm not sure if I was his—he was super popular—but that didn't matter. I'd rather have done stuff with him than anyone else. When I was back on Erf, Sam had just gotten his probationary driver's license. We'd go for drives, just the two of us. Maybe we'd pick up hamburgers and go up the mountain, or down to the old harbor or somewhere along the canal. And we'd talk. About everything. Our fears. Girls we had crushes on.

Victories and defeats. How we felt about Nia and Dad and Mom. I missed that all so much. When Noah was driving me crazy, I still texted Sam. When I hated Nia, I imagined Sam listening to me vent.

On my phone I still had all the music he'd given me, but I'd never have Sam again.

I could get used to a lot of things . . . but not everything.

It was a good half-hour walk from our cottage to the pond and we took turns carrying the puppy. ("We can't leave him all alone!" Noah had said.) We set out our towels on a nice stretch of grassy bank and Dad tied the leash around a tree. Noah couldn't really swim yet, but it never stopped him from hurling himself into water over his head. I jumped in after him and fished him out. He came up gasping and thrashing, a delighted smile on his face.

"You maniac!" I said.

I had to keep my eye on him. Luckily there was a good shallow bit near the bank where he could stand. Nia made him wear an old pair of my floaties and practice his doggy paddle and treading water.

We were all hot from the walk, so we had a swim first and horsed around. Nia was eleven years younger than Dad, and distractingly pretty in her bathing suit. I looked away. It bothered me that I'd seen her bare breasts when she'd nursed Noah. And then I felt angry that I'd never see anyone else's breasts. When I got out of the water, I stretched out on my towel and tried to empty my head. Over the last three years I felt like I'd spent a lot of time sandblasting away anger, resentment, or sadness.

It was a good thing so much of our lives here was spent outdoors. The cottage was tiny. It was meant to be lived in for a weekend, or maybe a week, tops. We were four people now, with just one bathroom, which, until not so long ago, usually smelled like ripe cloth diapers. Even now Noah sometimes wet the bed and the smell would wake me up. After he'd outgrown his crib, he'd started sharing my room and took my lower bunk; I moved up to Sam's. There was not a lot of space to be alone.

I put on my headphones and closed my eyes. Thank God for Sam's music. The first time I'd heard "Bizarre Love Triangle," the staccato opening notes and barrage of percussion had lit up my entire nervous system. It was like the music had been specially created to socket with my brain. Every time I listened to it, the ground fell away, and I was levitating.

Pathetic as it was, in the last three years, my most intense and satisfying emotional experiences had been through music. I felt like I'd fallen in love a dozen times and had my heart broken just as many. I yearned. I told girls they were my sun and aurora. I wanted nights to last forever. I had existential crises. I took good things and screwed them up. I lost my soul and found it as I walked home.

I texted Sam:

even after 1000x, BLT is still so good

(Not delivered.)

thanx for putting it on my phone

(Not delivered.)

I have the best alien abduction playlist

(Not delivered.)

I knew my texts weren't going anywhere, but it made me feel a tiny bit less lonely, like I still had someone to share my feelings with.

I got through two more songs before my phone died. The battery was so old that it only held a charge for about half an hour. I didn't like to think about when it died for good. All my music and pictures, all my one-way conversations with Sam, gone forever.

8

I ate my roast duck, which was very good, and my sweet potato mash, which was also very good. The beets and beans: excellent. Dad let me have some wine. He'd started making it the first autumn we were here. The thing about grapes, he'd said, is that they practically want to become wine. After three years, the stuff he made was still not great (not that I was any expert; I was just going by what Dad said). But it was better than no wine. I drained my glass and poured myself another.

The puppy yipped and scooted around under the table, wanting to be picked up.

"Can he sleep with us tonight?" Noah asked.

"He'll whine all night," I said. It was enough I had to share my room with Noah.

"We'll make a crate for him in the kitchen," Nia said.

Nia had made Noah's favorite apple-and-pear cake, and lit three of the stubby candles still kicking around. We sang "Happy Birthday," and Noah looked so delighted that my heart softened a bit.

We gave him his gifts. Dad had made him a full set of wooden D&D dice. A twenty-sided, four-sided, eight-sided, ten-sided, and twelve-sided. They were larger than the plastic ones because our woodworking tools weren't very precise, but he'd obviously spent a lot of time on them. He'd done a great job etching the numbers into the sides.

Noah had become obsessed with D&D and kept asking me to play. I made excuses:

It's too complicated.

Maybe when you're older.

We don't even have the right dice.

Which was now no longer true.

Thanks, Dad.

I gave Noah an old slingshot of mine. I'd seen him playing with it, even though the strap was broken. So I'd fixed it up with two thick rubber bands and a new pouch.

"Thanks, Zay!"

He looked so grateful that I felt guilty. It was kind of a lame present, and one of the reasons I'd given it to him was just to see Nia's reaction. She did not approve of anything that might be called a weapon.

"That is very cool," she said, "but is it okay if I hold on to it for you?" This was not a question, and Noah looked crestfallen. "You can use it when Dad or I are with you."

I felt sorry for Noah, so I impulsively said, "And you know what else you get from me? We are going to make you your very own D&D character. Now that we have some dice."

Noah actually threw himself at me, and I hugged him back, wishing I were a better person.

When we finished eating cake, Dad said, "Let's say what we're thankful for."

I was hoping he'd forget this part. He'd started doing this our first Thanksgiving at the farm, and it had spread to birthdays and other special days. I knew it was supposed to boost our morale, keep us focused on the good things. But like all Jedi mind tricks, it only worked on the weak-minded. I didn't feel thankful at all. We took each other's hands—another part of this cringey new tradition. Erf Dad wouldn't have started something like this.

"I'm thankful for Kimmy!" said Noah, who had apparently just named the puppy.

Dad said, "And I'm thankful we're together. Because that's what home is, being together with the people you love. Doesn't matter where you are, as long as you're together."

I took another big swallow of wine and said, "What about Sam?"

I saw Dad's chest rise and fall.

"You know, your other son?" I reminded him.

I didn't expect him to mention Mom—even though she was still part of *my* family—but it was garbage to talk about togetherness without bringing up Sam.

Calmly, Dad said, "I love Sam, and I miss him more than anything. But I'm also very happy he is where he is."

"Where is he?" Noah asked.

"He lives somewhere else," Nia said.

"On Erf?"

"On Erf," I said.

"We could visit him!" said Noah. He knew that we used to live somewhere else, but he didn't know how we got here, or why we couldn't get out, or that we would die here.

"Fantastic idea," I said, pouring another glass of wine and turning to Dad and Nia. "Should we visit?"

Dad gave me a cautioning look.

"A road trip!" I said. "Just a little toodle back to old Erf?"

"Well, I'm thankful it's shaping up to be another great harvest," Nia said. "And to be here with all of you, safe and healthy." She gazed at Noah, then made sure to give me a quick smile to remind me that I was being a total dick, but she was being tolerant. "You guys are the best family anyone could wish for."

The puppy skidded against my leg and had a quick chew on my sneaker before moving on.

"How about you, Zay?" Noah asked.

"I'm thankful," I said, "that our zookeepers are so nice to us. They're the best."

Noah didn't get it. "What zookeepers?"

"The dudes who gave you the puppy."

"Zay's just being silly," Nia said.

"Amazing, isn't it," I said, "the way stuff just turns up for you?"

"Someone's had too much wine," Nia said to my father.

I took another slug before Dad reached for my glass. I didn't let go right away, and some wine spilled onto my plate.

"Ah, such a waste," I said. "A particularly fine vintage."

"Tonight let's focus on the good things," Dad said firmly.

"Agreed, sir," I said. "Will make efforts to improve!"

"What's so great about Erf anyway?" Noah asked, his forehead creased.

"Absolutely nothing," Nia told him. "We have everything we need right here."

I waited until Noah was asleep, then quietly got dressed. I checked that my phone had recharged, grabbed the binoculars, and was about to slide the window open when I heard Dad and Nia talking quietly. It was easy to hear things between rooms, especially if you pressed your ear to the wall.

". . . sixteen years old," Dad was saying. "He's full of hormones, and there's nowhere for them to go."

"Well, he needs to figure it out."

Figure it out?

"He's got a lot to be angry about, Nia."

"He'd better not take it out on Noah."

"He's good to him. They're good together."

"You have to talk to him; he won't take it from me. I'm not his mom."

"He knows that, Nia. It's another thing he's lost."

I heard Nia exhale. "You're right."

"We're lucky. We have each other. Who's he going to have?"

There was a pause. She said, "It's terrible. Poor Noah. He'll never have a partner or children." It sounded like she was crying. "What if he ends up all alone, the last person here?"

Poor Noah.

I opened the window and hoisted myself outside.

Our first year here, we'd tried everything.

We'd mapped our entire landscape, divided it into a grid, and scoured each square for exits. All this took a lot of time. Could we have missed something? Of course. But we couldn't spend all our time searching. Dad and Nia had a new baby. We all had a new farm. Goats! Chickens! There was always a ton to do, especially that first year, when we barely knew what we were doing.

We'd also tried to capture *them* on video. Nia's phone, which was the newest, would take about five hours of video before the battery died. We'd set up our phones in all sorts of locations: the hayloft doors, strapped to the trunk of a tree. Sometimes during the day, sometimes at night. Afterward we'd review the footage. Hoping to see *them*. Whoever they were. Whatever they were.

Once, something with horns lurched into view and we all screamed, but it turned out it was just Herk, who'd somehow gotten loose. He tried to eat the phone but gave up.

Even the times *they* had dropped off gifts for Noah, our cameras were never in the right place.

We'd also tried to scale the wall. I'd had the idea of hammering a series of platforms into it. We'd bang in wood pegs, then lay a couple planks across them. We'd climb onto the planks, haul the ladder up after us, climb the ladder, and build another platform. We could just keep doing this until we reached the top. Like a *Mario Bros.* game. I figured the wooden pegs and planks wouldn't bother the wall too much, or give us electric shocks.

It started out great.

But on the fourth platform we noticed something. Each platform overhung the one below by a little bit. From the highest, Dad dropped a weighted line to the ground. It touched down about two feet from the base of the wall.

Which meant the wall was gradually curving inward. It was pointless building more platforms. After a while they'd slide right off the wall. Dad did the math. Assuming the wall kept curving at the same rate, it would form a perfect semicircle over us.

Our own little snow globe.

That had been a bad day.

We'd already had to accept a lot of hard things. We'd been moved. We'd been imprisoned. Now we had to accept that we were utterly *enclosed*.

It meant the sun and moon, the stars and constellations, were all fake.

Maybe it shouldn't have mattered. But it really did.

If this was some kind of game, they were winning.

Our objective, to escape, had failed over and over again.

Dad and Nia had given up on finding a way out, but I hadn't.

My head ached slightly from the wine, and I hoped the night air would clear it. We still called it night even though we knew it was just stars projected on a giant dome. Who knew what time it was on the other side? But even if the stars and moon were fake, their light wasn't, and when I was in the open, I didn't need the flashlight. Where I was going was only about a twenty-minute walk. Maybe it was stupid, but I thought that at night I might catch something we'd missed in the daytime. Light coming from a hidden cave or a hatch in the trunk of a tree. Maybe I'd actually spot *them* and they'd lead me to their secret portal.

I wasn't scared of them, not anymore. Maybe I should've been. But they'd had three years to dissect us, or eat us, or turn us into batteries to power their tech. So far they seemed happy to let us farm.

Just keep farming, little humans—what joy it gives us!

I reached my tree and climbed up. Near the top I'd made a perfect spot where

I could sit securely against the trunk. I'd sawed away just enough branches to have a sweeping view of our domed world.

Lately I'd been thinking a lot about that fake sky, wondering if there were openings way up there. Our air had to come from somewhere. The clouds were real. It rained. Sometimes there was fog. Wind. Winter mornings we occasionally woke up to frost. There had to be tons of machinery somewhere, creating our atmosphere—and pumping it through vents in the sky.

And if there were holes, maybe light sometimes shone through them—because who said it was even night on the other side?—and that light would be easier to spot in the dark.

Or maybe I just needed something to do, so I wouldn't lose my mind.

It was probably all the gaming. Always needing to find a way in or out. Doors were everything. They made a promise to you: *There's something on the other side, something that might change your life.* When I gamed, I could get into castles and escape from dungeons, swim a river out of a cave system or parachute down the chimney of an underground city.

I got out my binoculars. The moon was high tonight and looked bigger than usual, probably because it was so bright. Sometimes I studied a specific part of the sky with my binoculars; other times I just let my naked gaze go wide, waiting for something.

Why us? It was always with me, that question. We weren't farmers. We were city people who happened to have a cottage. If it hadn't been for those two books we'd found, we might've starved. Or maybe *they* wouldn't have let that happen. Still, why choose *us* to subsistence farm in a dome? Was it totally random?

It was a mistake to think of this as a game. We were no closer to understanding the rules or the objectives of our opponents. I wasn't sure there were any. I'd get old here and wear manure-stained clothes and talk to goats.

I wondered why they even bothered with this fake sky. They must've known we'd figure it out pretty fast. Why not just go for it, show us where we really were?

New suns and stars in startling new constellations? Maybe a black hole boiling in the distance?

Had they thought the fake sky would make it easier for us when we first arrived? Give us time to get used to our new life? Now it just made me angry. This was not the same moon that Sam or Mom were looking at.

The moon. I squinted at a small, dark shape I'd just noticed in its face.

I focused my binoculars. The moon had lots of ridges and pockmarks. But these particular edges were very precise. This was an intentional shape, almost a perfect hexagon. I put my phone against the binoculars, braced myself against a branch, and took some pictures.

A shape could mean some kind of hatch.

A doorway in the moon.

No: a doorway in the dome's ceiling. The shape stayed in the same place as the moon slowly glided over it. I made a note of the time, tried to fix some reference points on the tree and ground, so I'd be able to find the shape again. Then I stared at it through the binoculars until the moon passed over it entirely and I couldn't see it anymore.

9

"Dad. I found a way out!"

I was whispering, hoping to wake just him, but Nia opened her eyes, too. I was sweaty from the run back, vibrating with excitement. Nia said we should go to the family room so we wouldn't wake Noah.

Dad and Nia sat down on the sofa. Nia stroked Kimmy on her lap to calm him down and keep him quiet. I was too wired to sit. My voice trembled as I told them what I'd seen. Dad rubbed the back of his neck. His first question surprised me.

"How long have you been going out at night?"

"A while."

"Every night?"

"Some nights. When the moon's bright enough."

He didn't seem at all excited. More than anything he looked concerned.

"I don't want you climbing that tree at night, Zay. It's not safe."

"I've done it a hundred times—"

"If you fell—" Nia said.

"I'm not gonna fall."

"Listen to me," she insisted. "Someone gets injured here, even a broken bone, we're in real trouble."

Since we'd been here, no one had even had a cold. We were always healthy.

"They'd just fix us, wouldn't they?" I said.

"I don't think we should count on it," my father replied.

"Dad! I. Found. A. Hole. In. The. Sky!"

He sighed. "Did you get any pictures?"

Finally, a real question. I dragged out my phone. "It makes sense. There's got to be ventilation, right? Ways of pumping in air, making weather?"

"True, but . . ." He and Nia were looking at my pictures, zooming in as much as they could before it became a grainy mess. "The moon's pretty scratched up. Hard to say what we're looking at."

I had to admit, the pictures were not impressive.

Dad said, "Let's suppose it's up there—"

"It is!"

"—at a height of five kilometers—"

"That's a guess."

"We did the math, Zay," said Nia. "Five kilometers straight up."

"Only at its highest point. This wasn't right overhead."

"We will never reach it."

The certainty in her voice stopped me for a second. I sat down.

"There must be a way to get up there!"

"If it's a door, it can open and close," Nia said. "And if it's made of the same stuff as the wall? We've seen what happens when we try to break through."

"Maybe this hatch is always open."

"Okay, let's work through this together," Dad said.

I looked at him warily. Nia always came out with all guns blazing, but Dad was more a soft power guy. He was quiet, a good listener; he'd ask questions rather than telling you what he thought. He wore you down with persistence and conviction.

"Imagine," he went on, "that you can get up there to this hatch. Imagine it's open. What do you do?"

"I go through the hatch!"

"You find yourself on a beautiful alien planet. The atmosphere is toxic, and you die in a matter of minutes."

I wasn't sure if he was doing it intentionally, but he was talking like a Dungeon Master, and I resented it.

"Okay, let's just back up," I said. "I'd look around for a space suit or something first."

"Nothing fits you. But okay, let's say you're free on an alien planet, the atmosphere is a perfect match, you can breathe the air. Even better, parked nearby is something that looks like a spaceship."

"I go inside and find a cockpit."

"You find it and sit down at the controls."

I felt foolish now. "I fly the spaceship."

"You have no idea how to fly this spaceship."

"I take an alien hostage and make him fly it for me."

"They say no."

"Who says we're even on a planet?" I could feel myself getting angry. "We might already be on a spaceship, or an orbital station."

"Same situation. How's your celestial navigation? Can you find your way back to Earth?"

"So we're not even going to try?"

"Here's what I've learned these past three years," Dad said. "Whoever is keeping us here, they have no intention of letting us go. They're smarter than us."

"We don't know that."

"C'mon, Zay. We know."

He was right, but it wouldn't settle with me. "You're lame."

"Zay."

"This is bullshit. I show you a way out and you just yawn and say *don't bother*. So goddamn lame."

I'd never talked to my father like this. Dad looked at me and said, "What you want is impossible. There's no point wishing for the impossible. We have a good home here."

"This is not home, not for me. How about Mom and Sam? They're probably still looking for us."

"If they're still alive."

It was like getting smacked in the face by the invisible wall all over again. "What d'you mean?"

"Come on, Caleb," Nia said.

But Dad kept going. "Who knows how far away we are. How long it took us to get here." He paused. "Decades?"

I imagined Mom and Sam back on Earth, wilting like plants.

"You never thought of that?" he asked gently.

"No."

I was supposed to be so good at running scenarios, solving problems. This had never occurred to me.

Dad put his hands on my shoulders, but I shrugged them off and walked away.

In my bedroom I texted Sam.

Dad said you might be 100 now, so I'm picturing you limping around on a walker. I, on the other hand, am 16 and totally ripped

(Not delivered.)

I could prob bench press you

(Not delivered.)

I miss you

(Not delivered.)

This sucks

(Not delivered.)

You were the best big brother

(Not delivered.)

I realized I'd written *were* instead of *are*—like I'd already accepted he was past tense. Then my phone died. I plugged it in and climbed into my bunk.

"Zay?" Noah asked below me. "Are you crying?"

"No," I told him. "Go back to sleep."

They let me sleep late.

When I opened my eyes, the room was already filled with sunlight, and Noah was sitting expectantly on the floor surrounded by my D&D manuals and his new dice. He'd even made his own piece of graph paper with wildly crooked lines. A couple stubby pencils rested nearby.

"Let's make my character!"

"I need to do chores."

"Mom and Dad said you have the day off."

Noah could call them Mom and Dad and not feel weird. But I already had a mom. A brother, too. I let my head drop to my pillow.

A hole in the sky that we'd never reach.

And if we reached it and it was closed, we'd never get through.

And if we got through, we'd never get home.

And if we got home, everyone we loved might be dead anyway, or the planet frizzled up like Mars because of climate change.

If Dad and Nia were right, there would never be *On Erf* for us.

There would only be *Up Here*.

From the kitchen I heard the familiar hiss of the pressure canner and remembered that Dad and Nia were doing preserves today. It was a lulling, comforting sound. I must've dozed off again.

"Zay?"

I opened one eye and looked down at Noah. How long had he been sitting there? He was so impatient and excited he couldn't keep his legs still. In his shorts and T-shirt he was all knees and elbows.

"All right," I said, "let's do it."

I heaved myself down the ladder. I didn't have anyone to compare him to, but I was pretty sure Noah was precocious. Maybe farm kids just grew up faster because of all their chores. More likely it was being around adults (plus a teenager) all the time—*and* Nia's rigorous homeschooling. Or maybe the kid was just a super fast learner. He had a pretty great vocabulary and could already read and write simple words, and do some adding.

He had the *Player's Handbook* open, with his finger planted on a picture of a Viking brandishing a huge sword.

"I want *him*."

"Well, first we have to roll for your abilities, right? You need to be strong to be a fighter."

"I'm strong!"

"But if it turns out you're super intelligent and dexterous, you might want to be a magic user or a thief."

His finger had not left the picture. "He's best."

I sat down on the floor and moved my phone out of the way. The screen didn't light up, which was weird because it had been charging for hours. I tapped the screen: still nothing.

"Did you mess with my phone?" I said, which was unfair because I could see it was still plugged in.

"No!"

It should've had some battery by now. But I wasn't even seeing the charging icon. Maybe it was my cable. I grabbed my phone and walked out.

"Where you going?" Noah called.

I went into Dad and Nia's room and plugged it into his charger. I sat on the edge of the bed, foot pumping against the floor, waiting for my screen to light up. It didn't.

"Shit!"

"What's wrong?" asked Nia, appearing in the doorway.

"My phone's dead!"

"Maybe it just needs long—"

"It's had plenty of time."

I'd been starting to have trouble holding clear images of Mom and Sam in my head. Without my photos and videos, how was I supposed to remember how they sounded and moved and smiled?

Noah appeared beside his mother, clutching the *Player's Handbook*. "Zay, you promised!"

"Maybe it's your charger," Nia said. "Do you want to try—"

"It's not the charger! It's the battery! It's dead!" I glanced at my phone just in case. Still dark. I thrust it toward her. "See!"

"Zay, try taking a breath."

"Don't tell me to take a breath!"

"Guys, guys," Noah was saying, patting the air with his hands.

"Shut up, Noah!"

"Hey," said Nia.

How was I supposed to write to Sam now? I knew those texts never reached him. But it made a difference, writing those words, imagining them oscillating through the universe toward him. Toward home.

Very calmly, like she was reciting a script, she said, "I can tell you're really upset. I get it. Music's important to me, too. But look, I've got a pretty nifty selection on my phone—"

"I don't want your old-people songs. I want *my* music!"

All the songs that had helped get me through the last three years. The songs that let me feel things—or *pretend* to feel things—that I'd never get to experience here, inside this cottage, this dome where I'd spend the rest of my life.

"That really sucks," Nia said. "You must feel super disappointed."

"Oh my God, stop trying to empathize with me!"

Her face hardened. "It was going to happen sooner or later, Zay."

I glared at her. "And thanks to *you*, none of us brought a laptop, so I couldn't even back up my songs and photos! So we could *decompress*. Are we decompressed enough now, Nia?"

"We can still do D&D," Noah said.

"Shut the fuck up, Noah!" I yelled.

"Zay, cool it!" Nia warned.

I pushed past them and left the cottage through the front door so I could slam it. Three times. I wanted to bang the house down. They had no idea how important that phone was to me. It was my journal, my heart's pacemaker, my memory vault, and it had been cracked open and everything was lost.

10

I walked and raged and cried myself out.

Then I went back and apologized to everyone.

But that night I couldn't sleep. My sadness was too big for the room. I felt like I was suffocating in my bunk. I got dressed and slipped outside. Didn't bring anything with me this time, no binoculars or flashlight. I just needed to be outside. I wandered to the edge of the orchard. Our little Garden of Eden.

I tried not to do the if-onlys, but what the hell. If only I'd stayed home that weekend, like Sam. If only I'd gone to Serena's instead. If only I'd told Dad no, I wasn't coming to the cottage this weekend, and hadn't let him calmly talk me into it, like an anaconda adding one coil after another to its prey. He'd told me how much he looked forward to our weekends. He said we'd get ice cream at Moo's and sit on the dock. He said that Sam and I would be part of his life forever, but Nia was part of his life now, too, and he wanted all of us to get along and be a family, especially when we had a little brother on the way.

Well, here we all were (minus Sam) and I was supposed to be grateful for what we had. It was easy for Dad and Nia—they had each other. It was easy for Noah; he had two parents, and thought this was the best place in the world, and didn't know what his future was going to be like. I did.

I took a piss against the trunk of an apple tree.

"You guys watching up there? Is it viewing time at the zoo?"

I yanked an apple from a low branch and whipped it at the moon.

"Assholes."

A spark flew from the moon's face. As it fell, it expanded, then fractured into many smaller lights, traveling together like a vast flock of birds, knotting then unraveling across the night sky. The lights divided again, then again, becoming ever smaller. I felt nailed to the ground. They were coming closer. Swiftly and soundlessly they passed high overhead like a blazing swarm of midges. They headed southeast, then dipped below the trees.

In three years, we'd never seen them. Was this even *them*? These tiny things? Or were these just machines? Whatever they were, they were inside with us now. I ran after them. My head was empty, except for the desire to catch up.

I bolted through fields and woods. Even though the moon was big, I stumbled and had branches whipping me. Above the tree line I saw the glow from the midges' light. For maybe fifteen minutes I ran, until I smelled warm sawdust.

Through the trees, the glow was brighter. I made my way carefully to the edge of a big clearing. It was blanketed with a brilliant white mist, which I realized wasn't mist at all, but a million midges hovering low over the ground. They emitted a faint, distinctive hum. Now, in a mass, the midges lifted into the air, coalesced into a single light, and disappeared like a bulb that had blinked out.

My heart knocked hard against my ribs. I leaned against a tree trunk, trying to slow my breathing. The midges seemed to have cleared this huge space of trees, tall grass, even rocks. Cautiously, I stepped out from the woods. Long stretches of earth had been neatly furrowed. Other sections were marked off with regularly spaced holes that seemed to await fence posts.

Near the center of the clearing was what looked like a concrete pad. I tapped it with the toe of my shoe, then walked onto it. Little trenches and pipe-sized holes had been sunk into the surface. I figured the pad matched the footprint of a small house. Not too far away I spotted a second foundation, barn-sized. As I turned full circle, it seemed to me that the layout was almost exactly the same as our farm's.

Suddenly the clearing was brighter than daylight. Squinting up through my hand, I saw a huge cloud of midges, busily fusing together. Their faint hum now became the buzz of an angry hornet's nest. Heat wafted off them.

Within seconds they'd formed themselves into an airborne anvil, spanning the entire clearing. It lowered swiftly, its underside bristling with tapered needles. I started to run, but they stabbed down around me, blocking my escape. I dodged as they jabbed and swirled in bewildering patterns, retracted, then plunged again. There were so many of them, and no way through. I cowered, covering my head.

Nothing impaled me. I peeked out. The needles were jetting out a maze of lines onto the concrete pad, layer after layer, all sorts of different textures and colors. I shouted as a pair of needles nudged me roughly to one side, and a third needle stabbed down where I'd just been, spraying a layer of what looked like wood.

A floor was being built, then tiled. I was shunted again. The needles were a frenzy of movement. A chrome disc was sprayed on the floor and before I could blink, it grew into a dog's bowl, filled with whisker-flecked water. I watched cabinets rise from the floor, along with a dishwasher and oven. I saw inside a big refrigerator, like an exploded diagram, as needles built cucumbers, a bottle of ketchup, a head of iceberg lettuce.

In the middle of the kitchen, I tried to make myself as small as possible as an entire house grew around me.

11

Overhead a ceiling was spun, an incredible spiderweb made solid in a matter of heartbeats. Sealed away from the blinding light of the midges' machinery, the kitchen was suddenly darker. On the other side of the ceiling I heard the needles still furiously working. They could've impaled me so easily. But they hadn't. They'd moved me out of their way. Slowly I stood, soaked with sweat, my legs wobbly.

The kitchen had two doorways, one leading to a family room, the other to an entrance hallway. I ran for the front door, unchained it, and staggered out onto a covered porch. From the anvil-shaped rig, needles thrust down, creating wooden fences, a goat shed, a chicken coop, a red barn just like ours. It was like watching time-lapse footage of a construction site, everything rising with freakish speed. Beyond the fields, now bristling with crops, an orchard bloomed from the busy work of the needles.

At the peak of the barn roof, a final needle, with a dramatic flourish, created a rooster weather vane. And then they were done. The aerial construction rig disintegrated into thousands of brilliant midges. They streamed high into the sky, contracted to a single flickering light, and disappeared.

I stepped off the porch and turned to look at the house. It steamed slightly, like something freshly baked from a fairy tale. Except this house wasn't made of candy and didn't look designed for bears or witches. It was a handsome two-story wood house with a pitched metal roof and a big stone chimney at one end.

It emanated the same chemical smell I'd noticed in our cottage the very first morning we'd arrived. I had no doubt our cottage, our farm, had been created just like this one, 3D printed in a matter of minutes. I walked into the main pasture and checked the goat shed. Empty. I peeped through a window of the coop. No chickens. Maybe the animals would come later.

And with them, people?

I looked back to the house. A lamp shone invitingly over the porch. I'd left the front door open. The urge to go back inside was overpowering. At the threshold I hesitated, remembering the dog's water bowl. I told myself that if the dog was already here, it would've barked its head off by now. I listened for the sounds people make when they're asleep. The silence was total. I stepped inside.

Four pairs of shoes on the mat. Judging from the sizes, and the small pink ones decorated with unicorns, I guessed: Papa Bear, Mama Bear, a preschooler, and maybe a teenager. Assorted hoodies and rain jackets hung from a row of hooks. On a narrow table was bug spray, sunscreen, a couple pairs of sunglasses, and keys for a Jeep that was definitely not parked outside.

I returned to the kitchen. Enough moonlight shone through the window to let me see the gray stone counters, a big island with barstools, and shiny chrome appliances. It seemed incredible that everything had been fabricated just seconds ago.

On the counter was a shallow wicker basket of odds and ends. I picked up a small flashlight and turned it on. The family room had a vaulted wood-beamed ceiling and a wall of windows that might once have overlooked a lake or a mountain valley. There was a wood-burning stove and lots of sofas and armchairs in what Nia would have called a "rustic" style. Cushions on everything. One of them said, THIS IS OUR HAPPY PLACE. On a coffee table was a half-finished puzzle of tropical fish. Above the mantelpiece hung a massive painting of a massive German shepherd. If this was their dog, I was glad it hadn't arrived yet.

At the far end of the family room were a couple doors, both ajar. Through one I saw a porcelain sink in the glow of a night-light. I walked to the other door and hesitated. This one had to be a bedroom. Cautiously I poked my head in, flashlight aimed at a corner of the ceiling. In the pale glow I made out a double bed, the covers humped into people shapes. The hair on my neck lifted. There were no heads resting on the two pillows, only dents. It was as if two people had been expertly removed, leaving the covers undisturbed.

On the night table closest to me, my flashlight beam picked out a copy of *Sportsman* magazine, a book called *Extinction*, and a box of the same breathing strips my dad used. Also on the night table was a wallet. I lasted two seconds before picking it up. I pulled out a Tennessee driver's license.

Riley Jackson.

He was a handsome white guy with a strong jaw, his hair combed very neatly back from his forehead. Younger than my dad by maybe five or ten years. He looked like having his photo taken was the last thing he wanted. According to his license, he was six two, had blue eyes, and lived in a place called Sage Creek. I put down the wallet, feeling a bit grubby.

Wouldn't anyone peek, if they hadn't seen another human being in three years?

I was just finding out who our new neighbors were.

The house had been built, but the people hadn't arrived yet. Had our cottage stood empty and expectant for a while, waiting for our bodies to be slipped back into our perfectly molded bedclothes? How long would the wait be?

On the far night table were some face creams, a box of tissues, and a Bible bristling with pink sticky notes. I left the bedroom and had a quick look in the bathroom. One side of the sink was messy with bottles and tubes of lotion and makeup and skin cleansers. On the other side was a washcloth, neatly arranged with a razor, a can of shaving gel, a toothbrush, toothpaste, and deodorant. Quite a neat freak, our Riley.

I knew I should leave now. But I paused at the bottom of the stairs. I knew about Riley Jackson from Tennessee; I knew he had a partner. I knew they had a dog, possibly a German shepherd. But I wanted to know about the kids, too, especially if there was one my age. *Especially* if there was a girl my age.

The stairs took me up to a gallery that overlooked the family room. I walked past a small bathroom to a bedroom. When I saw the single bed nearest the door, my heart sank. The covers, eerily ridged into the shape of a small human, were decorated with rainbows and unicorns.

On the floor nearby was a big plastic castle, opened at its hinges to display the pink interior. A princess was poised on the spiral stairs while another was doing time in the dungeon. In the royal chamber, a dragon and a knight were in bed together watching TV. A full-sized Barbie had been crammed into the throne room like a caged giant. Dangling from one of the turrets was a bra.

Not a Barbie bra. A real-person bra.

Heart pounding, I aimed the flashlight deeper into the room. A big chest of drawers, its top covered with more hair scrunchies and brushes and tubes of lip gloss than I'd ever seen. There were some of those leather bracelets that your friends make for you because you're popular. I saw a slim bottle of something called Minx. Beyond the chest of drawers was a second bed.

Scattered around it were a couple sundresses, a pair of skinny jeans, and underwear that was definitely not little-kid underwear. A paperback was splayed face down on the floor. Its cover showed a frightened teenager looking back over her shoulder. Written in scary lipstick was the title: *Don't Pretend You Didn't.*

On the bed itself, within easy reach of the dented pillow, was a phone. I'd already rooted around in someone's wallet, so I figured why not look at someone's phone. Purely for informational purposes. As I lifted it, the screen lit up with a picture of a pretty girl about my age. She had wavy blonde hair, a big smile, and very white teeth. The quick line of her cleavage sent a startling surge of blood between my legs. My hand trembled. The first girl I'd seen in three years.

I cooled off when I shifted my gaze to the guy on whose lap she was perched.

One of his beefy arms encircled her waist. His other hand rested comfortably on her bare thigh, just below her shorts. He looked smug. Probably I'd look smug if she was sitting on my lap. I decided his eyes were too close together and that he'd never had a grade higher than a B.

Across the bottom of the screen was a text from someone called Lucas.

U all good?

The phone was locked, or I would've looked for more texts—and photos, which was creepy and wrong, but I would have done it anyway. I looked at the girl again and wondered where she was right now. I pictured her sleeping body—in a tube? a vat of goo?—being ferried across galaxies. On a spaceship? Or were her atoms being transmitted like radio signals, to be glued back together later?

She and her family might be arriving any second, along with the dog. I knew I should hurry. I tried to put the phone back exactly as I'd found it, then saw something plastic poking from the covers. I carefully peeled back the sheet to reveal a narrow white cartridge. It was face down, so I couldn't see any markings. It reminded me of an antigen test, and I felt sick, wondering if there was another pandemic back on Erf.

U all good?

Three years had passed since we'd been Up Here. They'd been saying that pandemics would become more common. Was the girl sick? Her whole family could be sick, bringing it into the dome. To all of us.

I turned the cartridge over. It was a pregnancy test.

I slipped it back under the covers. Downstairs I put the flashlight back where I'd found it.

I ran home as fast as I could and woke the whole house up.

12

We waited till midmorning before we set out for the Jacksons' house.

We didn't want to startle them awake—if they'd even arrived yet.

Nia wasn't convinced we should go at all. She said they'd be completely freaked out and might think we were responsible for their abduction. Better, she said, to give them a little time to freak out on their own, figure things out, and calm down before bringing a welcome basket. Dad said he would've been pretty grateful if there'd been other people around when we'd arrived, to explain things. And then Nia asked, "Would you have trusted them, though?" Which I thought was a fair point. But in the end, it hadn't stopped any of us from heading out.

As I led the way through the woods, the same playlist of thoughts shuffled through my brain:

People.

The girl.

The Jacksons.

The girl.

Not alone anymore.

The girl.

The girl with the pregnancy test.

I hadn't told Dad and Nia about that part. It was none of their business. It was none of *my* business, and I was ashamed of myself for looking. It wasn't like I could take back what I'd seen, though.

"Zay, wait up!" Noah cried.

With every step, my anxiety grew. What if the farm wasn't there? What if the midges had decided to take it away as quickly as they'd built it?

I was so relieved when we came out from the trees and it was there.

The pastures were still empty. No chickens, no goats—and probably no people.

"Hello!" Dad called out as we neared the house.

He stepped onto the porch and knocked politely. There was a rocking chair and two regular chairs, all with cushions that looked new. When no one answered, Dad knocked again, then came down.

"We aren't going inside?" Noah said in astonishment.

"No," Dad told him. "Not until we're invited."

"Zay got to go inside!"

"I didn't *go* inside," I reminded him. "They built the whole thing around me!"

"I know it's hard, Noah," Dad said. "We're all excited to meet the Jacksons, but we need to be patient."

Noah glared so hard at the house, I thought he might cry. I probably shouldn't have told him about the toy castle.

"Can I sit in the rocking chair?" he asked.

That made me laugh. Dad smiled and said, "I can't see why not."

Noah pulled free of Nia's hand and bolted onto the porch. I'd never seen anyone happier on a rocking chair. It made a creak on its backward swing.

"Is it weird they're not here yet?" Nia asked, looking at the empty pastures and the silent chicken coop.

"There might've been a lag before we arrived," I said.

I looked into the sky, the area where I figured the hatch was. How would they do it? Would the midges just form themselves into magic carpets and fly the sleeping bodies down, along with a few goats and chickens?

I realized the rocking chair was no longer creaking, and turned back to the porch. The rocker was empty and the front door was wide open.

"Oh boy," I said, hurrying inside.

"Noah!" Dad shouted as we all piled into the house.

I was pretty sure where Noah was headed, and took the stairs. Sure enough, he was kneeling in the girls' bedroom, playing furiously with the castle, like he knew his seconds were numbered.

"Noah, you weren't supposed to go inside!"

From the doorway, Nia said, "These aren't your things, Noah."

"But there's lots of them!"

"I'm sure they'll share after they arrive."

"They're not even *using* them," he muttered.

"Let's go, Noah," Dad said in his firm-dad voice.

"Fine!" Noah rolled his eyes and took a long time putting the toy princesses back in their rooms.

"This is someone's house," Nia said, taking his hand and leading him out of the room. "It's private."

Guiltily, I glanced back at the older sister's bed. But now that we were all inside, none of us seemed in a big hurry to leave. Nia and Dad paused on the gallery, looking over the family room.

"A dog painting over the fireplace," she murmured. "Worrying sign?"

"Only about their taste in art, maybe," Dad said.

They leisurely descended the stairs. I could tell they were as curious as me. Dad's eyes lingered on the master bedroom and I knew he wanted to go in, maybe peek at the night tables. Nia didn't hold back. She went straight to the bathroom and I heard the magnetic click of a mirrored cabinet opening, the soft rattle of pill bottles, then the snap of her phone taking pictures.

"What?" she said when she came out and saw me and Dad staring at her.

"Why was that necessary?" Dad asked.

"You can learn a lot from someone's medicine cabinet. Our new neighbors are quite the pill enthusiasts."

Somehow we'd lost Noah again. From the kitchen came a crinkling sound. We hurried in to find him holding a bright red cereal box and fisting Cap'n Crunch into his mouth.

"Did you *know* about this stuff?" he asked in wonderment.

Laughing, I reached for the box, but he plunged in his hand for one last fistful, scattering cereal across the floor.

"Why don't *we* have this?" he demanded.

"Oh, Noah," Nia said mildly, "that stuff is so bad for you!"

I put the box back on the counter, then helped pick up the spilled cereal. Riley Jackson seemed like the kind of neat freak who'd notice a Cap'n Crunch nugget under the fridge.

"Okay, we're leaving now," Dad said.

In the entrance hallway was a door I hadn't opened. Nia opened it now. It was a large storeroom. Inside I spotted skis and winter clothes and boots, camping equipment, bulk containers of detergents and food. I looked at the pack of toilet paper with more longing than the bag of sugar. Stacked on the floor were sacks of dog food that promised to satisfy the hunger of even the biggest of canines. The German shepherd was definitely theirs.

A deep freeze hummed at the back of the room, and Dad opened the lid. A puff of cool air wafted out. The only time I'd seen so much meat was at the supermarket. Each freezer bag was carefully labeled with the cut and date. There were also lots of frozen dinners and pizzas, as well as two tubs of ice cream and a box of Popsicles smushed against one side.

"Wow," said Dad. "These guys are well stocked."

"I'll say," Nia said. She wasn't looking at the freezer.

Behind the door was a locked gun rack with two hunting rifles and a crossbow.

13

"We should take them," Nia said outside.

I was shocked, but I had to admit, the sight of the rifles and crossbow freaked me out, too. It was the first time I'd seen real ones. We were city people who sometimes went to a cottage in the country, which wasn't really that far from the city. We'd never owned guns. I didn't know anyone who did.

We'd parked Noah on the rocking chair and walked off a ways so he couldn't hear us.

"Lots of people hunt," Dad said quietly.

He was trying to be reasonable, to stay positive. His personal view on guns, I knew for a fact, was that basically no one should own them except people who needed to hunt for food or keep wild animals away from their livestock and crops. Nia's views were more absolute.

"Guns get used for more than just hunting," she said.

Dad said, "We have no reason to think the Jacksons—"

"Tennessee. White people. Big attack dog. Guns."

"That's a lot of assumptions, Nia."

She gave him a look. "Sometimes it's best to make assumptions. Just in case."

I knew that look, and what it meant.

"We should take those weapons," she said again, "and destroy them."

I already felt weirdly loyal to the Jacksons. The fact that they were *human beings* automatically made them good things. They were new people who were going to be *here* with us and one of them was a girl my age.

"Taking the guns would be a very bad idea," Dad said.

I nodded. "They'd know it was us. I mean, who else would've done it?"

She gave us both a withering look. "Maybe the same people who moved them here while they were unconscious?"

"Like you said, the Jacksons might think that was us, too," Dad pointed out. "At first anyway."

"Even if they didn't," I said, "they'd probably always suspect us."

"And then they'd never trust us," Dad added. "We need to get along with them. Our whole lives."

Nia thought about this. "Maybe they're great people. But the fact is, great people *with* guns are still one hundred percent more likely to shoot someone than great people *without* guns."

I watched as she and my father locked eyes. Nia was not one to give in, but I sensed Dad wasn't caving on this one.

"Caleb," she began.

"We're not doing it," Dad said.

"I hope we don't regret this."

From his pocket he took the note he'd written in case the Jacksons hadn't arrived yet. He left it in their mailbox, jutting out. I'd watched as he'd written it. It was pretty bare bones. He didn't mention aliens. He drew a simple map of the dome. The Jacksons' place. Our place. Basically it said:

We're the Oaks, four of us. We were abducted like you. We're sealed inside a dome. We can't find a way out. We've been here three years. We've never seen anyone else. We have a farm exactly like yours. Come find us when you're ready.

Back home, Nia wanted Dad and me to check out her photo of the Jacksons' medicine cabinet.

"What's diazepam?" I asked, looking at a slim bottle with the name Charleze Jackson on it. Was she one of the daughters, or the mother?

"A sedative," Nia said. "For anxiety. And it seems Riley has trouble sleeping." She pointed at another prescription bottle. "The doctor gave me these once, when I had a bout of insomnia." She looked at my father meaningfully. "People who are anxious and sleep-deprived don't make the best decisions."

"We were anxious and sleep-deprived when we arrived," Dad said.

"Yeah, but the Jacksons haven't even arrived yet. Throw in an alien abduction, and they might be a hot mess. And Riley's got another one over here . . ."

She zoomed in on a third bottle. I squinted at the label and tried to say the long name, probably mangling it. "What is that?"

Nia shook her head. "No idea. But three renewals. Sounds like a chronic condition."

"Could be anything," Dad said.

We got busy with our work around the farm. I thought it would distract me, but the Jacksons were all I could think about. The eldest daughter mainly. As I milked the goats, I thought about how we'd hang out together. As I weeded vegetables, I ran conversations we might have. As I scattered chicken feed, I wondered how long it would take for her to forget about Kronk, or Lucas, or whatever her boyfriend was called, and fall in love with me. It wasn't like she'd have any other options. I was lovable, wasn't I?

When I finished up my chores and came back to the house, Kimmy was whining and scratching at the closed door of my bedroom. I scooped him into my arms and knocked.

"Hey, Noah, what's up?" It wasn't like him to avoid the puppy.

"He'll just mess it up," came Noah's voice.

I put Kimmy back down and slipped into the room. Noah was sitting cross-legged on the floor, his back to me. My D&D manuals were open around him. I watched as he rolled a six-sided die, carefully wrote down the number in a crooked column, and tried to add them up. With a sigh he wrote the sum (it was wrong) beside the word *Dxitry*, which I figured was *Dexterity*. I'd never helped him make his D&D character, so he was doing it himself.

I sat down beside him. "How's it going?"

"My strength's no good," he said, pointing to his score of eleven.

"What about your other attributes?" I asked, reading them over. "Intelligence is solid. Your constitution's not bad."

"Yeah, but my strength."

"Were you rolling just three dice?" I asked. When he nodded, I said, "You're allowed to roll four times, and get rid of the lowest number."

His eyes widened with astonishment. "Really?"

"Yeah. You better do these all again."

"Okay," he said, gleefully scribbling out all his scores. He started rolling the die. "Four. Three. Six! Six again!" He looked at me. "What's my score?"

"Toss the three, and you've got four plus six plus six is sixteen, dude!"

"I can be a warrior?"

"A very good one."

"Thanks, Zay!" He carefully wrote the number down, then gave me a big hug. I hugged him back and was disappointed when he pulled away to keep rolling dice. It was so easy: a number on a piece of paper and everything was right with the world.

The Jacksons didn't visit that day or the next.

"When're they coming?" Noah asked at dinner. He'd been asking about every half hour.

"Maybe their trip's just taking a little longer than we thought," Nia said.

"From Erf?"

"Right."

Noah and I weren't the only ones on tenterhooks. I often caught Dad and Nia watching the horizon. Inside, their eyes strayed to the windows. We were all waiting for a shouted hello, the knock at the door.

By lunchtime on the third day, the Jacksons still had not come.

"Should we go check on them?" I asked.

"We wait," Nia insisted.

I was starting to worry something had happened. Some kind of interstellar accident en route. Their house sitting empty forever. The thought was unbearable. Dad said they might already be here, and just trying to figure things out before coming over. It didn't make sense to me. We'd left them a note. Why wouldn't they come right away so we could answer all their questions?

After I finished afternoon chores, I asked Dad if I could go have a look.

He told me not to.

I went anyway.

Through the tall grass and into the trees. I'd left without telling anyone. At a fast walk, it would only take twenty-five minutes. I'd had an extra-long shower this morning, scrubbing with our homemade soap that was supposed to smell like rosemary but didn't really. The shampoo was long gone. So was everyone's deodorant. I'd picked the cleanest clothes I could find, which wasn't saying much. That weekend three years ago, I'd hardly brought any clothes with me. Luckily the dresser drawers had been filled with cottage clothes going back many years, including quite a few of Sam's. I'd grown into my big brother's clothes. *Out*grown some of them.

The creek marked the halfway point. Six hops—four small, two big—and I was across. On the other side, I hesitated, remembering the crossbow and two rifles. I told myself to stay positive.

I kept walking. Maybe I should've brought some of Dad's raisin cookies.

Welcome to our outer space dome; we're your friendly new neighbors!

I was only a few minutes away. I sniffed my armpits: not great. But at least I didn't smell like goat. I didn't think so anyway. I didn't trust myself to know anymore.

Then I heard real goats, and my heart kicked.

If the goats were there, it must mean the Jacksons were, too.

The moment I stepped out from the trees, I heard barking. It was a throaty bark with a serrated growl at the end. I hoped I hadn't made a terrible mistake. Maybe the dog was barking at the goats or the chickens. But the sound was getting bigger. Over the vegetable plots, a huge German shepherd hurtled toward me. I snatched up a stick.

"Patt!" I heard a voice shout. "Heel!"

My heart pounded all the air out of my lungs. Not just because of the German shepherd, but also at the mere sight of Riley Jackson. I'd seen his photograph, but the simple *fact* of him was now undeniable. Here he was, another person, finally. The dog circled back and trotted alongside him as he approached. He wore khaki cargo pants and a black T-shirt, short sleeves tight against his biceps. Around his neck was a pair of binoculars.

The dog growled at me ominously.

"Quiet," snapped Riley. He was clean-shaven. He'd taken the time to shave, even though his eyes were shadowed from lack of sleep. "Who're you?"

"Xavier Oak."

He looked me over. The dog gave a contemptuous sniff. Riley seemed far from glad to see me.

"We left you a note," I said.

"We got it." He jerked his head toward their house. "Come on, then."

I noticed he made me walk ahead of him. I almost felt like I should raise my hands in the air.

"Take a seat," he said on the porch.

I sat in the nearest chair, which was the rocking chair. Riley Jackson remained standing. The German shepherd stood at his side, emanating a meaty heat, watching me with a gaze not dissimilar to its owner's.

"You've been here three years?"

"Yes."

Monosyllabic answers seemed best. His easygoing accent was at odds with his posture and gaze. The chair creaked and I realized I was rocking myself a little. I stopped.

"Never seen another soul?"

"No, sir."

He seemed like the sort of person who'd appreciate a good "sir."

His eyes bored into mine. "There's marks on all of us, low down on our backs."

"Us too."

His eyes drilled a little deeper. "Show me."

Creak went the rocking chair as I stood. He wanted to make sure I wasn't one of *them*. Nervously I turned and lifted my shirt. "They're pretty faded by now, but you can still see them."

I heard Riley sigh. "Yep. I see them."

Gratefully I sat back down.

"Where's the rest of your family?" he asked.

"My dad thought we should give you time, wait till you came to us. But I thought . . . well, you might need some help."

"You know how to get through that invisible wall?"

So he'd found it. I wondered how much time he'd spent bashing away at it. Presumably enough to know it hadn't been built by humans.

I shook my head.

"Then I don't see what help you could give me."

The only time his gaze left me was to look off at the goats, bleating their hearts out in the pasture.

"With the livestock maybe," I said. "Or maybe you have questions?"

The screen door opened and a woman with lots of blonde hair came out. She seemed kind of glamorous, maybe because she was made up. I hadn't seen makeup since Nia ran out almost three years ago. The woman wore green leggings and one of those cropped workout tops that Nia wore for exercise, except Nia's stomach wasn't as flat and ridged.

"Riley, this boy looks scared half to death. Quit grilling him." Her smile was strained but friendly. "I'm Charleze Jackson and this is my husband, Riley."

I stood and introduced myself. Her skin had a slightly parched look to it, like it had maybe seen too much sun. Around her eyes was a little pouchy. I remembered how sleepless our first nights had been. I sat back down.

"Meheheheheh!" went the goats.

"Thank you for leaving that note—that was very thoughtful," Charleze said. "You didn't say where y'all are from."

Erf, I almost said. "Montreal."

"I thought I detected a French accent."

"Well, I'm Anglophone, but I can speak French."

"That is so wonderful. I have always wanted to get on up there, but I just cannot tolerate the cold. We're from Tennessee."

I nodded politely.

"Would you like something to drink, sweetheart? I'll get you something to drink."

She cut Riley a look that might have meant, *Go easy on the boy*, and went inside. I wondered if their older daughter was in there, out of sight and listening.

Riley rapped his knuckles against the side of his house. "I'm thinking this isn't my real lodge."

I was impressed. It had taken us forever to realize that our own cottage was fake, even though it was the only logical conclusion. Probably I hadn't fully accepted it until I'd seen the Jacksons' 3D printed.

"It's a replica," I said. "I saw them build it."

Riley's eyebrows lifted. "*Them?* Your note said you'd never seen anyone."

"It was their machines, I think." I described the midges that had cleared the land, then formed themselves into a massive aerial rig. It sounded incredible even to my own ears, and I worried Riley might think I was lying. "They 3D printed your entire place."

"And everything inside?" asked a teenaged girl as she came out the screen door with a glass and a plate of cookies.

Creak went my rocking chair. I stopped moving. Her tanned boots went halfway up her calves, which were snugly encased in tight jeans. She wore an unbuttoned plaid shirt over a white tank top. Her hair cascaded down her back in a loose braid. Like her mother, she wore makeup, mainly around her eyes. She'd outlined them and darkened her brows so that she looked like an ancient Egyptian queen. She did not look like someone who would choose to spend her time at a hunting lodge—or inside a space dome. She put the glass and plate of cookies on the little table in front of me, then stepped back beside her father.

"Yeah," I said. "Everything inside, too."

"This is my daughter Mackenzie," Riley said.

She stared at me warily. I suddenly saw myself as she must've: a lean kid who needed a haircut, in clothing that was frayed, badly mended, and stained with all the things that could come out of a chicken or goat. I felt my face heat.

"Even our food?" she asked.

"I saw your fridge get made. Like, the ketchup bottle with the ketchup. The milk carton and the milk. It was crazy."

"How'd you see all that from a distance?" Riley asked.

"Beheheheheh!" cried the goats.

Creak went my chair.

"I was inside," I admitted, and felt the temperature on the porch dip.

"In-side," repeated Riley slowly, like it was two words. His left hand absent-mindedly stroked Patt's head, and the dog's ears sharpened a little.

Charleze came back out and stood beside her husband. I was the only one seated, with a glass of juice and a plate of cookies in front of me, like a six-year-old who was about to lose his treats.

I tripped over my words as I backtracked. "I was standing on the foundation. I thought the midges had all gone, but they hadn't, and they started all of a sudden. I couldn't move. It was like needles pounding down everywhere, blocking the way."

I kept going, and when I finished Riley sniffed and scratched his nose, like my words had left a very bad smell in the air.

"Well, I imagine you had a good old snoop around afterward," he said.

"Oh, no—"

"Were *we* there?" Mackenzie asked, horrified. "Sleeping?"

"No, you guys weren't—"

"How'd you know?" Riley asked. "Unless you had a peek in our bedrooms?"

He had me. Again.

"I did look in the bedrooms. I'm sorry, I wanted to see if you'd arrived."

"Strange word to use," said Riley.

"But you weren't there, any of you," I reassured Mackenzie. "And that was it. I just left."

Riley's level gaze was still on me. I felt like he was mentally reciting all the other things I'd looked at: his wallet, deep freeze, gun rack. His daughter's phone and pregnancy test.

"Heck, I would've had a good snoop, too," Riley said.

When he smiled, his face became much kindlier. His cheeks dimpled and his eyes narrowed to playful crescents, crow's feet radiating from their corners.

"I knew someone must've been inside," Riley said, "given our chain wasn't latched."

I nodded. "I had to open it to get out."

"I appreciate your honesty."

Not complete honesty. Still, this didn't seem like the best moment to mention the second time we'd all trooped inside and gone through their medicine cabinet.

"So this place got built when, exactly?" Riley asked.

"Three nights ago."

Charleze crossed the porch and took the chair beside me. I was relieved I was no longer the only person sitting.

"We must've gotten here the next night," she said.

"You see that part, too?" Riley asked me.

I shook my head, relieved I didn't need to lie.

"Must've been quite a production," Riley remarked. "Sorry I missed it."

I chuckled nervously. I still wasn't sure how much of all this he believed. My mouth was dry, so I took a long drink. Cranberry juice—something I hadn't tasted in years.

"Beheheheheh!" said the goats, and Riley glared at them.

The screen door opened and a little blonde girl in a unicorn T-shirt walked out and asked me, "Do you have a car?"

I shook my head. "Sorry."

"Meheheheheh!"

The goats must have seen us all out on the porch and were hoping to get fed, or milked.

"This is Alyssa, our youngest," said Charleze.

The girl looked ruefully at her mother. "Am I going to Suzie's birthday?"

"We'll see."

"They're doing bracelets!"

"I know, sweetness."

Alyssa walked over and took one of the cookies off my plate. "He's not going to eat *four*," she told her mother preemptively, then turned to me. "You're not going to eat four, are you?"

"No," I said.

She gave her mother a sassy grin.

"Meheheheheh!" went the goats.

"Since you've been here three years," Riley said to me, "you know how to shut those goats up?"

"Have you milked them?"

"Yesterday."

"We *tried*," Charleze corrected, "but I don't believe we did a very good job."

"They almost kicked her in the face," said Mackenzie.

"Do you want me to check on them?" I asked.

"Can I milk them?" asked Alyssa, her hopeful expression reminding me of Noah.

"Xavier's going to teach us how," Charleze said.

I asked for a bucket of hot soapy water and a cloth, and we all trooped out to the barn, leaving Patt, the German shepherd, inside the lodge. The barn was identical to ours, including the milking platform. The two goats were not happy, and I had a bit of a time calming the first doe. She gave a shiver of relief as I gently cleaned off her teats with the warm cloth. Her udders looked painfully full.

"If you let them go too long," I said, making the first few squeezes, "they can get mastitis."

"What's that?" Mackenzie asked.

"A breast infection," her mother told her.

Mackenzie shuddered. I'd been hoping to impress her with all my farm know-how, but she looked like this was pretty much the worst day of her life. We were close enough that I could smell her coconut shampoo—and I felt a little dizzy.

"Anyway," I said, "if they don't get milked, they eventually dry up, and no milk."

"We won't be here that long," said Riley.

"Still, we'd better get the hang of this," said Charleze. "If we want any peace."

"I'm so glad I'm not a goat," Mackenzie said, watching me. "Nothing personal. I'm sure you've got a nice gentle touch. But imagine being milked every day."

"Twice."

"Ouch."

After I gave them a quick lesson, I showed them what to feed the goats and chickens. Riley muttered something about this being no concern of his. As we walked back toward their lodge, I said, "Looks like we have the same crops. I can give you a rundown on—"

"Thanks, but we've got plenty of food," Riley said. His eyes made a slow sweep of the horizon, then came to rest on me. "Three years." Mixed with his amazement was a hint of disdain. "And you've never even caught a glimpse of them, huh?"

I shook my head. "We have no idea what they look like."

"Oh, I got a pretty good idea who they are," Riley said.

I laughed.

"Why's that funny?" he asked.

"Sorry, it's just . . . you make it sound like you know lots of aliens."

Riley's head pulled back in astonishment. "Aliens?"

He exchanged a glance with Charleze, who said to me, very politely, "Well. Lots of folks believe in space aliens, and God bless them, it's a free country. Personally, we don't think there's one bit of evidence that's half-decent."

I had this weird, floaty sensation, like my head had just lifted off my shoulders on a string. The Jacksons were looking at me pityingly, like they'd spotted me waiting in the desert on a lawn chair, wearing a tinfoil cap.

"Sure, before this," I said, "I would've agreed one hundred percent. But their technology. That wall—"

Riley held up his hands. "Am I impressed? Yes. But the government has all sorts of tech we don't know about. They don't *want* us to know. We haven't been abducted by space aliens. Make no mistake, you are right here on Earth. Now, better get back before your folks worry. Tell them we'll pay a visit tomorrow afternoon."

14

The whole way home, the idea pulsed in my head like one of those bioluminescent jellyfish, trailing light and hope.

Not a billion miles away, but on Earth all along.

Maybe not so far away from Mom and Sam and my old life.

When I reached the cottage it was a whole other interrogation.

"What if he's right?" I said. "About being on Earth?"

"He's not right," Dad said.

"We might be ten minutes outside Montreal!"

"Zay—"

"In some underground bunker!" My balloon head lifted off again. "Why's that any crazier than thinking we've been abducted by aliens? Even saying *aliens*, it sounds kind of ridiculous, doesn't it? Riley made me feel like all this time we've been wrong."

"Did you get to go inside?" Noah asked.

I squinted at him in confusion. "What?"

"Did you see the toys?"

My head bounced back on its string and settled on my shoulders. I took a breath. "No, Noah, I didn't see her toys this time."

Noah's expression became philosophical. "Will she share?"

"You can find out tomorrow when the Jacksons come over," I said.

When I said *Jacksons* all I was thinking was *Mackenzie*, and a giddy wave of excitement washed over me. Someone here, my age. A very appealing someone. The photograph on her phone had told me so little. It hadn't shown me the forceful intelligence in her hieroglyphic eyes. It hadn't told me the lilt of her voice making a sarcastic remark, or how her braid swayed when she walked. I felt like I could still smell her shampoo.

I wanted tomorrow now.

Even if Riley was dead wrong about where we were, everything was suddenly very different, and there was no denying that.

The next day, we got on with things as usual. We didn't know exactly what time the Jacksons would be coming, and I wanted to stay busy so I didn't go crazy.

"You gonna help?" I said to Noah over my shoulder. I was hoeing the zucchini beds, and he was supposed to be collecting the weeds in a basket. But he just trailed after me, playing with Rumpety and another small toy that I hadn't seen properly—until now.

"Noah, did you take that from the Jacksons?"

It was a pointless question, because of course he had.

"She had *three* princesses!" he said, like this was an ironclad justification.

"That one was her favorite! It was on her bed. Give it here."

"Why?"

"You need to give it back to them."

"But then they'll know I took it!"

I almost laughed, then realized that they'd also know about the second trip inside their house—the one I'd decided *not* to tell them about. Riley struck me as the kind of guy who got suspicious pretty easily. It might be best to keep the princess after all.

In the distance came Patt's telltale bark.

"Is that them?" Noah asked, standing very straight.

"Yes. Put it away!"

He crammed the princess into his pocket but left his fist in there, like this would hide it better. The barking got louder. I hoped the dog was on a leash this time. The tall grass beyond the orchard thrashed as something hurtled through it. In a reedy voice Noah asked if I'd pick him up. Then the dog burst into view and Noah threw himself at me and climbed my body.

"Patt!" came Riley's voice. "Heel!"

The dog stopped short and circled back to Riley Jackson as he came striding across the orchard, ahead of his family. He looked more relaxed today, and when he gave his dimpled smile, he looked like a movie star.

"He's all bark," he said, seeing Noah's face pressed against my chest. "Don't be afraid of Patt. Wouldn't hurt a fly."

"And this must be Noah," Charleze said, though she looked confused for a second, maybe because we didn't have the same color skin. "What a sweetheart."

In a lordly manner, Noah said, "Put me down," probably because he'd just seen Alyssa, who was not being held. In her lilac dress and sun hat she walked hand in hand with her big sister. Mackenzie wore a baseball cap the same color as her shorts, and a distractingly tight top—not that she could be any more distracting to me.

"Hi," I said as I lowered Noah to the ground.

"Hey," she replied, her eye makeup giving her a baleful look.

Noah regarded the German shepherd warily and said, "Why's he called Patt?"

"Short for Patton," Riley said. "The greatest American general there ever was."

"You found us," I heard my father say, and turned to see him approaching with Nia.

"Your map was good; Patt was better." Riley nodded to his dog. "Picked up the scent a ways back."

There was certainly lots to smell on a farm—goats, chickens, manure—but Riley made it sound like we were the prey. As everyone said hello, Dad had a huge smile on his face, as if he was greeting friends he hadn't seen in forever. Even Nia was smiling. I was grinning, too. We couldn't help ourselves. We were castaways, overjoyed to see another boatload of shipwrecked people.

"I was a bit hard on your boy yesterday," Riley said, then turned to me. "Hope it didn't seem like an interrogation."

It had absolutely been an interrogation, but I shook my head and said, "Nah. I had juice and cookies," and everyone laughed.

"We've got juice and cookies, too," Noah said hospitably.

Nia asked, "Would you like to come inside? Have something to drink?"

"That's kind of you," said Charleze.

"Zay told us you've already been to the wall," Dad said as we headed for the house.

"Indeed we have," said Riley. "Had a good go at it."

"Give you a jolt?" I could tell Dad was trying to get all manly with Mr. Jackson. Riley looked fit and muscular, like he spent a lot of time at the gym, or outdoors chopping wood.

"Yes, sir, it did."

I was surprised he called Dad "sir." Maybe it was because Dad was a bit older and had some gray in his hair and beard, or maybe it was just a Southern courtesy.

"I was making some headway with the chain saw," Riley said, "and then the current just fried it."

"It was like lightning," said Charleze. "I thought he'd been electrocuted."

It sounded pretty badass to me, Riley going at the wall with a chain saw. It must have been very satisfying.

"You must have questions," Dad said.

"A fair number."

"Your goats are nice and quiet," Mackenzie noted as we went by their pasture.

"We've got happy goats now, too, thanks to Xavier," said Charleze.

As we approached the cottage, Kimmy was yipping behind the patio doors. I saw the German shepherd's ears prick up.

"Patt won't tangle with him," Charleze said. "He's real well-trained."

"Kimmy's not!" Noah said cheerfully.

I scooped up the puppy as we opened the door and went inside. I noticed Riley hesitate just a second on the threshold, checking out the room like he was counting doorways and measuring the distance between things.

Nia had tidied. It wasn't often we got company in our dome. Riley chose the sofa against the wall, where nothing could sneak up behind him and he had a view out the big windows. His wife sat next to him, and Alyssa climbed into her lap. There was room for Mackenzie, but she sat in my favorite green armchair, which I chose to believe was significant. She looked ticked off, like she'd been dragged along on some terrible family outing. Riley snapped his fingers and Patt settled instantly at his feet.

"It's okay to put the puppy down," he told me.

Patt patiently allowed Kimmy to crawl all over him, lick him, and chew his feet, only occasionally nudging the puppy away. What was going on inside the German shepherd's head was a mystery, but I sensed he took comfort knowing that he could eat Kimmy with one quick snap of his jaws.

"There many dogs around here?" Riley asked.

"None," Dad said. "This one appeared just last week."

"They give us things sometimes," Nia said.

"For me!" Noah chimed in before anyone could get into who *they* actually were.

"That right?" said Riley.

"And why not?" Charleze said. "How old are you, sweetheart? Four, five?"

"I just turned three!"

Charleze looked at Nia with raised eyebrows and said, "I had him pegged the same age as Alyssa. He's a bright boy, and a good height for three."

I'd never thought of Noah as unusually tall, but then again, this was the first time I'd been a big brother.

Something else seemed to occur to Charleze. She leaned closer to Nia and in a lowered voice asked, "Was he born here?"

Nia nodded. "A few days after we arrived."

I caught Mackenzie listening, riveted.

Charleze's face radiated sympathy. She whispered to Nia, "You poor thing."

"Oh, it all worked out."

"Well, Noah's not the only one who gets gifts anymore," Riley said. "We've brought you a few little things."

Charleze had made up some packets of coffee, sugar, and flour as well as some store-bought cookies and things we hadn't seen in years. From his backpack, Riley produced a bottle of Tennessee bourbon and presented it to my father.

"I'm thirsty," Alyssa said.

"Manners, missy," said Charleze.

Nia said, "We've got water, fresh pear juice, milk—but it's goat milk."

"Pear juice!" said Noah, and Alyssa concurred.

"Noah," Nia said, "I bet Alyssa would like to see your toys. Why don't you show her your room. If that's okay?" she added, deferring to Charleze.

"That's a grand idea," Mrs. Jackson said, and I knew they wanted to get rid of the little kids so they could talk seriously. "Alyssa's brought some of her own things to show you, Noah."

From a backpack Charleze pulled out a clear plastic purse stuffed with toys and jewelry, and passed it to her daughter. "Scoot now."

Alyssa slid off her mother's lap and followed Noah down the hallway. I could see Noah's fist still clenched in his pocket. I hoped the little thief didn't do anything dumb.

Nia turned to me. "Would you mind taking them their drinks? Some cookies, too."

"Lend a hand," Charleze told Mackenzie, who got up with a barely audible sigh.

I wondered if they were trying to get rid of us, too. But I'd been living this situation for three years now, coming up with good ideas, doing the same work as the grown-ups, and I wasn't about to be demoted.

The kitchen was small, and I could tell Mackenzie and I were both trying hard not to bump into each other. I stuck my head inside the fridge, hoping to cool my cheeks, and took my time rummaging around for the pitcher of pear juice. This was my first time sort of alone with her, and I realized I was only taking little glimpses of her, in case I fell into a kind of trance and couldn't look away. In the living room Riley was already asking Dad about the wall and the ways we'd tried to break through it.

"Glasses up here?" Mackenzie asked, opening the cupboard above the sink.

"Thanks. Just grab anything. Nothing matches, we've broken so much stuff over the years."

As she got down two plastic cups, she whispered, "Daddy checked you guys out, even before you visited yesterday."

"Really? He came over here to spy on us?"

"Yeah."

He must have been very stealthy. I imagined Riley commando crawling through the undergrowth, watching us through his binoculars. Or was it his rifle sight?

Mackenzie continued, "I think he's still half convinced you're in on this whole thing."

"Oh no." I poured two cups of pear juice. My hands trembled a bit.

"Planted here to keep an eye on us."

Her eye makeup was so dramatic that I hadn't noticed her actual eyes until now. Her blue irises were encircled by a thin, dark ring, making the color all the more striking. I forced myself to look away.

"*You* don't think that, do you?" I said quietly.

"No. You *look* like you've been here three years."

I laughed. "That bad, huh?"

"I figure if you can milk a *goat*, you're legit. And you look kind of like a farmer. A very *fit* farmer anyway."

I liked that she'd noticed I was fit. I also liked the conspiratorial way we were talking. I put some cookies on a plate. I hoped our homemade ones wouldn't taste like garbage compared to the Jacksons'.

"Daddy's always been a touch on the paranoid side," Mackenzie said, then raised her thick eyebrows and added, "but at least he doesn't think we've been abducted by space aliens."

She was mocking me, and I could hardly blame her.

"He might change his mind," I said.

She took the plate of cookies, and I brought the cups. My bedroom was average messy, and I could see Mackenzie's eyes sifting through it. Noah was introducing Alyssa to the wonders of his toy farm.

"Let's play farm animals!" he said with more enthusiasm than I thought humanly possible.

Alyssa's shoulders lifted and dropped with a resigned sigh. "All right. Do you have princesses?"

As I put their drinks down, I caught Noah's eye and sent him a look that meant: *Keep the princess in your pocket.* Riley already thought we might be spies; we didn't need him knowing we'd been filching toys and rifling through his medicine cabinet.

Part of me wanted to get back to the living room to hear what they were talking about. But I wanted to be alone with Mackenzie more. We drifted toward the doorway and paused. She didn't seem in any hurry either.

"You really think we're in outer space?" she asked.

"I mean, if the universe is as big as they say, seems like there's got to be other life out there."

She seemed to consider this. "It isn't in the Bible, so my parents don't want to know about it. God made us in His image, and that's that. Not with four arms, or beaks."

"You guys are super religious?"

"*They* are. Mom especially."

I remembered the well-read Bible on her night table. Pink sticky notes.

And then I thought about the pregnancy test in Mackenzie's bed and tried not to blush.

"Well," I said, "good luck explaining how your house got built in two seconds. Or that wall."

"Oh, Daddy's got some ideas about all that," she replied, almost wearily.

"I hope he's right. 'Cause three years is long enough for me."

"Oh my God, I don't think I can last here three *weeks*. I didn't even want to come for the weekend."

I smiled. "Me neither. I should've stayed in Montreal with Sam and my mom."

"Nia's your stepmom?"

I nodded.

"And Sam . . . that's your other brother?"

"Yeah, he's a couple years older than me. And Noah's my half brother."

"That really sucks, to lose your mom and brother like that. I am so awfully sorry, Xavier."

Her condolences sounded so heartfelt in her southern accent that I couldn't help smiling. But mostly it was just the pure pleasure of getting all this sympathy beamed at me.

"What're you smiling for?" she asked.

"Your accent."

"You're the one with the accent!"

"Yours is nicer."

She seemed mollified. "A magazine said we had the fourth most charming accent in the country."

"What were the top three?"

"Doesn't matter," she replied with an insouciant smile. "They're not as good."

Over at the toy farm, Noah was offering Alyssa the chicken.

"You can be Mrs. Chicken-nucker if you like."

"I want that one," Alyssa said, pointing at Rumpety.

I saw Noah's hand hover protectively over his favorite toy, but then with a determined frown he said, "Okay."

"What even is this?" Alyssa asked, squinting at it.

"It's a bakzhilshek," he said indignantly, and I assumed he'd lifted the name from the *Monster Manual*.

"Sometimes I think we're in some kind of zoo," I told Mackenzie quietly.

"Seriously?"

"And they replicated our houses so we'd have a familiar habitat, to make the transition easier."

"If this is a zoo, where are the visitors?" She shivered. "Oh my gosh, I just gave myself goose bumps."

"Even if we can't see them, maybe they can see us."

I was probably talking too much, and worried I'd freaked her out.

"Mackenzie!" Alyssa whispered loudly, pointing at her pear juice. "It's got *bits* in it."

"Well, I'm sure it's delicious anyway." Mackenzie went over and took a sip. "It sure is." She drained the glass.

Alyssa watched, bewildered, and said, "What about me?"

"There's goat milk," Noah said.

Alyssa looked like she might cry.

"Cookie?" Mackenzie said, swooping the plate under her nose.

With the tip of one finger, Alyssa pushed a raisin cookie out of the way and took a store-bought one.

"I'll get you a glass of water in a bit," Mackenzie promised, walking back to me. Lowering her voice, she said, "So. A zoo, huh?"

"And the zookeepers take really good care of us, but they're never going to let us go."

"Okay. Wow," Mackenzie said, and headed back to the living room.

The bourbon was open, as was a bottle of our pretty terrible wine. Nia was finishing the story of Noah's birth.

"Next thing I know, I wake up in bed with my baby. He's warm and alive and nursing. Everything's tidied up. Caleb's beside me, and Zay's standing in the doorway, both of them looking totally bewildered. None of us have any memory of what happened."

Charleze touched her fingertips lightly to her throat. "I am so relieved for you and Noah. But that's terrifying, to think how quick they can knock you out and do whatever they want with you."

"In this case, they saved our lives," said Nia.

Mackenzie sat down in the green chair.

"Sounds like they had a crack medical team standing by," Riley said.

Dad was about to say something, but Riley held up a hand in truce.

"I know we have a difference of opinion on who our captors are, but there's something I want to show you." He pulled a laptop from his backpack. "Only wish I had internet, but I've got some photos that might be helpful. I was thinking of those machines you described, Xavier, the ones that built our house. Midges, you called them."

Our egg timer went off in the kitchen, and Riley sat up straighter, his gaze instantly welded to the source of the noise. I saw Charleze give his leg a little pat. Riley nodded and took a breath.

"Sorry," said Nia. "We put it on for the puppy. You want to take him out, Zay?"

"He'll be okay for a bit." I wasn't going to miss this.

Riley fired up his computer and we all gathered round. Everyone except Mackenzie, who looked like she'd seen and heard all this before. Riley navigated a maze of folders, then opened one filled with photos of the tiniest flying machines I'd ever seen.

"They call these nanodrones," he said. "They were contracted by the Air Force.

You believe these little guys can carry weaponry? Four of these can take out a tank. So you can pack *a lot* into these. I'm thinking: not much of a stretch to repurpose them to do 3D printing."

Nia looked skeptical. "All the different materials, though. Wood, stone, iron, organic materials for the food. And the quantities."

"I agree, way more complex. But your boy said there were millions of them. Shame you didn't catch one," Riley said. "Would've given us a chance to see what made them tick."

Trying to put one in a jar had been the last thing on my mind. I'd been terrified.

"And there was that subdivision they just put in," Charleze said, touching Riley's arm. "Outside Swift Rapids."

Riley nodded. "They 3D printed the cement shell of all the houses: foundation, floor, walls. Much simpler job, sure, and yes, it took them a lot longer than a couple minutes."

"And they didn't do food," Charleze said, preempting me.

"My point," said Riley, "is that human technology can do this."

I glanced over at Dad and Nia for their reactions. I hadn't known about these nanodrones. They were a long way from the midges I'd seen, but still.

"What about the wall?" I asked.

I noticed that Mackenzie was now gazing at her phone. Probably looking at pics of Kronk, or reading over their last texts. *Me gonna miss u. Me not think good when u r gone.*

"Got something interesting there, too," Riley said, opening another folder.

On-screen appeared a structure that looked like an igloo made of gooey gray blocks.

"Again, a military application," he said. "It's a biomaterial to make shelters for troops in hostile environments." He showed us a few more photos. "Basically, this stuff grows itself. It gets hit with a bullet or an RPG, it *fixes* itself."

"Our wall here," Dad reminded him, "swallowed me. It was like muscle, moving me around. It could've crushed me."

"The brightest minds in America are working on this kind of stuff," said Riley.

I wondered what kind of person kept things like this on his laptop. Dad must have been wondering the same, because he asked:

"Are you in the military, Riley?"

"Law enforcement," he replied, closing his laptop.

"Daddy, you're a prison guard," said Mackenzie without looking up from her phone.

"Your father is associate warden of operations," Charleze said sharply.

Riley smiled. "Which, I must say, seems a bit ironic at the moment."

"The jailer, jailed," Dad said.

"Indeed." Riley poured a little more bourbon into Dad's glass, then his own. With his free hand he made a circle in the air. "But this here is just a cage, and I know a lot about cages. Every one of them, no matter how ingenious, has a way in and a way out. All we have to do is find it."

"And where does that get us?" Dad asked.

"Outside the cage, Caleb!"

"We have different ideas about what's outside."

"Open air, the world, freedom!"

"Not if we're in outer space."

Riley sipped his drink. "None of my pictures did the trick, huh? Not a dent?"

"A very small dent," admitted my father good-naturedly.

"What if I told you we weren't the only people in this situation?"

I leaned forward. "How d'you know?"

"Has it been in the news?" Nia asked.

"Mainstream media wouldn't cover it," said Riley. "But we overhear things in Corrections. The government's set up lots of places like this."

"Which government?" said Nia. "We're Canadian."

"I'm talking about *world* government," Riley said. "And they don't care who they take. Whole families sometimes."

I felt my balloon head lift off again. "Why would they do that?"

"You've been out of the loop for a bit," Riley said. "Things have only gotten worse on planet Earth."

"You mean the climate emergency?" Nia said.

Riley frowned. "Don't get me started on that nonsense."

"It's not nonsense!" Mackenzie said, looking up now. "Nobel Prize–winning scientists all agree on it! What about that heat dome over Florida this spring?"

"Yeah, it got real hot."

"Twenty thousand people died, Daddy!"

"Mostly the elderly."

"And the sickly," Charleze added, taking a sip of wine.

Mackenzie kept at him. "The wildfires all across the Midwest?"

I was pretty impressed by her, standing up to her parents like this. I'd grown up being taught that people were responsible for the climate emergency: a doomscroll of missed reductions targets fueling more extreme weather events, rising sea levels, fatal temperatures. But Mackenzie obviously wasn't getting that from Riley or Charleze. She'd had to fight for it.

"People like to make a lot of noise," her father said. "Whip it all out of proportion. Have there been droughts? Yes. Wildfires? Sure. Always have been, always will be. We adapt and keep going. That's what the human species does."

"It must be even worse overseas," Nia said, looking stricken.

"I don't follow them much," Riley admitted.

"Seems it's always one thing or another with those poor souls anyway," Charleze said.

"Guys, there was a big flood in Pakistan just last month," Mackenzie said. "Most of the country's still underwater."

"It's called right-sizing," said Riley. "Planet can't handle so many people, so we get a correction. What's that term you like, honey?"

"Benevolent disaster," said Charleze.

It was weird hearing the two words together like that. The good and the terrible, destined to join forces.

"There must be so many climate refugees," Nia said.

"Huge problem," Riley agreed. "But honestly, all this is a distraction. Like the pandemic."

"There's a new pandemic?" I exclaimed.

"So they say," Charleze replied.

"Oh my God, you guys!" said Mackenzie. "The World Health Organization said it's already started, and it's going to be a big one."

"All of five cases, last I heard," said Riley. "But already the government's hunkering down for another lockdown. It's all a big show." He paused, and I sensed he was winding up. "The climate emergency, the pandemic—these are just excuses to strip away our freedoms. To put us in places like this."

My head was at the end of its string, snapping in the breeze.

"So the government put us here to . . ." Nia prompted.

"To quarantine and reeducate. To see how much we'll take. And, with respect, Oaks, it seems some people are willing to take an awful lot. They put a bubble over you, you stay put. They put a hoe in your hand, you farm. Three years, you've been doing exactly what they want."

It felt like an insult, and my eyes slid over to see how Dad was taking it. His face was calm. I heard the air whistle softly in his nostrils as he took a breath. This must be how he looked in boardrooms when he was getting a lot of pushback.

"What we've been doing, Riley, is surviving. And what you're talking about sounds like a conspiracy theory."

"Everything's a conspiracy theory till it's proven," Charleze said.

"Yours is a bit of a doozy, too," Riley told Dad with his dimpled smile. "But I'm willing to listen. Why would aliens do this to us?"

"I don't know," Dad said, which was honest, if underwhelming. "We're obviously of interest to them. Another intelligent species across the universe. Maybe they're observing us. Studying us before they interact directly."

"We're specimens, is what you're saying."

"Don't like the sound of that," Charleze murmured.

In the early days I'd worried a lot about whether we'd be used in some terrible lab experiments. We were helpless, after all. Mackenzie's nervous eyes flitted from her mother to me, and I gave her what I hoped was a reassuring smile. She didn't look reassured.

"Maybe they just want to observe us," Dad said.

Riley scoffed. "Sooner or later, they'd do stuff to you."

"They've never hurt us," said Nia. "They've always made sure we have whatever we need. We've never gone hungry. Their intentions seem kindly."

"Except you're here and can't get out." Riley ran a fingertip around the rim of his glass. "Well, I am a huge fan of facts, and your theory seems a little light on them. You've seen some technology that you think could only be alien. You've been here three years, and have you *seen* any aliens? No. You think you're in outer space, but have you seen any new stars or planets? No. If it looks like Earth, I'm thinking it's probably Earth."

I was worried that the string on my balloon head might snap altogether.

"Here's another reason I know all this is the work of humans. They're scared of us. They want us docile and defenseless. Why else would they disarm me?"

Charleze glanced over at him, looking as startled as I felt. Last I'd seen, Riley had plenty of weapons. Had the midges returned and taken them all away?

"What're you talking about?" his wife asked.

"First morning we got here, I checked my ammunition locker: all my cartridges and arrows, gone."

His words stained the air like firework smoke. No one said anything for a few seconds. I worried he thought we'd done it. Nia had certainly *wanted* to. I risked a glance her way. Her expression was neutral, but she must've been relieved our captors had done her work for her. They'd 3D printed everything in the Jackson house except the ammo.

"I have a couple hunting rifles and a crossbow," Riley told the rest of us.

"Why didn't you say anything?" Charleze asked.

"Didn't want to upset you."

"Maybe they want a gun-free community," Nia remarked.

Which I didn't think was the best thing to say, but luckily at that moment Alyssa came rushing in, her face bright with joy.

"Look, Mama! Noah found Leonella!" She waved a small lilac princess in front of Charleze's face.

"Isn't that wonderful!" Charleze said.

Taking the slowest steps I'd ever seen, Noah followed Alyssa into the room.

"Noah, she's been searching for that for days," Riley said. "Where'd you find it, son?"

Dad and Nia were looking at Noah with confusion. He stared at me with utter helplessness. I should've taken that stupid princess away from him. My anger waned when I saw him struggle to fill his little chest with air.

Then, with a flare of defiance, Noah said, "*Well*, she was *hogging* Rumpety, so I—"

"It was in Alyssa's purse," Mackenzie said, looking back at her phone. "I saw it while I was packing up her toys."

Riley lifted his whiskey glass with a grin and said, "Well, here's to good news, no matter how small."

15

When I got up to take Kimmy for a pee, Mackenzie said, "Mind if I come?"

"Sure," I said, trying to hide my surprise. I wanted to believe she liked my company, but probably she wanted to grill me about the princess toy.

"Stay close," her father said, and gave me a look that told me that if anything happened to his daughter, he'd hold me accountable.

The puppy scampered around the side of the cottage to his favorite place. He sniffed all over but didn't seem particularly interested in peeing. I didn't say anything for a bit, hoping Mackenzie would talk first. She didn't.

"Thanks for doing that," I said eventually.

"How many times you guys been inside our house?"

"It was just the one other time. When we came to leave the note, Noah ran inside and we went after him. I didn't even know he took the toy until today."

"You steal anything else?"

"We only steal toy princesses."

She didn't smile. "The ammo?"

Her stare reminded me of her father's. I tried not to look away or she'd think I was guilty.

"We did not take the ammo."

"I want to trust you, Xavier, but it is very creepy, imagining people going through my house, especially if I was there in a drugged sleep."

"You guys were not there, I promise."

"Tell me absolutely everything you did."

I figured this was some kind of test, to see how honest I was. So I told her about looking inside her father's wallet. I told her about the storage room and seeing the guns. When I casually mentioned that Nia had peeked into the medicine cabinet, her eyebrows lifted, but she didn't ask for details.

"And you were in my bedroom. Twice?"

"Yes."

"Did you look at my phone?"

I exhaled. "Yes."

Her gaze hardened. "What did you see?"

"There was a picture of you and . . ." I almost said Kronk.

"Lucas?"

I nodded. "And there was a text from him."

"What did it say?"

She must have known, but she wanted every detail out of me.

"U all good?"

"Anything else?"

"No! Your phone was locked."

Her shoulders relaxed a bit. Half jokingly, she said, "And you didn't do anything creepy like get into my bed or anything?"

"No!"

"Why're you blushing?"

"It's a pretty weird question!"

"Did you see anything else, Xavier?"

"Yes."

"What?"

"A pregnancy test."

Her face became very still. She waited.

"It was face down," I said.

"Did you turn it over?"

"I thought it was an antigen test. I thought maybe . . ."

"So you turned it over."

I nodded. I'd seen the single pink line, and wouldn't have known what it meant if the legend hadn't been printed right on the case: NOT PREGNANT.

"Well. You certainly had a good look around."

We said nothing for a bit. Kimmy had his pee and tugged at the leash.

"I could tell," she said. "Yesterday on our porch, just your face."

I was startled, thinking I was so easy to read.

"Can you get rid of it for me?" she said.

"What?"

She reached inside her shirt and pulled the pregnancy test from under her bra strap. "If I put it in the garbage, they might find it."

"Can't you just bury it outside somewhere?"

"When? I'm not even allowed on the porch alone. I've been carrying it around with me the whole time. Can't you just?"

Her face was too imploring to resist. I took it.

"Did you tell your parents?" she asked, watching my face carefully.

I jammed the test into my pocket. "No."

She gave me a good long look. "I trust you. You'd make a terrible spy, by the way."

I didn't know what to expect when we went back inside, but it seemed like the magical reappearance of the princess toy hadn't raised any awkward questions.

"We all like facts," Riley was saying pleasantly. "And there's plenty we agree on. Here we are, together, in this predicament. We have been locked inside this place. We have been deprived of our freedom. But we're all agreed we want to get out, yes?"

Dad gave a tired little laugh and said, "Well . . ."

"Just humor me, Mr. Oak, and entertain the tiny chance that we are actually here on Earth, maybe under a potato field in Idaho."

I couldn't help chuckling. That glowing jellyfish of an idea flared up: Earth, right here, right now.

Riley went on. "Let's figure we can get out and return to our homes. You said you have another son. Xavier has a mother. All of us have loved ones waiting on us. We owe it to them to try to break free."

It was intoxicating, even the *chance* of it. *Riley might be right*, I thought. And even if he was wrong and we busted out of the dome just to discover we were somewhere far from Earth, at least we'd *know*, once and for all. Wasn't that worth something?

"We've just doubled our manpower," Riley said. "We have a lot more resources now."

"Our families need to work together," Charleze chimed in.

My father said, "We've already tried everything. Unless something changes, unless they *decide* to let us out . . ."

I suddenly felt embarrassed by him. He seemed defeated compared to Riley's fire and resolve.

"I get it," said Riley. "They've had you in here three years, and that would beat anyone down. It's exactly what they want. Compliance. Don't let them break your spirit, Caleb. This is worth fighting for. I promise you, there is a doorway out of here."

"I found a hole in the sky," I said.

"Now that," said Riley with a grin, "is a very exciting bit of information."

16

The Jacksons stayed for dinner, and we all shared cauliflower-and-chickpea stew, a fresh loaf of corn bread, and goat cheese. The grown-ups got through the usual grown-up questions about what everyone did for a living. Riley seemed interested, and not at all surprised, to learn that both Dad and Nia worked for NGOs. Charleze was an elementary school teacher. "Education is so important," she said. "How're they supposed to grow up and make decisions if their little heads are filled with nonsense?"

We tried to keep the conversation general, so we wouldn't upset Noah or Alyssa, but I couldn't help asking what year it was, because Dad had freaked me out earlier, talking about how long it might've taken for us to get here. I was super relieved when Riley confirmed it was just three years since we'd been taken from our cottage. And then we all had questions about what was going on back on Erf. The current president? Canadian prime minister? (They weren't quite sure.) Were there any wars in Europe? Peace in the Middle East? Riley gave us football stats, but he didn't follow hockey, which was all my father cared about, being a lifelong Habs fan.

The Jacksons were very polite and complimentary about the food, but sometimes I caught Nia's expression and knew that she was not finding the fourth most charming accent in America irresistibly charming.

After the meal, Riley said he wanted to get going before they lost the light. I offered to guide them back, but he said he knew the way well enough—and I wondered just how many times he'd crept over to check us out. After they left, my cheeks were flushed and my head noisy, but we couldn't talk properly until Noah had been put to bed.

"Of all the people to end up with," said Nia. "A conspiracy theorist."

"What if he's right?" I said.

"*And* a climate change denier."

Dad shook his head. "He's not right, Zay."

"But those pictures—"

"Terrifying how sure of himself he is," said Nia.

I said, "We could be on Earth right now!"

"You'd think he was an undercover agent," Dad said, "not a prison guard."

"Associate warden of operations," Nia said in a mocking southern accent. "Another very bad sign."

They were being pretty mean about him. "You're against prisons, too?" I asked.

Nia said, "My problem with prisons is the inmates are disproportionately people of color. Black in the US, and Indigenous in Canada. It's a deeply racist system. Did you hear what he said about right-sizing and climate refugees?"

"What'd he say?" I asked, confused.

"Huge problem."

"Well, isn't it?"

"It was the way he said it. It's obvious he thinks we should be building bigger walls to stop them entering our countries. Not helping them, but keeping them *out*. The poorest, most desperate people on the planet. It's disgusting."

She looked at my father for corroboration, but he seemed reluctant to give it. I was with him on this one. I wasn't convinced Riley had meant it that way. But I could tell Nia was dead set against him.

"You didn't take his ammo, did you?" I asked.

It came out more accusingly than I'd intended, but I couldn't think of a smoother way to ask. I noticed Dad was waiting for her answer, too.

"No. But I'm glad someone had the courage."

That last line was definitely directed at my father.

"Let's hope Riley doesn't suspect us," he said.

Nia scoffed. "They're way too invested in their deep government plot."

"Mackenzie's not like that," I pointed out.

"No, she seems to believe in science, at least," Dad acknowledged.

"I hope this new pandemic's not super bad," I said.

Nia sighed. "At least we're out of harm's way here."

"Not so great for Mom or Sam," I said coldly.

"Sorry, Zay. I wasn't thinking."

"What if we've been on Earth all along?" I demanded. I felt like I kept bringing this up and no one was even considering it.

Dad shook his head. "Even if we are, our situation hasn't changed. We still can't get out."

"Riley thinks we can."

Amid all the confusion in my head was a drumbeat of hope. I didn't know why Dad couldn't feel it, too. Maybe he really had been beaten down.

"He wants me to show him the hole in the sky tomorrow."

Dad rubbed at his eyes, like he was already regretting the whiskey. "It's going to take Riley a while to come to terms with this."

"So you're not going to help him?"

"He'll want to try all the same things we did. It's understandable."

"Maybe he'll have some new ideas."

It seemed so closed-minded, so mean-spirited, to not even consider that Riley might be right. More than that, it seemed arrogant. Nia was disgusted by how sure of himself Riley was, but were she and Dad any different? They were alien abduction; Riley was deep government facility.

"Sooner or later," Dad said, "he'll accept the facts. So no, I'm not going to help him."

"Well, I am."

For three years I'd done what I was asked. I'd never said no. My only rogue act had been scouting for a way out. Everything else was for the family and the farm.

"Harvest is going to get very busy soon," said Nia.

"I'll do everything that needs doing," I said.

Nia looked at my father, wanting him to weigh in.

"We can't neglect the farm," he told me. "And the Jacksons can't afford to neglect theirs either."

"I can help with that, too," I said quickly. "It's not fair for Mackenzie and Alyssa to starve because you don't like their parents."

A smile softened Dad's face, and I think he understood the stronger source of my enthusiasm.

"Maybe we should all go over," Nia said. "Make sure their animals are okay. Show them it's not so hard."

"That's the best way we can help them," Dad agreed, looking at me.

When I walked inside the Jacksons' house the next morning, Alyssa was eating a bowl of Cap'n Crunch in front of the TV.

"What *is* that?" Noah exclaimed, pointing at the screen blaring with noise and color.

He'd never seen a television. It startled me, too: not the technology, but the sheer normalcy of it. *Kid With Cereal and Cartoons*. The Jacksons had a TV with an old disc player because they weren't maniacs like Nia. Noah sat down beside Alyssa, staring awestruck at the animated unicorns. They were singing about how you were beautiful, no matter the size or shape of your horn.

"This show makes me want to put a bullet in my head," Mackenzie whispered. "They sing *everything*. They are never *not* singing."

"What else do you have?"

"Aside from every single episode of this show? Take a look." She gestured to a drawer below the television. "Noah, you want some Cap'n Crunch?"

Noah turned to her wide-eyed, rendered speechless by his good fortune.

"Gonna say that's a yes," she said, and went to the kitchen.

I crouched over the drawer so I didn't block the TV. The selection of discs was mostly cartoons, some of which I remembered. It made me think of Sam, the stuff we'd watched together when we were kids, me watching his favorite shows, even if I didn't really like them, because I wanted to level up. He was never very far from my thoughts, same as Mom. The smallest things would sometimes surface: a shared joke, an expression on their faces.

Mackenzie brought Noah his bowl of cereal and knelt beside me. She sifted through the discs. The smell of her hair and skin made me happy.

"*Jaws*!" I said, picking up the case.

"So good! When Brody's chucking bait into the water, and the shark comes up!"

"When Hooper gets into the cage!"

"Or the beginning, and the girl gets tugged under, just a little, that first time!"

We shook our heads in shared admiration.

"It ruined an entire summer for me, though," she admitted. "I wouldn't go swimming, even in the pool."

"There's a pond here," I said. "No sharks, promise."

Earlier this morning, I'd buried her pregnancy test behind the barn. I was wondering if she was going to ask about it. Or maybe she trusted me, and never wanted to discuss it again.

"We should have a movie night," she said. "It must be forever for you guys. Do you even have a laptop with you?"

I shook my head.

"Oh man. Anything on your phone?"

"Mine just died. Like, for good."

"No!" She looked utterly stricken. "Your music, too?"

Finally, someone who truly shared my anguish. "Yes! And my photos."

"That is absolutely tragic."

The way she said it really did make it sound tragic, and I almost smiled.

"You bring that phone over here. Daddy might be able to fix it."

"I don't think it's fixable."

"He's real good with machines. Bring it next time."

"Mackenzieeeee, I can't seeeee!" Alyssa whined.

On-screen, Rainbow or Pluck or some other unicorn had just lit a candle (how, with those hooves?) under an orange paper lantern. It filled with warm air, then lifted into the sky to join a flotilla of other fire lanterns.

"All right, all right, we're moving," Mackenzie said.

We went over to the big windows and she looked out forlornly at the fields where Nia and my father were showing her parents the lentils. I'd come inside to get Noah settled and bring Mackenzie out for the farm briefing, but I could tell her heart wasn't in it. Anyway, I liked having her to myself.

"How come we're all supposed to be farmers?" she asked.

"Keeps us fit? Gives us something to do?"

"I'd rather have takeout."

I smiled. "I would not mind a pizza one bit."

"Favorite toppings?

"Ohhh. Hawaiian. Canadian invention, by the way."

"No way!"

"Yep. Greek guy who immigrated to Ontario."

"Fake news!"

"You could check . . . if we had internet. How about you?"

"Pretty basic. Pepperoni, green olives, mushrooms. I guess you don't have much meat here."

"I miss olives more," I said. "We don't grow those."

"Well, you're in luck, my friend."

She took my hand—which caused me to have a minor stroke—and led me to the kitchen. Opening their enormous fridge, she extracted a jar of olives, unscrewed it, and held it out to me.

"Go for it."

I fished one out with my fingers. They were the plump green ones with a bit of red pepper in the center. I put it in my mouth and smiled. "Yeah. That's it." I chewed very slowly, and gave a sigh when I swallowed the last morsel.

"Have another one!"

"Oh, no, that's okay."

"Go on! It was fun watching you!"

I popped another one into my mouth and put on a show, making appreciative noises.

"Okay, now it sounds like you're having sex."

I stopped, mortified. As if I'd ever had sex.

"Oh my God, you're blushing again!" she said.

"I can't help it!"

"Well, you make a great case for olives."

I handed back the jar. In the living room, the unicorns were chewing someone out for not collaborating.

"I still don't get why they don't just give us our food," she said. "People in jail get meals."

I had a theory about that. "When we were little, Sam and I had these fire-bellied newts. I'd wanted a dog, but my dad didn't want the hassle, so we got newts. They were cute. In the pet store they were zipping around in the water, catching crickets. Our parents weren't crazy about bugs getting loose all over the house. The pet store guy said we could feed the newts pellets instead. So they ate the pellets the first couple weeks, then they just sat there and watched them sink to the bottom. After a couple months two of the three died."

"You're saying they lost the will to live."

"Yep. They needed to chase their food. They needed to hunt."

"I think we're a little smarter than newts."

"We still need a purpose."

Outside, Dad was now coaching Riley and Charleze on how to use the manual plow.

"Well, I have plenty of purpose," Mackenzie said. "And it does *not* involve farming with my family. Daddy's positively embarrassing the way he can go on. And Mama's almost as bad. I swear to God I wonder sometimes if I'm their child. They love it up here—I mean, the lodge. Where it used to be. They both hunt. They both fish. You know how they met? Parachuting. There's a place they go nearby." She caught herself again. "Near the old lodge, I mean. They keep trying to get me to come. They even bought me a parachute of my own. As if I'm ever strapping that thing on."

Patt wandered into the kitchen and looked at me skeptically. Mackenzie scratched the German shepherd between his ears.

"Patt's about the only one I can tolerate. I don't even have my own room. Alyssa keeps crawling into my bed and playing with her dolls and picking her nose. When I tell her I can't sleep with all her fidgeting, she says I'll just have to try my best."

She was good at making me laugh. Dad could sometimes make me smile, and Noah's antics could crack me up, but there was something different about laughing with someone your own age. I felt like my happiness had been sprung from its cage.

Mackenzie said, "Daddy has some crazy ideas, but I trust him to get us out of here."

Even the idea of Mackenzie leaving, of me being separated from her, gave me a sharp pang.

"It'd be great if I didn't miss too much school," she added.

It took me a second to realize she was serious.

"Oh, you'll be fine," I said. "They'll have a spacebus waiting for you right outside the dome."

"Ha ha. We have a difference of opinion on our whereabouts."

"Fine. But who worries about missing school?"

"Me! I'm vice president of the student council next year. Also, I need to keep my grades up for college. Lucas and I have plans."

I never even got to start high school, and she was already planning the rest of her life with Lucas.

"He's probably been texting me. Thinking I'm ignoring him." Her eyes were suddenly shiny. "I want to be back there with him, especially if things get bad with this new pandemic." She yanked a tissue from the box on the counter. "My parents have their heads in the sand about the whole thing, and I hope they're right. But who knows?"

"Yeah," I said, imagining Kronk taking his last breath in a hospital bed, and Mackenzie collapsing helplessly against my chest.

She blotted the edges of her eyes. Stepping closer to me, she asked, "Is my eyeliner messed up?"

"No, it's good." My heart thumped, being so near her.

"Do you have a girlfriend back home?"

A grainy image of Serena flared in my mind. "Not really," I said, and then, because I didn't want to seem like a total loser, added, "Something was just starting maybe, until, yeah, *this* happened."

She shook her head sympathetically. "We're gonna get you out of here, Xavier Oak."

From the living room the unicorns sang deliriously about how teamwork had saved Hornville.

"With just a little help from the Unicorn Squad," I added.

We were still giggling when Riley came into the kitchen. I thought he might chew Mackenzie out for missing the farm briefing, but his mind was elsewhere.

"That's enough farming for me today. I don't even like lentils. Xavier, you want to show me this hole in the sky?"

17

Riley climbed up the tree after me. At the top there was some jostling around to get comfortable, but we found good perches against the trunk. It suddenly occurred to me that Dad had never climbed a tree with me—not even to see the hole in the sky.

I was worried that we wouldn't be able to find it in daylight. I'd only caught sight of it when it was backlit by the moon's glow. I had Mom's birding binoculars, but Riley's pair looked much more hard-core, with lots of focusing rings and buttons. As we scanned the sky, we talked. He asked me the usual grown-up questions, which were especially funny since they all had to do with Erf things. What I wanted to study at college. My plans when I finished school. My dream job.

"I don't think that's in the cards for me," I told him.

"Sure it is," he said, with such conviction that I almost believed it. "It's been hard for you folks, but you, Xavier, you've got fight in you. I can tell."

Maybe he was right. I'd been the only one still searching for a way out. Nia and my father had everything they needed here, but there were plenty of things on the other side I wanted. Although . . . now that Mackenzie was on the scene, they didn't seem nearly as urgent.

"It's great we've got some company now," I told Riley. "I mean, I'm sorry this happened to you, but . . ."

"Understood. People need people."

"Just having someone my own age," I added.

I found him surprisingly easy to talk to, especially with both of us looking elsewhere.

"I remember sixteen real well. These last three years must've been tough. Hang in there just a little longer."

As though in a matter of days I'd be partying it up in high school. But his confidence had gravity, and I wanted to be yanked out of my three-year orbit.

"Mackenzie could use some of your fortitude. Hasn't even been a week, and she's carrying on about her young man."

"Lucas."

"See, she's already moaned to you about him. Fine young man, but he'll wait for her."

I wondered if Riley was gently trying to warn me off.

Too late for that.

"Ah! Think I got it," Riley said. "It's faint, but you said hexagonal, right?" He held the binoculars out for me to take a look. "Bearing 143."

I didn't know what he meant until I looked though the eyepieces and saw the digital readout of the internal compass. I found the right bearing and after a few seconds nodded. "Yeah, that's it!"

I was incredibly relieved and ridiculously proud when he clapped me on the shoulder and said, "Good work. Not many people would've had the sense, or patience, to search for that."

"That must be where the midges come from," I said.

"Looks open. Did it look like this when you saw it?"

I nodded. From a clasped pocket on his pants, he took out a small notepad and pencil and jotted down some numbers.

"It's four or five kilometers up," I said.

"Only if this is a dome."

We'd always assumed it was a dome, because of how it curved and because it just seemed like the most natural shape for a sky. Planetariums had domed ceilings, why not alien snow globes?

"You think the walls only curve for a bit, then flatten out?" I asked.

I looked up at the scattered clouds, the sun. I remembered Mom telling me about palaces and churches she'd seen in Italy. They had flat ceilings painted to look like a sky filled with angels and cupids. The artists were so skilled at faking perspective that they could trick you into thinking some things were much farther away than others. *Trompe l'oeil.* Those paintings had been done hundreds of years ago. Whatever technology *they* were using now to mimic a sky, it would be a million times better.

"Doesn't really make sense, a dome," said Riley. "Waste of space. Three miles high at the peak? They don't need all that clearance to ventilate this place. End of the day, these people have budgets."

"Maybe aliens have bigger budgets."

"Nice one," he said with a grin. "Wish we knew how high it was. If I had my crossbow bolts, I'd fire one straight up."

"How high can it go?" I asked.

"Maybe fifteen hundred feet. If it stuck, we'd know our ceiling was no higher. Height of the Empire State Building."

It was a tantalizing image. Could we build our own tower? Then I shook my head. "Pretty sure you can't make anything that high out of wood. Even if we knew what we were doing. And climbing the dome wall, we tried that already. Even the best mountaineer in the world couldn't do it, not with the wall spitting out anything you hammer into it."

"I like the way you think an idea through," Riley said. "You're a problem solver."

"Probably because I played a lot of Dungeons and Dragons."

"What's that?"

He actually seemed interested as I explained.

When I was done, he asked, "So if this were a game, how would you get up there?"

I laughed. "I'd find a Grygax. They're like big goats with wings. You can ride them."

"Wouldn't that be something," he said, staring off.

"Don't suppose you know how to make an airplane?" I meant it as a joke, but almost right away the possibility of flight took hold of me. "Like one of those ultralights—"

"Too many parts we don't have," said Riley.

A new idea inflated inside my head.

"You've got parachutes," I said. "Three of them, right?"

"Four actually." He looked at me thoughtfully. "You're thinking we could sew them together somehow."

"Hot-air balloon," I said.

He shook his head in admiration. "A hot-air balloon. You, Xavier Oak, are one smart kid."

"Might've been better to keep that idea to yourself," my father said later as we walked home with Nia and Noah.

"The Jacksons seemed to like it," I said.

Riley had been singing my praises after we returned from the tree. Charleze had given me a squeeze and called me a hero. Mackenzie looked genuinely impressed—and hopeful, maybe already thinking about her reunion with Lucas. Alyssa had asked if they'd be back in time for Suzie's birthday party, then turned glum when her mother replied, "We'll see, darling."

"Where's the balloon going to take us?" Noah asked now.

"There's not going to be a balloon," Nia said.

"You don't know that," I countered. "It's something we never tried."

We crossed the creek on the rocks. Dad swung Noah up onto his shoulders.

"Does he even know anything about ballooning?" Nia asked.

"He parachutes."

"I wouldn't get in that thing," Nia said.

"Will we all fit?" Noah asked, which I thought was a relevant question.

Dad said, "Getting enough fabric is just one step."

"He knows, Dad."

"He needs a burner, and enough fuel to—"

"Dad, he knows all that!"

Nia said, "All he's going to do is waste time and energy. If he messes up his harvest, they won't have enough food for the winter, which means we'll have to share so they don't starve. A very shitty winter for all of us."

"Shitty!" Noah said, delighted. "Shit-tit-tit-titty!"

"You don't say that word, Noah," she told him mildly, then shot me a look like it was my fault.

"I don't get this!" I said. "A week ago you said we'd never reach that hatch in the sky, so why bother. Now we have a way! Because I had a great idea that might actually get us out of here. You're not even a little excited?"

"The opposite," said Nia.

"We're not on Earth, Zay."

"We might be."

Dad looked more disappointed than angry. Maybe he thought I'd been infected by Riley's conspiracy theory.

"Either way," Nia said, "if *they* want to keep us here, why would they let us succeed?"

That was the best point yet, and I didn't have an answer. Even if the balloon got off the ground, *they* could stop it. Like any good Dungeon Master, I'd already run the scenario. They could send their midges to puncture the balloon. They could close the hatch and leave us bumping against the ceiling.

They could render us unconscious and carry us back down to Earth.

"Maybe they want us to succeed?" I said half-heartedly.

Nia's raised eyebrows were deflating. "It's doomed," she said.

The terrible thing was, part of me wanted her to be right. Because if my idea actually worked, Mackenzie would literally float out of my life forever.

18

"It's kind of like watching Noah build his ark," Mackenzie said to me a week later, as we pushed more hay into the goats' feeder. "Daddy keeps muttering about cubic feet and rushing off to measure things."

Riley had not been idle. In the last seven days he'd made his own circumnavigation of the wall, just to satisfy himself. He had a go at digging under it, then scaling it. He admitted those were dead ends... so now it was full steam ahead with my hot-air balloon idea. He'd cleared out their barn loft for a workshop. He was still at the planning stage. Before he made the first cut, he wanted to calculate every last square inch of material. The four parachutes, each with a reserve chute, would yield the most. Then there were their jumpsuits, a big nylon camping tent, a couple tarps, and assorted rain gear. He'd sew it all together with fishing line, which was very strong, and which he had a big supply of.

"This will work, right?" Mackenzie asked as we pushed the last of the hay into the feeder.

Like I was suddenly an aviation expert. "In principle," I said cautiously. "I mean, he probably won't be able to bring two of every animal."

She laughed. I didn't want to get her hopes up. How was I supposed to know? I had an eighth-grade education, and physics had never been my forte. It might work. The only certainty was that it would take months. Months in which I'd get to hang out with Mackenzie and let her forget about Lucas.

"Daddy can get awfully stressed if things don't work out," she said.

I wondered what happened when Riley got stressed.

Every day now when I finished up work at my own place, I'd head over to the Jacksons' to see what needed doing. They'd started collecting the eggs at least, and milking the goats first thing. Often I did the second milking for them. There was weeding to do, and I showed them how to scythe grass for hay feed. Mackenzie usually helped, and sometimes Charleze, who, at the end of the day, would always try to give me something from their deep freeze. I'd say it was all right, and she would tell me not to argue, it was pointless. Then she'd thrust some wild boar into my hands.

"Who even knows what it'll be like when we get back," Mackenzie said gloomily. "If this new thing spreads?"

"They probably have good vaccines ready to go," I told her, worrying about Sam and Mom.

"Hope so. Not that my parents would take them. And I read this one's pretty different from the last one. A lockdown would totally screw up my college plans. I wanted to study at NYU and Lucas was going to get work modeling and acting."

"Oh yeah?"

"He's going to make it," she said, like she was used to people challenging her. "When you see him onstage, you just know. He has that *thing*."

Eyes too close together? I thought.

"Presence?" I said, trying to be generous.

"Presence, yeah." She looked away with a little frown of annoyance. "He knows it, too. He can be such a jackass sometimes. Anyway, New York might go down the drain. Even without a pandemic, the city's pretty messed up."

"How?"

"You heard about the seawall they were planning? Because of all the flooding?

Anyway, it got canceled after the last election because the governor said they didn't need it and it was just an 'ideological joyride' and too expensive anyway. So now there's nothing protecting the city from sea surges."

"It sounds pretty bad." Lately I'd been thinking less about things On Erf, mostly because I was so happy that Mackenzie was Up Here. But my thoughts still strayed to Mom and Sam, and what life might be like for them.

Mackenzie shrugged ruefully. "It's like the scientists said: sea levels rise, the oceans get more acidic, and species become extinct. There's smart people trying, and some good things are happening, but it's not nearly enough. Most people think if they get a heat pump, problem solved. Like my parents. And I used to be the same. When everyone around you believes something, *you* believe it. All our friends, the people at the church. Thank God for Ms. Taylor."

She told me about her ninth-grade history teacher, who'd made the students read newspapers and investigate current events. She'd taught them how to find good information on the internet. Mackenzie loved her, and had even started a fossil fuel divestment club at school.

"There was me and two other kids," she told me.

I'd just inherited all my opinions; Mackenzie had earned hers, which I thought was pretty amazing.

"Lots to go back and fight for," she said.

But I thought: *Out of harm's way.*

Nia's words. And I felt ashamed. Because I wanted to tell Mackenzie, just *suggest*, that it kind of made sense to wait things out here awhile. *Why not just do lockdown with me?*

"We should probably get the chickens inside for the night," I said.

They'd had a good afternoon forage and seemed content being waved back toward their coop.

"Thanks for helping us out so much," Mackenzie said as she closed the hatch. "I like it."

Her trademark Egyptian eye makeup didn't seem quite as heavy today. I wondered if she was conserving it or if this was her attempt to adapt to farm life.

"You tried goat milk yet?" I asked.

Mackenzie wrinkled her nose. "It tastes like foot."

"You're right! I've been trying to find a good comparison, and you just did it."

"Alyssa's feet smell that way at the end of the day."

"You get used to it." I laughed.

"Her feet?"

"The milk."

"Hope so."

"We can teach you how to make yogurt and cheese if you like."

"Hooray."

"Your parents made a decision about kids yet?"

She looked at me, startled.

"Sorry. Kids, like baby goats. As in, do you want your female goats to keep producing milk next spring?"

She looked miserable. "You don't really think we'll be here that long, do you?"

"It's just something you have to decide in the fall if . . ."

I realized I was about to say *if you want to get the females pregnant*, and figured she wouldn't want to hear the word *pregnant*.

"Thanks, Zay," she said, and surprised me by giving me a hug.

"For what?"

I realized this was the first time I'd put my arms around a girl. It was all so new, all the contours and warmth of her. She told me how grateful she was that I was here, and how she would've gone crazy if I wasn't. I hugged her back and said that everything would work out fine. When she pulled away she looked a bit embarrassed. With mock Southern belle melodrama, she said:

"I simply don't know how I'd endure this trial without the kindness of a handsome stranger like you."

I laughed, but she had no idea how I'd clasp that compliment to me, even if it was said in fun.

She elbowed me. "You, sir, are blushing."

"Fourth most charming accent in America."

When Patt started barking, I knew my family must've arrived, and brought Kimmy. The Jacksons had invited us all for dinner. Mackenzie called the German shepherd over and shushed him, and we headed for the porch, where Charleze was greeting everyone.

Noah was having a good ride on the rocking chair, which was still a novelty to him. Alyssa squished in beside him, and they both giggled, seeing how fast they could make it go. I caught the way Nia smiled at them; Dad was grinning, too. Their son was playing with another child close to his age. He had a friend. I had a friend, too, and wished she was more than that, but she already had a boyfriend who was going to be a failed actor.

"Mackenzie, will you fetch your father from the barn?" Charleze asked.

"I want to wash up. I smell like farm."

"I'll go," I said, but didn't need to, because Riley was already crossing the pasture toward us, hand held high.

"Hello, Mighty Oaks!" he called out. "Welcome!"

19

"No idea how good this is," said Riley, uncorking a bottle of wine as we sat down around the table. "Someone gave it to us a couple years back, and I can't think of a better occasion."

"The finest wine that can be 3D printed," Mackenzie joked.

"Believe me, anything's better than Chateau Oak," said my father.

Riley poured everyone a glass except for Alyssa and Noah, who got some of the Jacksons' dwindling supply of cranberry juice.

Charleze had made the table look really nice with ironed napkins and candles. In front of each of us was a plate with a T-bone steak, a steaming baked potato topped with sour cream, and carrots and peas gleaming with butter.

"If it's all right with you folks," Charleze said, "we like to say grace."

"Oh. Of course," said Dad.

All the Jacksons reached out to join hands with the people next to them.

Sorry, Mackenzie mouthed to me, but I didn't mind taking her hand one bit. Charleze closed her eyes and bowed her head as she thanked God for the meal before us, for bringing us together in our time of need. She mentioned all of us by name, and asked God to continue to look over us.

"Amen to that," said Riley.

"Caleb—now that is a wonderful name," Charleze said to Dad. "Do you know its meaning?"

"I'm not sure I do."

"Caleb was one of the twelve spies that Moses sent out to Canaan, to see if it could be the Promised Land."

"Ah."

I knew Moses was from the Bible, but that was not a book that had played any role in my life. The spy part actually made me a bit paranoid. I still worried that Riley didn't entirely trust us.

"And now I'd like to make a toast," Riley said. "To our great new friends, the Oaks. And to Xavier, whose idea is going to win us back our freedom."

I blushed because it was such a weighty claim, and no one outside my family had ever toasted me before. As we clinked glasses, I made sure to grin at my father: *Little bit of a hero over here.*

"How's it going so far?" my father asked Riley as we ate.

"Good. Nearly ready to start stitching. Could sure use some extra hands once we get going. Nia, how's your sewing?"

"In our house, Caleb's the one who sews on buttons."

"Ha! Well, both of you, then."

They smiled, noncommittal, which I thought was stingy.

"How's your steak?" Charleze asked. "Imagine it's been a while."

It had. I'd gone so long without beef that the texture seemed strange, and the taste of blood made me feel like I'd bitten the inside of my mouth. I took another swallow of wine, which was amazingly fruity and smooth, almost oily, compared with Chateau Oak.

"Any idea how you're going to heat the air in the balloon?" Dad asked.

"I've got a full tank of propane. I'm hoping I can rig it up as a burner."

"Will that be enough, you think?"

I didn't see why Dad had to grill him right now, when the Jacksons were giving us dinner and being so friendly. I knew my father didn't think the thing would even get finished. And if he was serious about fixing possible problems, there'd be plenty of chances without everyone around the table. It had to be jealousy. Dad wanted, literally, to burst Riley's balloon.

"Not nearly enough, no," said Riley. "We'll need a big wood fire for the launch; we'll need the propane to keep it hot during the flight."

"Can me and Noah watch TV?" Alyssa asked.

"Noah's not finished his meal, darling."

With extra speed Noah started forking food into his mouth.

"Caleb, you have any experience with metal work?" Riley inquired.

"None, I'm afraid."

"I'm thinking of a lightweight frame to support the burner under the envelope. I figure some of our tools can be reshaped if we heat them in a makeshift forge."

"You'll miss those tools, especially at harvest," Nia said.

Riley lifted his hands. "I need the metal."

"You're going to need food, too."

"Our deep freeze is large."

I was starting to worry Riley might be overestimating just how large. Luckily the conversation moved on. There was a little talk about how high the hatch was, and what the air pressure and temperature might be like. Riley didn't think any of that would be a problem.

At least he and my father seemed to have called a truce over our captors' identity: humans or aliens? Maybe they both knew there was no point arguing it; neither was changing his mind. Riley wasn't worried about ballooning into another galaxy.

And then Charleze shifted to friends and relatives who she wanted to see as soon as she got home.

"So, Nia, where are your people from?" Riley asked.

"Montreal."

"I meant originally."

I could see Nia sit up just a touch straighter.

"Same as you, Riley. Africa, three hundred thousand years ago."

Which I thought was a pretty cool reply, but Riley didn't seem to get that he was being told to knock it off. He gave his dimpled smile and said, "I guess I meant a little more recently."

"Canada for three generations. Before then, Haiti."

"Riley loves to know where *everyone* comes from," Charleze said.

"I find it interesting, is all," said Riley. "What a big old mix the world's become."

"Would you like to know where I'm from?" Dad asked pleasantly.

"I'm sorry if I've given offense," Riley said.

"It's fine," said Nia.

Charleze said, "Riley, honey, we need more wine."

"Chateau Oak next," he announced, going to the kitchen.

"Can we watch TV *now*?" Alyssa asked.

Charleze nodded. "Not too loud."

Alyssa and Noah bolted from the table and had a passionate discussion about which *Unicorn Squad* episode to watch. Noah had quickly become a convert. All he talked about now was Pluck, Spirit, and Rainbow, and their various skills, including robotics and origami.

I noticed that Nia had left quite a bit of her steak, and was concentrating on the vegetables. Even though it was making me feel a little sick, I was determined to work my way through the entire T-bone, so I didn't hurt anyone's feelings. I did manage to discreetly drop a few pieces for Kimmy, who was scampering around underneath the table.

Riley returned with our bottle of bad wine and something else, which he placed beside me.

It was my phone. I'd brought it over a few days ago after Mackenzie kept insisting. When I touched it, the screen lit up.

"You fixed it!"

"Well, we got very lucky," he said, squeezing my shoulder. "I found an old phone kicking around, and I swapped out the battery. Yours was well and truly dead. Can't promise how long this one'll last."

"Thanks so much!"

Changing a phone battery was no easy feat. It must've taken him a long time. He had no idea how grateful I was. He'd just returned my music, my Sam songs, and my photos. In the past three years, my Earth memories had gotten grainier and further away. Riley had given me a better set of binoculars to see them through.

"That was very kind, Riley. Thank you," my father said, and I hoped he felt like garbage because he wasn't doing anything for the balloon project.

Mackenzie smiled at me. "Let's hear some of this prehistoric music of yours." To her mother, she said, "We'll go upstairs where we can't hear unicorns."

I'd never been invited to a girl's bedroom, and I didn't look at anyone as I left the table, in case I looked smug. *Just heading upstairs with Mackenzie Jackson, vice president of the student council.* Maybe I was imagining it, but I felt Riley's eyes burning into the side of my head.

She kicked clothes out of the way, and we sat on the floor with our backs against her bed. I'd been in her room before (twice) but this was the first time we'd been in it together, and it felt fundamentally different and altogether more exciting.

"So, what've you got?" she said, hooking my phone up to a portable speaker.

I was suddenly nervous. Music was really personal. I didn't want to play my favorite song first, in case she hated it. With Sam we'd just volley music back and forth and call it crap, or okay, or freaking amazing. I didn't even know what Mackenzie liked, and everything I had was at least three years old. I searched for something uncontroversial and decided on "Pumpin Blood" by NONONO. It would probably end up on a car commercial (maybe it already had) but it was still a crowd-pleaser.

"Oh, I know this one," she said after the first few notes. "It's good."

Her shoulders swayed lightly to the beat, and I relaxed. By the end she was singing along to the chorus, and even did that whistling bit. I tried not to stare too long at her mouth.

"Your turn," I said afterward, eager to get a sense of her taste.

She scrolled through her library, pausing occasionally, pulling her mouth thoughtfully to one side. "Okay. I was into this one last month. I don't think it has staying power, but I got a kick out of it."

It started with a simple acoustic guitar riff, and then a guy with a feverish voice came in, talking about how messed up he was, and how he destroyed everything he cared about. A second voice came in, hoarse and tormented, wailing about how he couldn't sleep, couldn't think, and nothing helped. I didn't think much of the lyrics, but the song had a raw energy to it, and I definitely felt my nerve endings spark. I wondered if it made Mackenzie think of Lucas.

"It's supposed to be about saying no to drugs," Mackenzie said, amused. "But if you watch the video? They are definitely *not* saying no to drugs. You've probably seen it."

"I'm a little behind on my videos," I said.

"Oh, right. Sorry. You're up."

We each took a couple more turns. We were lying side by side on the floor now, looking at each other's song lists, pointing out stuff we liked or hated. It was the best time I'd had in years.

"Okay, this one's pretty old but it's still a favorite," I said, not letting her see what I was choosing.

As the first notes of Chappell Roan's "Super Graphic Ultra Modern Girl" pumped from the speaker, I had no idea what she was thinking. She shook her head and my heart sank. Then she turned it up.

"I love this song." She sprang to her feet and pulled me after her. We jumped around the room. It was a jumping kind of song. Our arms thrashed like branches in a gale. The beat seemed hell-bent on capsizing the whole song, but never did. Mackenzie whipped her hair from side to side. She did moves I'd never seen; I did moves that should never be invented. She shimmied and poured herself around the room. I kicked off the wall. We hollered and cheered each other on.

When the song ended, I dropped to the floor, hands folded under my head. I closed my eyes. The song reverberated in my mind, now forever choreographed to Mackenzie's moves. I'd danced to one of my favorite songs with her. I didn't think it was possible to feel any happier.

The touch of her lips against mine was so startling I stopped breathing. Every particle of me was focused on the soft warmth of her mouth closing around my lower lip, her hair brushing my face, the intoxicating scent of her shampoo and skin. Finally I opened my eyes. She gave my lower lip a tiny bite and drew back.

I breathed again and my fingertips instinctively went to my mouth, like they were trying to keep the kiss there. She was lying beside me, propped up on an elbow.

"You just looked so happy," she explained. "Also, you haven't been kissed in three years, and I figure you've earned it."

I wasn't sure how she meant *earned*. Because of my balloon idea? Helping out on their farm? Burying her pregnancy test? Or just because she felt sorry for how long I'd been trapped here?

"So should I call this a pity kiss?" I asked.

"More a good-job-hang-in-there kiss."

I'd been hoping it was because she found me irresistible, but I knew that was a long shot.

"Thanks," I said. "I think maybe I could use another one."

Her eyebrows lifted.

"Three years is a long time!" I said.

She laughed. For a giddy second, I thought she was going to kiss me again, but then her face changed and she sighed. "That was already one kiss too many. I'm in a relationship. Sorry."

I wasn't sorry. Hands down, this was the best night of my life.

"It's cool," I said. "What happens in the dome stays in the dome."

20

Five days later I was doing the weekly cleanout of our chicken coop when I heard Mackenzie call my name. It was midmorning, not the time I usually saw her, and I felt like I'd just been given a surprise gift. She was out of breath, her face lightly flushed. I wanted to hear her say she'd come because she couldn't stop thinking about me, because she had to feel my lips against hers again.

Since that first kiss, I'd been living in a haze of happiness. The kiss had not been repeated, but that didn't stop the days feeling sweeter. The mornings smelled more intense; everything looked gilded. Even when I wasn't around her, she was with me, having conversations in my head. Whatever I did or saw, I wondered, *What would Mackenzie think?* and I'd hear her voice answer. I even imagined a day when she'd say, "You know what, I've just realized Lucas isn't the one for me, Zay—because *you* are."

"Hey," I said, stepping away from the chicken coop because, even in my ecstatic state, it smelled like shit, and I worried I might, too. "What's up?"

"Did you guys lose power?"

I felt myself deflate. "No. Don't think so." I glanced toward the cottage, which told me nothing. "When did it go out?"

"This morning."

We walked to the cottage and I checked a few light switches in the main room, which were fine.

"How about your fridge?" she asked.

When I opened the door, the light went on, and I was greeted by a wave of cool air.

"Sure you didn't blow a fuse or anything?" I said.

"Daddy checked that."

In three years, we'd never lost power, not so much as a flicker. It wasn't like there were power lines to blow down. The source of our electricity remained a mystery.

"I'm sure it'll come back on," I said.

"Daddy's worried everything's going to thaw."

Now I understood why she'd run here. I pictured the depths of their freezer chest: the frozen pizzas and vegetables, the endless cuts of meat. Riley was counting on that food to last them a long time, or at least until they sailed out of here. I checked our own crammed little freezer. "We can maybe fit some of your stuff..."

"He wanted to move the whole chest over, if you guys had power. Is that okay?"

"Yeah, but how much does that thing weigh?"

"He says we can use the wagon."

Like us, the Jacksons had a wooden cart with four metal-rimmed wheels, because *they* apparently thought it was fun to give us the tools of nineteenth-century farmers. It wouldn't be fun maneuvering that thing through the woods.

I found Dad in the fields and told him the situation. Nia stayed behind with Noah, and the three of us set out for the Jacksons'. Mackenzie walked ahead, fast. She seemed on edge. *Daddy can get awfully stressed if things don't work out.*

When we reached their farm, Riley was pacing on the porch. He reminded me of the man who'd greeted me that first day.

"Still no power?" Dad called out as we approached.

"Nope. You?"

"They've got power," Mackenzie reported.

"Interesting," said Riley.

I cut a look at Dad. I hoped Riley didn't see this as evidence we were colluders with evil government forces. *Only sheeple get power.*

"How can we help?" Dad said.

Riley mustered a smile. "I know it's a lot to ask, but I figure with four of us, we can move the freezer to your place for the time being."

"Let's do it," Dad said, surprising me with his enthusiasm.

"Thank you so much for this," Charleze said inside as we emptied the contents of the chest into coolers and ice-filled plastic bags. "Alyssa and I'll walk on ahead with the first load."

Empty, the freezer was lighter than I thought. Getting it onto the cart was the easy part. Pulling the cart across open fields was work. Hauling it through the woods was nearly impossible. It was very slow going. Dad and Riley pushed, and Mackenzie and I stayed up front to pull and steer. Patt trotted alongside for a while and then raced on ahead to Charleze and Alyssa.

The cart wasn't built for uneven ground, and tilted wildly over roots and holes. The freezer slewed around and nearly toppled off several times. We pushed and pulled and heaved that cart, and between us we went through every obscenity there was. I was quite impressed by Mackenzie's vocabulary. Toward the end, one of the wheels was more square than round and we had to drag the thing on the final stretch to our cottage.

When we finally shoved the freezer onto our deck and through the sliding doors, Nia and Charleze were waiting with glasses of cool water, which we drained gratefully. I could hear Noah and Alyssa playing farm animals in the bedroom.

"That was a beast of a job," said Riley to me and Dad, "and you two are true gentlemen to make it possible."

It didn't take long to realize that the deep freeze wouldn't fit in our kitchen without blocking the counters. So we moved furniture and pushed it against a wall in the family room.

"We can't just leave it smack in the middle of their room, Riley," Charleze said, with an apologetic look at Nia. "I'm so sorry about this."

Dad plugged in the deep freeze and said, "It's fine, it's just temporary."

Kimmy scampered over, sniffed at it, and promptly peed on it.

"Should we go back and get the rest of the food?" I said.

Frowning, Riley held up his hand for silence. "Should be able to hear the compressor." He bent to peer at a small panel on the deep freeze. "Light's not even on. This outlet busted?"

"Don't think so," said Dad. "The lamp worked."

Noah wandered in to watch as we pushed the chest around the room, trying two other outlets. Neither made the freezer work.

Noah said helpfully, "You could try it in my room."

Riley glared at the chest, chewing his lower lip. He had the look of someone who was trying very hard to hold it together.

"It was a pretty rough ride," I said. "Maybe it got damaged on the—"

"No, that's not it. They're sending me a message. This is punishment."

I saw Nia glance worriedly at Dad. I could tell she thought Riley was overreacting.

"They don't want me working on the balloon," Riley said. "They want me farming. Yep. Out there tending my veggies." His smile seemed slightly crooked. "Like an obedient little citizen."

He opened the sliding door, and I thought he was stepping out to let off some steam, but he turned to grab the freezer.

"I'll just clear this out of your way." He yanked it so hard, the cord snapped from its socket.

"Riley, sweetheart . . ." Charleze said.

Mr. Jackson hauled the freezer roughly onto the deck, swiveled it, and sent it careening down the steps. He went after it, grabbed a metal rake leaning against the cottage, and started swinging at the deep freeze. It was almost funny at first, a cartoon man taking out his frustration. But he kept going.

"He's going to break it," Noah said.

I glanced over at Mackenzie, who stood frozen, watching. There was something in her face that made me wonder if she'd seen other incidents like this.

Nia went out onto the deck and said, "Riley, take it easy, you'll want that freezer later."

"No, ma'am. They don't want me to have it." The metal tines of the rake punctured the side. He yanked them out and struck it again.

Nia returned, looking grim. I'd often heard her say she wished she had a deep freeze. It would've meant way less preserving every fall.

"Noah, go play with Alyssa," she said.

"I want to see if he breaks it."

"Go."

With an exaggerated sigh, Noah stalked off.

Riley was still swinging. Patt snarled and barked at the deep freeze, amplifying his master's rage.

Charleze said, "He's been working so hard. He didn't need this."

Riley cursed as our rake splintered in two. He took a couple kicks at his broken-down cart, then stormed over to the pasture fence. He planted his hands on the top rail and leaned against it, his back to us. His shoulders lifted and fell, lifted and fell. One of the goats took a few steps closer and said, *"Beheheheheh,"* and I thought that goat better watch it.

Mackenzie's face was taut. Charleze went outside. Riley didn't look at her as she stood beside him and rested a hand on his shoulder. She leaned in close, tipped her forehead tenderly against his, talked to him. Eventually I saw Riley nod a few times.

When he turned and walked back to the cottage, I think everyone tensed a little bit. But when he came inside, he wore a sheepish grin and said, "I have a bit of a temper and I do apologize." He scratched at his neck. "Well. How much meat do y'all reckon we can eat the next few days?"

That night the Jacksons had dinner at our place. We cooked two packs of their thawing beef ravioli and I helped make a fresh tomato-and-basil sauce. It was the first time I'd had pasta in three years, and every mouthful felt like a celebration.

"My bet?" Riley was saying in good humor. "If we start farming, after a week or so they'll give us back our power. A reward for good behavior. Can't say I'm inclined to give them that satisfaction."

"Riley," Charleze said in gentle chastisement. "We need electricity."

I caught Nia exchanging a look with Dad. She was already very ticked off that Riley had destroyed the freezer and broken one of our rakes.

"It was well played," Riley said. "I'll give 'em that. They want to force us onto the land, so they wipe out our food surplus."

When he put it like that, it made me wonder how kindly *they* really were. We'd arrived without a deep freeze to tide us over, so we'd had no choice. We'd needed to start farming right away. Maybe Riley was right: We received kind treatment as long as we followed their playbook.

"You're not going to lose all your meat," Nia reminded them. "We're going to can it."

Our pressure canner had become one of the most important machines we had. Before we'd arrived Up Here, it had lived unused in the back of a cupboard. Now it was the reason we could have vegetables and fruit through the winter. After every harvest, we froze what we could in our small freezer and preserved the rest in jars.

"That sounds like an awfully big job," Charleze said.

"It'll be worth it."

"You're very kind," Charleze told Nia, and to her husband she said, "See, we can have your venison stew in February after all."

Riley grunted. "I doubt they want us eating meat at all."

"Oh, Daddy!" Mackenzie said, rolling her eyes.

"Want us filled with soy and all that nonsense. Keep us a little weaker. Humans need meat. That's how we evolved big brains. Scientific fact."

Under the table Mackenzie dug her fingertips into my thigh in exasperation. Even through my jeans, her touch was electric. I'd wanted to be touched all day. I took a chance and slid my hand over hers. Both of us were looking straight ahead. She turned her hand over and twined her fingers through mine. All the electrons in my skin went into overdrive, lighting up my entire body. I suppressed a sigh when Mackenzie gave a quick squeeze and slipped her hand free.

"I love Erf food!" Noah said, forking more ravioli into his mouth.

"Look at that happy little face," Riley said. "Here's a boy who likes his beef!"

"Erf food, Erf food!" Noah chanted.

Mackenzie smiled. "I love the way he says Erf."

"I do not!" said Noah indignantly.

"Go ahead and say it, then: *Earth*."

"*Erf!*" Noah said. "See?"

Then he glared at everyone because we were all either laughing or trying hard not to.

"You said it perfectly, sweetheart," Charleze told him.

"Noah," said Riley, "you can eat all the Earth food you like after we finish our balloon."

"Zay, could you pass the water, please?" said Nia, trying to change the subject.

"It's going to take us all the way to Erf?" Noah asked, wide-eyed.

"That's the plan."

"And then we'll come right back," Noah said matter-of-factly.

Riley chuckled, then stopped when he realized Noah was serious.

"I like it here," Noah said, forehead creased anxiously. "We're coming back, right?"

"Absolutely," said Dad, who was sitting beside him.

"We're not going anywhere," Nia added.

I felt a squeeze around my heart. We'd tried to keep Noah out of these conversations, but I hadn't thought about what it would mean to him, to actually leave this place. It was the only home he'd ever had. He loved it here. What would it do to him to leave?

"When will we get TV back?" asked Alyssa, which distracted Noah. He sat up straighter, only now realizing he'd lost his favorite television show.

"Bit of a blessing, huh?" Riley said, winking at his wife and Mackenzie. "No singing unicorns."

"Darling," Charleze said, "there'll be a whole lot of crying, and you know it. We need electricity. We need our kitchen. We can't impose on the poor Oaks forever."

"Honey, I'm not the one making the rules here. But all right. We'll put on a show for them. Tomorrow, you start canning, and I'll go out and till our fields. How's that?" He looked at Nia. "Think that'll get our power back?"

"Can't hurt," she said.

"Well, I think it's double helpings of ice cream for everyone tonight," Riley said with a grin. "Unless you know how to preserve that, too, Nia."

21

"I hope they're seeing us being good farmers," Mackenzie said. "How am I doing?"

"Great. Maybe a little too close to the zucchini."

We were out in the fields, and she was pushing the cultivator, weeding.

Riley and Charleze knew about things like hunting and parachuting, but when it came to farming, they were starting from zero. There was a lot I could help them with, and it made me feel good. Earlier in the week I'd shown Riley how to use the scythe, and he was out in the alfalfa right now, doing a cutting. True to his word, he'd agreed to take a break from the balloon project and tend to his farm. Charleze was canning with Nia, while Alyssa played with Noah. The two of them were getting along famously—even without *Unicorn Squad*. They had blended the princess castle and farm and all their assorted toys into a complex feudal society with endless possibilities for drama.

"You think they're watching all the time?" Mackenzie asked. "Your space aliens?"

"You still betting on evil government agents?"

It confused me that she pushed back so hard against her parents' denial of climate change and pandemics, but she agreed with them about a deep government conspiracy.

She pulled her mouth to one side. "Well, all through history, governments have done terrible things to people: made them slaves, put them in labor camps, reeducation camps, concentration camps. They've experimented on people. Even in the US—you've heard about MK-ULTRA?"

"The one where they tried to turn people into super soldiers?"

"Yeah! The CIA gave them drugs. So we have proof about stuff like that. And none about aliens."

"Except where we are now."

She suddenly looked glum. I sensed she needed to believe she was still on Earth; she needed to believe her father could rescue us.

Six days, and the Jacksons' power still hadn't come back. I was thrilled, because it meant I got to see Mackenzie even more. They were eating most of their meals at our place. There wasn't any way to preserve the Jacksons' frozen meals, so right now we were working our way through pizzas and pasta and burger patties. Between the canning and the cooking, our house smelled like pork and venison and steak and chicken all the time. After being a virtual vegetarian for three years, it took some getting used to. I couldn't deny I liked it. It was also nice having different things. I felt like we'd tried pretty much every variation of the foods available to us Up Here.

I remembered how reassuring meals were, those first days. They made me less panicky, reminded me that I was in my body, taking breaths. I was still *me*, even if everything around me had gone to hell. A solid meal made things seem a lot more manageable, even hopeful. It was like that now, having the Jacksons eating with us. And I could tell they felt it, too. I saw their postures relax, especially Riley's.

"Whoever they are," Mackenzie said as she weeded, "you think they can see us even when we're inside our houses?"

"They knew when Nia was giving birth."

"Doesn't creep you out?"

"It did. For a long time. I've mostly stopped thinking about it."

"It's like what they tell you in Sunday school, how God sees everything."

She put down the cultivator and turned to me with mischief in her eyes. She moved her hands up my chest. "You think they see this?" she asked, and kissed me, sliding her tongue past my lips. I felt like my brain had short-circuited, like pleasure was the only thing I'd ever experience for the rest of my life. It was a long kiss. I didn't care who saw it—God, aliens, or bored government agents with cigarette ash on their jackets.

"I'm sorry, Miss Jackson—aren't you in a relationship?" I asked, delighted.

"I seem to be taking a break from my relationship. I'm pretty ticked off with Lucas, more I think about it."

This was excellent news. She looped her arms around my waist. This, even more than the kiss, made me inflate with happiness. I felt claimed. I put my arms around her, too, hungry for this embrace to last as long as possible.

"Why're you ticked off with him?" I asked. I was genuinely curious, but I also wanted her to get even angrier with him.

She rested her cheek against my shoulder. "We only started doing it a little while ago," she began, and I tried to keep breathing normally. "And each time I said I wanted him to use protection, but he'd always go, 'No, no, no, I'll pull out, it's one hundred percent totally safe, I read up on it.'"

She put on a slightly dim-witted voice I assumed was her Lucas impersonation.

"'We don't need condoms, darlin', I'm super careful, don't you worry. It'll be so much better this way, and I want it to be so special for us.'"

I listened, stunned. I'd never had anyone confide in me like this. I didn't know anything about sex firsthand. Anything I'd learned was from Sam and grade-eight sex ed. It wasn't like my father had given me a crash course Up Here. Who was I going to have sex with? But even I knew that you were supposed to use a condom.

"So I let him," she said. "And that made me angry with myself, too. And when my period didn't come on time, I freaked out. We were already up at the lodge, so I had to make up some lame excuse to go into town to secretly buy a pregnancy test. And Alyssa wanted to come into the pharmacy with me."

"Oh my God, what'd you do?"

"I told her to go look at the rack of stuffed animals and I'd buy her whichever one she wanted. That gave me time to buy the pregnancy test first."

"That sounds super stressful," I said.

"When it was negative, I was so relieved. But then I got furious all over again. That stupid text of his. *U all good?* 'Oh, sure, Lucas, it's all real good. I was just a teensy bit worried I was going to have a baby in high school. Just a bit of a drag, is all.'" She shook her head angrily. "I mean, I could've said no. I should've insisted. It's not like it's all his fault. Still. He should've been more careful. It was selfish, to put me through something like that. He treated me bad."

I just nodded. *Yes, he treated you badly.* She put her hand on the back of my neck and ran her fingers through my hair.

"I want our power back," she said into my shirt, and we both laughed. "I'm tired of having cold showers."

"I could use a cold shower right now."

She tickled me under the ribs. "I'm serious, Zay. Once it gets dark, I have to read old books with my phone light. And Alyssa is bored because she can't watch TV, so I've been playing a ton of Candy Land with her."

I remembered that one. "The most boring game in the world."

"She is the only person in the world who does not find it boring."

"At least there's no *Unicorn Squad*."

"The one blessing." She looked up at the sky. "Where is it?"

"The hatch?" I wondered if she was thinking of sailing on out of here. I tried to find it. "I can't see it today, too hazy."

"You're nice to hold," she said, running her hands down my torso.

I brushed her warm cheek, the corner of her mouth. This was so new to me, all of it. I kissed the spot behind her ear where her hair started growing, and breathed in her skin.

She said, "So it's just too bad for Lucas if I found myself a bubble boyfriend."

I laughed. "I feel so temporary."

But I didn't care. I'd be Mackenzie Jackson's bubble boyfriend any day. Sometimes bubble boyfriends turned out to be permanent.

The next day, as I neared the Jacksons' farm, Patt came running to greet me as usual. He didn't bark anymore, but I was never sure if he was happily greeting me or just *intercepting* me like a good sentry. I gave his head a scratch, which he tolerated with a sniff before heading back toward the lodge. From its open windows, I heard the faint but unmistakable sound of *Unicorn Squad*.

They had their power back. I felt a stab of disappointment. I'd miss our meals together, and all the extra time with Mackenzie. On the porch she greeted me with a big smile.

"I never thought I'd be so happy to hear those unicorns sing," she said. "I got a hot shower this morning!"

"Your reward for good behavior."

I could smell her shampoo and felt my usual urge to hold and kiss her. When I came closer, she looked back nervously at the window. Whatever it was we were doing together, I got the sense her parents didn't know, and she wanted to keep it that way.

"We also got our first little gift," she said. "Not so little, really."

She led me to a small back pasture, where Riley was filling the feeder and water trough, keeping a careful eye on a new billy goat. The goat strutted and stomped, knocked his head against the fence, and made an obnoxious snorting sound like someone blowing a raspberry.

"Is that normal?" Mackenzie asked.

"He's in rut. He's frustrated."

Her eyes widened in horror. "What's he doing now?"

"He's peeing all over his head."

"Why would he do that?"

"They just do. When they get excited. Doesn't Lucas do that?"

She looked at me in shock, then started laughing.

"Oh my God, I think I can smell him from here!" she said. "Is that him?"

"The females dig it. They find it very romantic."

"Don't get any ideas." She wrinkled her nose. "I'm worried I smell like goat now."

"You smell really good," I said quietly, because her father was heading toward us.

Riley let himself out through the gate, chuckling to himself. "Even if I was planning on breeding goats, I'm not sure this fella's the best candidate."

"We won't be here that long anyway," Mackenzie said, and I wasn't sure if she truly believed this or was just trying to be supportive.

"Exactly," said her father.

Since the deep freeze freakout, Riley had been nothing but cheerful. Even without electricity, he'd worked good-naturedly on his farm. He kept thanking us for all the help we were giving them, especially for the jars of preserved meat.

"You want to see the balloon?" he asked me.

"You've been working on it?" Maybe I shouldn't have been surprised. It wasn't like he'd made any promise to give up on it for good. But he hadn't mentioned it all week, and I was starting to wonder if he'd lost interest.

"Man's allowed some spare time. Mostly nights when I can't sleep."

From Mackenzie's expression, I could tell she hadn't known about this either.

"Don't look so alarmed," he said. "Our kindly overlords haven't noticed, or if they have, they still saw fit to give us power back."

He took us up to the loft and showed us how the balloon was coming together. All the pieces had been cut to shape and were draped over rafters. On the floor were two pieces that he'd been sewing together. The stitching was tight and straight.

"Slow work," he said, "but we should be able to speed things along now."

"Daddy, I don't want to lose power again."

"Oh, I'll still be farming," Riley said with a grin. "But I'll gradually cut back."

I doubted it would be that easy to trick *them*, but Riley seemed filled with energy and confidence.

"Want to try your hand?" he asked, holding up a needle and a spool of fishing line.

I hesitated. I knew that my father and especially Nia would think it was reckless to persist with the balloon. But did they need to know? This thing would probably never get finished anyway (*or maybe it would*, said the competing voice in my head). Most likely they'd run out of material, or botch it up somehow (*or maybe it would fly us out of here, back to the real world, to Mom and Sam*). From the corner of my eye I saw Mackenzie watching me.

"Sure," I said.

Riley clapped me on the shoulder. "I knew you'd keep the faith."

Which made it sound a bit like I was part of a religious cult. But if Mackenzie was a member, that was okay.

22

A few days later, I woke to the sound of something I hadn't heard in years. Birdsong. Only now did I realize how much I'd missed it, especially at dawn and twilight. I lay in bed, listening to the small symphony, and thought: *happiness*.

After three years of the same routines, I now had a new one, and I loved it. Mornings I worked on our farm, and then after lunch I headed over to the Jacksons', often bringing Noah so he could play with Alyssa. Mostly I helped with their farmwork, sneaking off sometimes with Mackenzie. Not just to fool around, but to talk and laugh and *be* with each other in our own little bubble within a bubble. Riley spent more and more time up in the loft with the balloon, and often he'd ask one of us up to lend a hand with the stitching. Technically I was working more than usual, but nothing I did with Mackenzie felt like work.

"What's that noise?" Noah said, hopping out of his bunk and running to the window.

He dragged the curtains open and drew in his breath. A big spiral of birds expanded and contracted across the sky.

"Let's go see!" Noah said.

We got Kimmy on his leash and took him with us so he could have his morning pee. The grass was still dewy. The birds could have come from only one place: the hatch in the sky, which meant *they* had released them. Their music felt like a gift. They made life seem *more*. They flew over the farm and settled on the trees in the orchard, filling the branches. Noah wanted to go closer. Their plumage wasn't actually black but dark iridescent green. They had narrow yellow beaks.

When I realized what they were doing, I started shouting and waving my arms to drive them off. Such small birds, but their beaks were sharp. They pecked at the apples and pears, just a few punctures in each piece of fruit, before hopping to another.

My noise didn't do much to scare them away, but it brought Nia and Dad.

"Starlings," Nia said grimly. "They're the worst."

"They're only eating a little," Noah pointed out.

"Once it's pecked, it starts to rot," Nia said.

We ran around the orchard, trying to get rid of the starlings, but just drove them from tree to tree. There wasn't one left untouched. It seemed almost malicious.

"We can cook and preserve it, can't we?" I asked.

"Some of it, maybe."

"We've never had birds," Dad said. "Why now?"

Nia raised her eyebrows at him. "You have to ask?"

"You think they sent the birds to punish us?" Dad asked.

"What'd *we* do?" I demanded.

"Riley's working on the balloon again, isn't he?" Nia said.

I didn't think this was really a question. I certainly hadn't mentioned it, but maybe Noah had passed on something Alyssa had told him. It wasn't a secret in the Jackson household. And Dad and Nia were bound to find out sooner or later.

"Yeah, he's working on it a little," I said. "But what's that got to do with us?"

The starlings lifted off and coiled through the air, until we lost sight of them.

"I think we're collateral damage this time," said Nia.

I knew things weren't right when Patt didn't rush to meet me. Crossing the orchard, I saw that the Jacksons' fruit trees had been ravaged, too. The goats were making a god-awful noise because they obviously hadn't been milked or fed. Nearing the main pasture, I noticed that the chickens hadn't been let out of their coop.

From inside the barn, I heard Patt barking, then Riley shout, "Get outta here!" A stutter of gunfire made my body go weak. Where had the ammo come from? A few starlings streamed from the loft doors, swirling above the barn before settling on the roof. There was another staccato barrage—not gunshots but fireworks, I realized with relief. More starlings flew out. Colored smoke eddied after them, and then the doors slammed shut.

When I entered the barn, Mackenzie was just coming down the stairs, and she shook her head at me in warning.

Upstairs I heard Riley shouting, "They pecked holes in it!"

Charleze said calmly, "You scared them all off. It's fine now."

"Look at all these goddamn holes!"

"We can patch them up. Honey, did you take your pill today?"

"That's got nothing to do with it!"

Mackenzie looked miserable. She took my hand and started to lead me out of the barn.

"You need to take them, Riley," Charleze persisted from the loft.

I thought of the medicine cabinet, the drug whose name we didn't recognize.

"They make me foggy. How many times I have to say it? I can't be foggy, not here!"

Outside the barn, Mackenzie nestled against my chest and said, "Take me swimming?"

We spread out our towels and stripped down to our bathing suits. Back at their lodge, Mackenzie had given me a pair of her father's trunks. When I'd changed in the bathroom, I worried they were a bit big on me and that I wouldn't look as beefy as Lucas. But Mackenzie had given me an approving nod and said, "Nice!"

She wore an emerald-green bikini. There was an awful lot of bare skin and interesting curves, and I must've stared too long because she said, "Well, I feel duly appreciated and objectified," but she was smiling.

I dived into the water because I was blushing, and I still thought I looked dumb in the trunks, and also I had a hard-on. I surfaced a ways out and treaded water.

She was wading in, wrinkling her nose. "It's kind of muddy."

"Just swim out."

A few ducks quacked and paddled out of my way. The water was perfect, cool and silky. Sunlight filtered through the overhanging branches.

"You're sure nothing spooky lives in here?" she asked, up to her waist.

"Yep."

I pretended to get tugged under, and came up looking terrified.

"Not funny!" she said, splashing me.

"How could I resist?"

"You are such a jerk! I'm going back."

"No, don't! Please!"

"It's pretty nice actually," she said, and floated on her back with her arms spread out.

It was suddenly summer. Swimming in a lake with a girl.

Afterward we lay down on our towels and talked about everything *but* her father and our general predicament. We talked about books and movies, favorite places, smells, and foods. I reached out and took her hand. I felt kind of intimidated, knowing she was way more experienced than me. I was glad that, so far, she'd been the one to make the first move, kissing me. I wanted to kiss her pretty much all the time, but I figured it was best to leave it up to her.

"Daddy didn't used to get angry like that. Just since he's been on leave."

"Why's he on leave?"

She looked a bit sick, like she worried she was being disloyal.

"You don't have to tell—" I began.

"He has PTSD."

"Oh, wow. I'm sorry."

"There was an incident at his prison. A big fight, and Daddy went to break it up. A prisoner got violent with him, and Daddy had to tase him. Turned out the prisoner had a weak heart, and died."

"Oh my God, that's awful."

I tried to imagine a person dying because of something I'd done, even in self-defense. Tried to imagine carrying the nightmare weight of it.

"It was a complete freak accident. It wasn't Daddy's fault, but they've put him on leave without pay until they finish the investigation. It's not like he *shot* anyone. And that guy was no angel. My father did nothing wrong."

"I believe you."

"So, yeah, he freaks out sometimes. No wonder."

I was amazed by how buoyant Riley seemed most of the time. He must've been so worried about his future, and his family's, and what everyone thought of him. And then to end up here. Anyone would flip out. We'd been freaked out and we didn't arrive with PTSD.

"They gave him pills," Mackenzie said. "Mood stabilizers, Mom calls them, but he's stupid about them." She sighed. "Don't tell your father or Nia, okay? I know how Daddy comes across sometimes, but he's a good man, and I'd hate it if they held it against him."

"Yeah, of course."

Nia would go nuclear if she knew about this. Anything to do with prisons was a flash point for her. She'd instantly assume the inmate's death had been Riley's fault. She wouldn't want *anything* to do with the Jacksons. Probably she'd convince my father to stop me seeing them, including Mackenzie.

"Thanks, Zay."

We turned to face each other and kissed for a long time. She came even closer so I could feel her whole body against mine. She put her hand on my chest and moved it slowly down to my stomach, and then lower.

"We're going to need you around here a bit more," Dad said after dinner.

"A lot more," Nia added.

"Yeah, sure," I replied, smiling. I'd been smiling pretty much nonstop since getting back from the pond.

It was late August and harvest was our busiest time of year. I knew that. I could work harder at our farm, I could work harder at the Jacksons'. I could handle anything now that Mackenzie was in my life. Extra work, starlings blighting our fruit, Riley with PTSD: all manageable.

I was in a euphoric daze. At the pond, Mackenzie had made me feel so much better than what I'd been doing alone for years. I'd never had anyone touch me like that. How had I lived so long without this? Why didn't people just spend all their time doing this? I'd also felt kind of embarrassed afterward, the messiness of it on her hand. She'd just shrugged and invited me back into the water so we could wash off.

"We want you to stop helping the Jacksons," Dad said.

My smile disappeared. "Why?"

"You really need me to spell this out?" Nia said. "Why do you think the sparrows did that to his balloon?"

When I'd gotten home, I'd told them about how the birds had wrecked the Jacksons' orchard—and pecked holes in the balloon. I didn't know what normal starling behavior was. Maybe the birds were just attracted to the material's bright colors. Maybe they thought it was fruit. But Nia and Dad had obviously discussed it and decided that the birds had, somehow, been instructed by our captors to destroy the balloon.

"Riley's still farming! Sort of. Anyway, the farmwork's getting done! Isn't that what they want?"

"I'm not sure it was ever just about the farming," Dad said.

"Sure, they want Riley to farm," said Nia. "They also *don't* want him making that balloon. That's when all this started. First the power outage, then the starlings."

"If they really wanted to get rid of the balloon," I said, "why didn't they just send the midges to eat it?"

It might've been the best thing for Riley, to see the midges himself. Maybe he would've realized how tiny and powerful they were, how they couldn't possibly be human-made.

"The starlings are a warning," Nia said. "And who knows what they'll send next? It's like the plagues of Egypt."

Even without going to church, I'd heard of those. Locusts, famine, then all the firstborn children getting killed. My heart felt chilled.

"Why're you getting all biblical?" I asked.

"I'm just using it as an example. These are punishments."

"What have *we* done wrong?"

She gave me a hard stare. "Have *you* been helping with the balloon?"

"A little stitching sometimes, no big deal."

"That was a mistake, Zay."

"So this is my fault?" I demanded.

"Nia—" my father began.

She lifted her hands. "It's all of our faults. We've *all* been helping. When they lost power, we cooked their meals for them; we canned their frozen meat." She nodded at me. "Every day, you farm for them."

"If I stop helping out, their harvest is going to suck. How's that make anything better?"

"It might force Riley to step up and do more," said Dad. "And give up the balloon."

"He's not going to give up!"

They had no idea how determined Riley was. Maybe the balloon wouldn't even hold air. Maybe it wouldn't fly or get through the hatch. But Riley wouldn't be able to think straight until he'd tried.

"Zay, we don't want you helping anymore—period," Nia said.

"Too bad! No way am I giving up my time with Mackenzie."

"She seems like a nice girl," said Nia, "but your life is bigger than just her."

I stared at her in disbelief. "Are you kidding me? Before her I had *zero* life. She's made my life a million times better."

"We're not asking you to stop seeing her," said Dad. "Just stop doing their work for them."

"Oh yeah, that'll go great. Super neighborly. She'll like me so much when I ditch out on her family."

"That balloon is making trouble for all of us."

They were both looking at me, waiting for me to make a choice.

"Fine. I won't work on the balloon. But I'm still helping with their farm."

"Which gives him more time to finish the balloon," said Nia pointedly.

"You guys don't even think it'll fly. So let him go ahead and fail."

"That might come at a very high cost," Dad said.

Nia looked at me severely. "I just hope no one ends up getting hurt."

I wasn't sure if she was talking about a balloon accident or some new kind of punishment, sent from above.

23

There was no sign of the starlings the next day. I hoped they'd been spirited back up into the sky for good. We spent the morning harvesting the damaged fruit. It looked like we'd have less than half our usual amount to preserve.

With all the other work to do, I got to the Jacksons' later than usual. When Alyssa opened the door, her smile collapsed in disappointment.

"Where's Noah?"

"He's not coming today. Maybe tomorrow."

Nia had kept him home, saying she wanted him to help and that we needed all hands on deck. I hoped she wasn't going to stop Noah seeing Alyssa permanently. Angry as she was with Riley, did she want Noah to go without his only playmate?

Alyssa's body slumped a little. In the background I heard the ululating of unicorns.

"They're all in the barn," she told me. *"Again."*

When I climbed the steps to the loft, Riley called out a cheerful hello. They were kneeling on the balloon fabric, working with needle and fishing line. I wondered if they'd been at it all day.

Mackenzie gave me a smile that made me remember everything we'd done yesterday at the pond. I tried hard not to blush, which was pointless.

"Xavier," said Charleze, "you are so good to always come."

"He sure is," said Mackenzie, watching me blush even more, with amusement. "He comes, and helps all the time."

"Just patching all those holes the birds pecked," said Riley, head bent over his work. "Not nearly as bad as I first thought."

"That's great."

Riley seemed his usual self. Maybe he'd taken his pills, or maybe he'd just needed to blow off steam yesterday.

"I hear the starlings made an appearance at your place, too," he said to me. "Surprised they troubled you folks."

It hurt me that Riley still thought we were somehow favored by *them*.

"They wrecked our fruit trees, too," I pointed out.

"Sorry to hear that."

"Nia thinks it's because of the balloon."

"Now, that is something she and I agree on, one hundred percent."

When I told him how Nia called it a plague, Riley laughed.

Charleze said, "As a believer, I take exception to that. The plagues of Egypt were a righteous use of power against the wicked. Whoever's up there"—she pointed at our fake sky—"that is not our God, Xavier."

Riley stood up and stretched. "Know what it tells me, though? That we've got a chance. They wouldn't bother punishing us if they weren't worried. They think we've got a good shot at escaping. And that is a very encouraging thought." He walked over and clapped me on the shoulder. "We're shaking things up, Xavier Oak. They're gonna have to try a lot harder to discourage us."

That confidence of his. Its gravitational pull. I felt it again as I looked at the progress they'd made on the balloon's envelope. He showed me the drawings he'd done of the frame, and told me the materials he was thinking of using, and how he could shape them.

"You're not worried they'll do something worse?" I asked him.

Riley regarded me thoughtfully. "Seems you don't think your alien keepers are quite so kindly anymore."

"Maybe not."

Dad and Nia assumed that *they* wanted the best for us, that they'd never harm us. But it hadn't stopped them wiping out our orchard—which was completely unfair, in my view.

"Well, all we can do is our best," said Riley. "I'll be keeping the barn closed tight at night, and leave Patt inside to guard it. No one and nothing gets past Patt. He hears a peep, he'll raise Cain. And we should be done with the balloon before long, especially with you helping. Ready to do a little more work on USS *Xavier Oak*?"

I laughed, but he must've seen the hesitation in my face.

"Your folks don't want you helping with it anymore, do they?"

"It's just that it's harvest, and there's a ton to do."

My excuse was dishonest and they must've known it.

"You have done so much for us already," Charleze said.

"And I'm sorry," Riley added, "if I caused you to go against your parents. I've no business interfering in another man's family."

Since the Jacksons had come, I'd been walking a tightrope. Government conspiracy at one end, alien abduction on the other. Depending on who was talking, I could almost reach either end—but never quite. Both propositions seemed insane. Yes, I wanted to escape, to get home, to be with Mom and Sam. But yes, I also wanted to stay because Mackenzie was here and I was happy. I was happy to think my life could include her forever.

The Jacksons were all looking at me so kindly. Mackenzie gave me a sad smile. A terrible fear sprang into my head. I wondered if she only liked me because I'd kept her secrets and helped out. And I knew that, even if it was true, I didn't care. I liked her too much. The thought of not hanging out with her, not kissing her, made me want to crumple up.

"Let's finish this balloon," I said.

24

I worked harder than I ever had in my life. Most of each day I spent at our place, milking, feeding, watering, harvesting, baling alongside Dad and Nia. Afterward I'd go over to the Jacksons' to do the bare minimum with their livestock and crops before helping with the balloon.

The envelope turned out to be straightforward compared with the metal frame beneath it. That frame would support the weight of the propane burner—and all the passengers. Riley had decided a gondola was too complicated and too much extra weight, so he was going to have everyone wear harnesses that clipped onto the frame. We'd all be dangling from it like thrill seekers on some uncertified amusement park ride.

Riley and I moved their woodstove outside and converted it into a forge. We had no idea what we were doing. We made a makeshift bellows. It was a nightmare keeping the fire at the right temperature. Too hot and we'd melt holes in the metal, too cold and it would crack when we tried to work it. We wrecked a lot of farm tools and still didn't have the frame finished. We had no internet, no books to help us. We were like grunting cavemen, trying to break into the Iron Age.

In the remaining hours, I slept.

I'd been honest with Dad and Nia. I told them I'd changed my mind and was helping Riley finish the balloon. That was a pretty spiky conversation. First they'd tried to persuade me out of it. Then Nia said I was being selfish, that I wasn't thinking of the family. Dad tried to keep things civil, but I could tell he disapproved of what I was doing. That hurt way more. It also made me think he didn't have a clue what it was like being me. Being sixteen. Being *here*. Sometimes I thought he'd become one of those fathers from a fairy tale: they remarry, and their new wife wants to ditch the kids in the woods, or feed them to witches, and the father just dopily goes along with it because he's getting such great sex. Dad wasn't that bad, but still.

One afternoon he and I were harvesting the grapes, cutting bunches from the vines and filling the wheelbarrow. I pushed a load back to the barn. Inside, Nia was cranking the extractor, spinning the frames from the beehives to separate out the honey. That thing was a beast to use, and you needed to spin it for a long time before the honey pooled at the bottom. She paused to shake out her arm and rub her shoulder.

"You want to take over for a bit?" she asked.

It was obvious I was in the middle of another job, and I muttered irritably, "Get Noah to do it. He needs to start pulling his weight."

"You know he's not strong enough."

"I need to get the wheelbarrow back."

"And on the subject of Noah, you don't spend a second with him anymore."

"Well, you might've noticed, Nia, I'm a very busy farmer these days. At least I take him over to the Jacksons' so he gets to hang out with Alyssa. Since you haven't been arranging any playdates for him."

I knew I'd annoy her, but she surprised me by saying:

"You're right. Sorry. You work really hard, Zay."

I didn't know how to reply, so I nodded at the honey extractor. "I'll have a go."

While I cranked, she emptied the grapes into the nearby fermenting tubs.

"How's the balloon going?" she asked.

Another surprise. She hardly ever asked about its progress, but now she nodded attentively as I brought her quickly up to date.

"Eight people hanging from harnesses," she said, and let the image dangle for a few seconds. "Lot of weight for a small balloon. You think it'll launch?"

I took a break spinning the extractor, unsure where to begin.

Nia said, "You're a smart kid. You've run the scenarios."

I gave a little laugh. "Yeah, *lots* of them."

"And?"

"Undecided. You?"

I knew she must've thought it through, just like me. I didn't always like Nia, but I respected her. She was excellent at comparing assets and liabilities, watching the scales to see which side was overweight.

"That thing never gets off the ground," she said.

"Probably not," I admitted.

"Then why are you still helping them?" She smiled a little. "Aside from Mackenzie."

My cheeks heated. I didn't feel comfortable talking about it with Nia.

"Look, I get it," she said. "And I'm happy for you, honestly. I like Mackenzie."

"You like her?"

"Yeah. I wish she didn't buy into the deep government plot, but how she can even think straight with those parents, I don't know. She's got guts. I wish her dad would listen to her more."

All I could do was nod in agreement.

Nia said, "I don't want our family going up in that balloon."

Our family. Her family and my family had never been the same thing. Hers would never include my mother. When Nia had first come on the scene, Sam and I had looked at her like an intruder. But Up Here things were different: Now that Noah had come along, if anyone was an outsider, it was me.

"And this *family*," I said, "does it include me?"

She looked genuinely shocked. "Of course it does! Are you serious?" She put her hands on my shoulders, and I felt them tense. I was suddenly worried my eyes were going to tear up. I'd always been wary of Nia; I'd never gotten the sense she particularly cared about me. But her expression right now said otherwise. It made my chest ache to think how long it had been since my own mom had looked at me like this.

I cleared my throat. "So who made this decision about not going up in the balloon?"

"Your father and me."

"Well, I make my own decisions. And I haven't decided yet."

"Okay," she said. "But I don't want you to go. And if you truly care about Mackenzie, make sure she doesn't go either."

I exhaled. "You asked why I'm helping them. It's not just for Mackenzie. It's because there's a chance Riley's right."

"There really isn't."

"Have you ever thought you're kind of like Riley, not even admitting there might be other possibilities?"

"No. Because I know he's wrong."

I almost laughed. "Well," I said. We hadn't changed each other's minds, but things felt better between us somehow, like we'd cleared the air.

"You've done enough here for today," she said. "Go see Mackenzie. I'll help out with the grapes."

"You seen the pillowcase?" I asked Dad.

It was the next day and we were up in the loft, getting ready to do the lentils. It was way easier, we'd learned, to let the plants dry, stuff them into a pillowcase, then stomp all over them to crack the seeds out of their pods.

"Haven't seen it," Dad said.

We had another look without success.

"I'll grab another one from the cottage," I said.

When I went inside, the pressure canner was going full blast, and Nia was cutting beans. I rooted around in the linen cupboard for the oldest, rattiest pillowcase I could find, and saw one way at the back. When I grabbed it, it felt heavy.

I opened it. Inside were boxes of rifle cartridges and crossbow arrows.

I must've stared for ten seconds before my brain started hammering thoughts together. I'd thought this ammo had never existed inside our dome, purposely left "unprinted" by our captors. But all along, here it was. It must've been Nia. She'd wanted to disappear it from the start. Before the Jacksons arrived, she must've made a trip of her own to the empty house, found the key to the ammunition chest, and emptied it. And Dad? For a second I wondered if he'd been in on it, too. I figured no, or he wouldn't have let me go look for a pillowcase; he would've done it himself. It was Nia alone.

She'd lied to Dad and me. And it made a liar out of me, too.

No, I'd said to Mackenzie, *we didn't take the ammo.*

This pillowcase, the ammo inside: It was another secret I was supposed to keep. I felt like I was already keeping enough, dragging them around like a sack full of stones.

And why the hell should I?

I wanted to confront Nia, right now in the kitchen, dangle the pillowcase in front of her, see what she said. *You ever think*, I'd tell her, *that you've probably made Riley even more paranoid? Because he thinks this missing ammo is just more evidence that evil government agents want to disarm and reeducate him.*

But I stopped myself. I knew she'd fight. She'd insist it was still the right thing to do.

And I wasn't sure she was wrong.

A man with a temper, a man under investigation for killing an inmate. A man with PTSD.

I shoved the pillowcase to the back of the closet and took another one to the barn.

25

Just before daybreak we were woken by the goats shrieking. Noah was so scared he barnacled onto me the moment I got down the ladder. I told him it was okay, and had to pry him loose so I could pull my pants on. Kimmy was barking and wouldn't stop. I heard Dad in the next room, stumbling into his clothes. All four of us met in the hallway.

I'd never heard a sound like this before, a symphony of pure terror. It was hard to think. Nia wrapped her arms around Noah. Dad and I hurried outside.

Our flashlight beams skittered around, picking out the goats as they darted and jostled in panic. Then I caught the white flash of another animal's eyes. For a second, I thought: *Patt*. But this animal was leaner, yet powerful enough to be dragging one of the kids along the ground.

"Hey!" Dad shouted, and we both made as much noise as possible as we ran across the pasture.

By the time we reached the shelter, the animal had jumped the fence, leaving the kid behind. It was Stripey. I'd delivered her just five months ago, and Noah had named her for the white band on top of her head. Her throat had been ripped open. The mother was bleating at her lifeless body.

"I think it was a coyote," Dad said.

Another animal that we'd never had before. We checked to make sure the chickens were okay, then herded the goats inside the barn in case the coyote came back. We gave them some hay and water to settle them down, and closed the doors firmly behind us.

"What do we do with Stripey?" I asked.

"Bury her."

By the time we were done, the sun was floating above the horizon. At breakfast, Noah cried when we told him, and wanted to visit Stripey's grave. It wasn't a particularly nice spot, behind the barn near the manure pile. But Noah stood there for a few moments, murmuring quietly.

"Well, Riley's certainly *shaking things up*," Nia said to Dad and me.

I knew she'd call this another plague, sent down because I was working on the balloon.

"We need to talk to him," she told my father. I could tell this was not the first time they'd had this conversation.

"I have," Dad said with a touch of annoyance. "Many times. What more can I do?"

"You're a master negotiator," she said. "You convince people to do things they don't want to do. I've seen how you can turn a room. So *convince* him!"

"He's . . ." Dad shook his head. "He's impervious."

"If you don't, I will."

As we headed back to the cottage, we spotted Riley coming through our orchard. He lifted a hand in greeting, smiling, oblivious to Nia's seething animosity.

"Morning. Just wanted to let you folks know, we had a coyote last night."

"Oh, us too," said Nia. To Noah she said, "Go inside—we'll be there in a sec."

"They killed our goat, Stripey," Noah told Riley.

Riley's forehead creased in sympathy. "I'm very sorry to hear that. One of them got into our henhouse. Alyssa forgot to latch the little door. Patt was shut up in the barn, but he sniffed the coyote and made a ruckus. By the time I got there, six chickens were dead."

"Zay, you want to take Noah inside and start breakfast," said Nia.

I knew she wanted to get rid of us, so she could lay into Riley, but I wasn't missing this. I gave Noah's shoulders a little squeeze and said, "Go ahead. I'll be right in."

"Only wish I had my ammo," said Riley, when Noah was out of earshot, "and I could deal with this fairly easily."

"Well, you don't," said Nia. "So that's not an option."

I couldn't believe how self-righteous she sounded, when she was the one who'd stolen his ammunition.

"What is an option," she continued, "is quitting the balloon."

Cordially, Riley said, "You can't ask me to do that."

"Why not?"

"I'm not telling you how to live your life. I'm just exercising my rights."

"Well, *your* rights are getting in the way of *our* rights. Don't we have a right to eat? To have enough to feed our family? Your decisions are killing our crops and livestock."

"I'm sorry you feel that way. No one said freedom came cheap."

"If this keeps up, we could all lose our ability to feed ourselves," Nia said.

"Oh, they will provide for you Oaks," said Riley.

"The pattern's pretty clear," my father said. "They're going to keep squeezing *all* of us."

"Stop with the balloon. Please," Nia said.

"I can't do that."

Any reserve Nia had evaporated. "Well, Riley, I think things might get hard for you this winter, and if they do, we will not share our food with you."

I looked at her in shock. "Nia!"

"So think about that," she continued. "You will experience food scarcity, like all those sad, far-off countries that always have 'some problem or another.'"

"Nia," Dad said gently.

"Not a fucking lentil," Nia said, "unless you stop work on that balloon."

"Work's nearly done," Riley said. "With a lot of help from your boy here. So you don't need to worry about the winter. I'm assuming you're coming with us."

My father gave a weary sigh; Nia glared at Riley.

"In the meantime," Riley said, "the coyote, or coyotes, are a nuisance, no question. But I know coyotes. They're cowards at heart, no risk to us. So long as we keep our goats inside at night, they'll be fine."

The coyotes didn't return the next day, or the day after. For five nights, we stabled the goats, keeping Kimmy inside except for walks to do his business. Every morning we checked for tracks around the barn and coop, but found nothing. It seemed the coyotes were a one-off, like the starlings. Another little warning from *them*.

When I arrived at the Jacksons' in the afternoon, Riley was ebullient. The frame, finally, was finished. We tested its strength by hanging weights from it. We seated the propane tank in its cradle and ran the hose up to the burner that Riley had made by cannibalizing the barbecue. The burner sat right underneath the balloon skirt, ready to blast heat.

"Hot damn!" said Riley when we tried it out and it flared up perfectly. "Xavier Oak, we did it!"

With a whoop, he opened his arms and we hugged. We'd spent so long on this beast of a metal frame and, seeing it finished now, I felt a surge of pride. I could imagine how the whole thing would look: the balloon swelling overhead, straining at its tethers. My idea.

All that was left was the harnesses for the passengers, and Riley said he'd take care of that himself.

"Take a well-deserved break, Xavier," he said. "Take the girls for a swim, why don't you?"

Inside the lodge, Riley shared the good news with his family, and waltzed Charleze around the family room. Alyssa raced upstairs after Mackenzie to get changed.

"Is it safe?" Charleze asked Riley quietly. "For them to go to the pond?"

I was hoping Charleze would keep Alyssa home, so Mackenzie and I would be all alone, but Riley said, "The coyote? They're scaredy-cats. Won't see them during the day."

"You sure?"

"I think we've seen the last of them." Sensing that Charleze was still unsure, he added, "They can take Patt. No coyote would mess with him. And Xavier's as trustworthy as they come."

Alyssa asked if Noah could come, too. She hadn't seen him since the coyote incident, because Nia didn't want him walking through the woods, even with me. I wasn't sure if this was the real reason, or she just didn't want Noah being around the Jacksons too much. But Alyssa's face was so hopeful, I said:

"We can swing by our cottage and ask."

I didn't have high hopes. When we arrived, my family was out harvesting carrots and cucumbers, and Alyssa and Noah actually ran toward each other and hugged.

"Can I go, too?" Noah asked, when Alyssa said we were going swimming.

I could see Nia wrestle with it as she looked at her son's beaming face.

"What d'you think?" she asked my dad, and I knew her heart was softening around the edges.

"I think the four of them'll be just fine," Dad said. "And they've got Patt with them."

"You'll be extra watchful, right?" Nia asked me, so frankly vulnerable that I felt my own heart soften toward her. She was a really good mother, and it made me miss mine.

"Yeah, promise."

At the pond, Mackenzie and I stayed within easy reach of Alyssa and Noah while they paddled close to shore in their tiny life jackets. I was disappointed that Mackenzie and I wouldn't have a chance to fool around, although we managed a bit of underwater groping that left me with a pleasantly frustrated ache. It was a perfect September day, and the water seemed all the warmer in the cooling fall air. On the shore, Patt sat obediently, watching over us.

"I'm getting out," Alyssa announced.

Mackenzie helped her onto shore, dried her off, and settled her on a beach towel with some of her toys and books. Noah wanted to stay in a bit longer, dog-paddling in the shallows.

"Can I take off my jacket?" Alyssa asked.

"You keep it on," Mackenzie told her firmly. "House rules."

Mackenzie jumped back into the pond, swam out to me, and put her arms around my neck. We treaded water and kissed.

"I'm kind of afraid," she whispered, "of going up in that balloon."

Not for the first time, Nia's words haunted my head: *And if you truly care about Mackenzie, make sure she doesn't go either.*

Now that the balloon was finished, the next challenges suddenly came into sharp focus—all the things I'd kicked down the road to worry about later. Even if we got this thing into the air, could we fly it? How would we steer? Would it fit through that hatch in the sky? And the big one: If things went wrong, could we safely descend?

Before I could check myself I said, "I don't want that balloon to ever get off the ground."

She frowned and was about to say something when Patt started barking. He stood on all fours, pointed toward the woods, ears pricked high. Then tore off.

"Patt!" Mackenzie shouted. "Come!"

We swam for the bank, where Alyssa was sitting on her towel, looking in the direction Patt had disappeared. The German shepherd's distant barking became a vicious snarl, punctuated by another animal's yips and growls. It had to be the coyote. There were awful choking and tearing sounds.

"Stay in the water," I told Noah, making sure his feet could touch the bottom.

I was the first to scramble ashore, just as a second coyote silently appeared beside Alyssa. Most coyotes I'd seen looked like lean dogs; this one was more like a wolf. It clamped its jaws around her forearm and she screamed.

"Hey!" I shouted. "Get off!"

I kicked the coyote hard. It released Alyssa and snapped at my ankle. When I waved my arms to make myself as big as possible, it backed off a bit, snarling.

"Patt!" wailed Mackenzie, splashing out of the water. "Come, Patt!"

The German shepherd burst from the trees and sprang on the coyote. As the two animals tore at each other, Mackenzie ran for her little sister. Before she got there, another coyote, bloodied from its earlier fight with Patt, lunged from the undergrowth and bit Alyssa in the face. She stopped screaming.

Mackenzie and I pounded and kicked at it. I shoved myself between the coyote and Alyssa, and it sank its teeth into my wrist. I punched its nose and it let go. Then Patt suddenly had it by the throat. The two animals thrashed around, until the coyote broke free and ran. The other one was long gone.

I turned to see Mackenzie holding Alyssa, pressing the beach towel hard against the left side of her face.

"You're okay," she said to her little sister, but she was looking at me in helpless panic.

Mackenzie lifted the towel away for a second. There was so much blood I couldn't see Alyssa's eye. A jaw-shaped flap had been cut into her cheek.

"Let's get you home," I said, and lifted Alyssa against my chest, wrapped up in her beach towel.

Mackenzie helped Noah out of the water and put a towel over his shoulders. He was quiet, his eyes wide, as he trotted alongside us. I headed for the Jacksons'. It was closest. Mackenzie kept the towel pressed against her sister's cheek. The blood was soaking through, and she had to find new, dry places. Patt limped alongside, his muzzle bloody.

"I want a drink," Alyssa said thickly.

"Soon, honey," said her sister.

"It tastes like blood."

"Just a little cut. We'll get you fixed up."

"My arm hurts."

"You're almost home," said Noah.

"Am I okay?"

"You're fine," Mackenzie said. "Absolutely fine."

I walked as fast as I could without tripping. Alyssa was whimpering, her head rolling against my chest, her hair blood-streaked.

We called out as we approached the lodge, and when we entered, I got the sense Riley and Charleze had been having sex because they were both rushing out of the bedroom at the same time, looking rumpled.

They were both super calm. I passed Alyssa to Riley and he talked to her gently as he carried her to the bathroom. He called her his little chick, promised her she was safe now, and they were going to look after her. When she told him it hurt, he said, "I know, honey, but it won't for long." He made her promises that might have been lies, but what else could he do right now?

I hovered outside the bathroom, feeling so useless and terrible I could barely form words in my head. Riley and Charleze spoke to each other calmly, saying things like, "Her eye's fine, it was just crusted over with blood," and "We'll need to stitch that bite up," and "We have any antibiotics kicking around?" and "I can make a splint for her arm later."

"Is there anything I can do?" I said when Riley came out to sterilize some needles.

"Just go, Xavier," he said, walking past without looking at me. "Go home."

Dad, Nia, and I snatched anything useful from our medicine cabinet and first-aid kit. A tube of long-expired antibiotic cream. Half a bottle of hydrogen peroxide. Some butterfly skin closures. Alcohol wipes and gauze. A roll of medical tape.

Nia stayed behind with Noah, so Dad and I made the walk to the Jacksons' alone. We both brought just-in-case pitchforks. We didn't talk much. I'd made this trip so many times over the weeks, my feet had worn a path. Between the trees, through the fields. Walking this trail usually made me so happy, because I knew it would bring me to Mackenzie. Right now I felt sick.

When we knocked, Mackenzie answered, her eyes puffy, and stepped out onto the porch. I heard Alyssa crying.

"How is she?" I asked.

"She's got a fever, and it's hurting a lot. We cleaned the wound best we could, and Mom did the stitches. She did a really tidy job."

Her voice broke. We both knew how big that wound was, how there was no way it would heal tidily. I gave her a hug, but her arms hung limp at her sides. I stepped away and she wiped her eyes.

"We are so sorry," Dad said. "Is there anything we can do?"

"I think we're okay," she said. "She just needs us with her."

"We brought some stuff," I said, and handed her our first-aid kit. "It might be useful."

"Thanks."

"You're sure there's nothing we can do?"

"I'm going to go back in."

She'd been avoiding my eyes.

"We'll come back tomorrow to check on her, if that's all right," said my father.

Mackenzie nodded vaguely, said goodbye, and shut the door.

That night, I waited until everyone was asleep, then got dressed. I had to make things right. Riley had called me trustworthy. I should've stayed closer to the shore instead of fooling around with Mackenzie. I should've reached Alyssa faster, had a stick or something ready, just in case. I'd been afraid of the coyotes' teeth, the hunger curling back their lips. Mackenzie blamed me, I could tell, the way she wouldn't look at me.

As I opened the linen cupboard door, it creaked. I paused for a second, breath held, before quickly opening it the rest of the way. The ratty pillowcase was still at the back. Silently I lifted it out.

Outside the cottage, I zipped it inside my backpack. As I hefted it over my shoulders, I heard the metallic clink of the cartridges. My mouth went suddenly dry. For a second I thought I might throw up. Riley being put on leave and investigated. The pills he was supposed to take and didn't. And then I remembered how gently he'd held Alyssa, how calm he was. Her poor torn face.

I grabbed a pitchfork from the barn and started out. I knew the path to the Jacksons' so well by now I hardly needed any light. I used my phone to sweep the trees, watching for a pair of eyes to light up. But with the pitchfork in my hand and terror pulsing through my veins, I was ready to take on any coyote that came at me.

There was a steady breeze in my face as I approached the Jacksons', which was good because Patt would have a harder time sniffing me out. I saw a light on in the lodge, and wondered if they were up with Alyssa, comforting her, trying to make her pain go away.

I left the ammo in a neat pile at the bottom of their steps, where they'd be able to see it as soon as they stepped onto their porch in the morning.

Like it was a gift from *them*.

26

Next morning, we'd just let the animals out when Riley appeared at the far end of the pasture, holding a rifle.

I was filling the water troughs, my father was scattering garden scraps for the chickens, and Nia had just wheelbarrowed in some hay for the goats. I caught her look of bewilderment and fear.

Riley opened the gate and stepped inside the pasture. He was wearing a camo hunting vest with lots of pockets. Carefully, he closed the gate behind him and walked toward us. None of us moved. Dad was closest, then me, then Nia. Noah was inside the cottage, because Nia didn't want him outside, period. My gaze welded itself to the rifle. He held it two-handed, diagonally across his chest, pointing up at the sky. I told myself he'd only brought it in case he ran into coyotes on his way over.

"Someone saw fit to give back what they stole," he said. "Left the ammo on my doorstep."

I didn't dare look at Nia, could only imagine she was working very hard to keep her face from blazing guilt. Riley didn't look angry or accusing, just exhausted. I noticed he had a second rifle slung over his shoulder—and wasn't sure if this was reassuring or not.

"How's Alyssa?" Nia asked, her voice strained.

"Good as can be expected. Thanks for the supplies. Those butterfly closures keep the sutures together."

"Riley, we're so sorry," my father said.

Riley held the rifle out toward him. "You'll need this." When my father hesitated, he said, "Take it. I can't be two places at once. We need to kill those coyotes."

Dad took the gun. "Is it loaded?"

"Not yet."

Only now did I realize how hard my heart was beating. I took a few deep breaths and walked toward them.

"How's your wrist?" Riley asked, nodding at my bandage.

"It's fine."

"You cleaned it properly?"

"Yeah, it really wasn't that bad. Mr. Jackson, I should've done more."

Maybe he saw my eyes get wet because he put his hand on my shoulder and said, "Xavier, I'm the one at fault. I never should've let you go to the pond, especially with the little ones. Those animals must be crazed with hunger." He looked from me to my father. "Which is why we need to deal with them. I'm guessing neither of you've hunted."

"No," Dad answered for us both.

"Ever fired a gun?"

"No."

"Time to learn."

"You three go ahead," said Nia. I saw the disapproval in her face, and the anger when she turned to me. I held her gaze until she looked away. No way would she say anything to me, not right now.

We carried some lumber from the barn to the field we'd scythed recently. In the short grass, Riley stacked the wood into a coyote-sized target and backed us up about a hundred meters. From his pocket he took a box of cartridges.

"They'll either come to my farm or yours," he said as he showed us how to load the rifle. "Aside from the ducks, that's their only real source of food."

He made us load the gun ourselves until he was satisfied. His movements were calm, but I sensed rage roiling around inside him, thumping at the walls, searching for weak spots. He taught us how to hold the rifle, use the sights, the best way to squeeze the trigger.

"Charleze had a lot of miscarriages after Mackenzie," Riley said, firing a shot dead center into the wood coyote. "That's why there's such a gap between the girls. And when Alyssa finally came, she was like a gift from God."

My heart clenched. Dad and I exchanged a glance, and decided it was best to say nothing.

"And I am amazed," Riley went on, "that you've been content to remain in a place where your captors try to kill children. Caleb, take a shot." He handed my father the rifle. "But I suppose it hasn't been an issue for you. When Nia and Noah were hurt, they got fixed up lickety-split. Not my girl."

Dad fired the rifle. I didn't see anything hit the target.

"High right," Riley remarked. "Ease up with the heel of your hand next time." He passed the rifle to me. "A little girl gets mauled, and she's suffering right now. How's that just?"

"It's not," my father said. "It's terrible, what happened."

"Thank you, I appreciate that. If I were you, I'd be thinking pretty hard about the upstairs management. Go ahead, Xavier, take a shot."

I saw wood fly off the target.

"Your boy's a better aim," Riley told my father.

We each fired off several more shots. Afterward, as we walked back to the cottage, Riley stopped and looked around the farm.

"So. Where you gonna be?" he asked.

"The barn loft," I said. "Best sight lines."

"Good. Just after dusk or before dawn are the most likely times. I'd recommend killing a chicken as bait. You'll probably only get one shot before they bolt."

He left us two boxes of cartridges and set off for home.

* * *

Dad carried the rifle as we headed back to the cottage.

"Why would they give him back his ammunition?" he asked, bewildered.

I stopped. "You really don't know?"

"No."

"I found it in the linen cupboard, and I didn't put it there."

"Jesus," he said.

Nia and Noah were waiting on the deck. Noah must have heard our gunshots. Nia sent him back inside and walked to meet us.

"Zay, you had no right to do that," she said, fury leaking out around the edges of her clipped words.

"Nia—" Dad began.

"Maybe you had no right stealing from him!" I retorted.

"I have no regrets. It was the right thing to do. You saw what he did to the freezer. Someone who can't govern their temper should not have weapons."

"Zay did the right thing," Dad said quietly. "We need to kill those coyotes."

I was amazed he was actually backing me up on this. Nia turned to him with an expression of betrayal. "Your son has just armed that man!"

"They bit a hole in Alyssa's face!" I shouted.

"And I'm very sorry about that, but—"

"If it was Noah, you'd want a gun!"

She took a breath. "It's what else Riley might do with the guns."

"Oh, come on!" But I felt another stab of guilt. I still hadn't told them about Riley's PTSD, the pills he wouldn't take. "He's not going to hurt us, Nia!"

"We can't keep Noah inside the rest of his life," Dad told her gently. "We won't rest easy until those coyotes are dead."

"Well, it's not like we can take it back now," she said bitterly. She pointed at the rifle. "And *that* is not coming into my house. Keep it in the barn, somewhere Noah can't reach it."

* * *

That evening we killed one of the hens and left it in the pasture with a clear sight line from the loft. It was my idea to spike it to the ground, to make it harder for the coyotes to take off with it. With luck it would give us more time to take a good shot, maybe even two.

Dad took the first watch. His gunshot woke me. I heard a second shot as I leaped out of bed. When I reached the loft, Dad told me he'd missed. Most of the chicken had been torn from the spike.

"I got in a couple shots at least," he said. "They don't seem to be afraid of the sound yet."

I wondered if that would change. I got a bit more sleep, then took my watch. It was cooler at night now, and I wore a sweater, but still shivered for a while before warming up. Dawn came on, and the coyotes didn't come back.

Later in the morning, I went over to the Jacksons' because I figured they'd be too wrecked to tend to their livestock. I did the milking, and fed and watered the animals. I collected the eggs. I wanted to find out how Alyssa was doing. I wanted to see Mackenzie; I needed to know if she was angry with me. I was even tempted to tell her it was *me* who'd brought back their ammo—but that would mean revealing who'd stolen it in the first place. If Riley found out it was Nia, I didn't know how he'd react. He was already on the edge, and I didn't want to find out how far the drop was.

No one came out of the house while I was working, so I didn't want to bother them. I harvested some of their vegetables and left them in baskets on the porch, beside their eggs and milk.

Two nights later, the moon was almost full and there were hardly any clouds. At two o'clock my alarm woke me and I went out to the barn to relieve Dad. I settled in by the loft doors, letting my gaze drift around the periphery of the pasture. Just before dawn, I saw one of the coyotes dip under the fence and come for the chicken carcass.

I lined it up in my sights and squeezed the trigger. It was like firing a shot in a video game. It was like nothing. The coyote fell over and didn't get up. I lowered the gun. I hadn't even heard the noise of the shot, I'd been so focused. Now I heard our door slide open and saw Dad and Nia come out onto the deck.

"I got it!" I called, my voice obscenely loud in the stillness.

I hurried out of the barn and across the pasture. When I saw the coyote up close, I recognized its markings. It was the one that had bitten Alyssa on the arm. It looked smaller now. Like someone's pet struck by a car. I felt smaller, too.

"Good job," Dad said beside me, his hand on my shoulder.

Very faintly, I heard the sound of a distant gunshot.

"Bet he got the other one," I said. Riley was an experienced hunter; he wouldn't miss.

"Let's hope there's only two of them," Dad said. "We should probably bury this."

"What the hell is that?" Nia blurted out. She was looking up. I looked, too. A swarm stood out against the pale sky, and my first thought was: *locusts*. The cloud expanded toward us, toward our fields of corn, lentils, sweet potatoes.

The next plague.

Nia pressed herself closer to my father. Dad put his arms around both of us. My hand tightened around the rifle.

Then I realized it was the midges. I'd never seen them in the daytime and their light was diminished, but I recognized the way they contracted and unknotted through the air. As they passed low over our farm, they made a whispering sound. *Shhhhh*, they said, like they were asking us to keep a secret. They streamed over our crops, leaving them unharmed, and carried on in the direction of the Jacksons'.

I dropped the rifle and ran.

27

Pounding along the trail, five rocks across the creek, I slipped and got wet up to my knees. Scrambled out, running again. In my head: terrible images. Midges shredding Riley's balloon while he fired at them uselessly. The house ablaze, the crops withered, livestock slaughtered. Worse.

Shhhhh, said the midges, their sound floating on the air behind them.

I didn't understand their rules. Were they angry about the coyotes? Of course we had to kill them, after what they'd done to Alyssa. I'd shot one, too. I'd given Riley back his ammo. I'd been helping with the balloon. But the midges had just passed over me and my farm, grazing our crops like a blessing. Whatever they intended was only for the Jacksons.

When I arrived, there was no sign of the midges. The goats bleated inside the barn. The chickens were making a racket in their coop. In the early dawn light the crops looked fine. Nothing on fire. Had the midges just passed over, like they had at our place? Maybe their business was elsewhere.

Then, inside the pasture, I saw Riley sprawled on his side, his back to me. There was a small pool of blood beneath him. I called out his name as I vaulted the fence. I thought, *He's dead, they killed everyone.* His rifle was sticking out from under him, like he'd collapsed onto it. Had he shot himself? When I reached him, I saw the dead coyote against his chest, a bullet wound in its flank. The blood I'd seen was the animal's. Riley was breathing. But he wouldn't wake up even when I smacked his cheek.

I looked toward the lodge. Where was everyone? Patt wasn't barking. As I raced for the porch, I heard the midges' telltale humming inside. When I opened the door, it bumped against Patt's motionless body. I slipped inside. The German shepherd was unconscious on the floor, flanks quivering with his rapid breath. The house was noisy and hot. Warily I walked into the family room. The humming was coming from the master bedroom. Light blazed from the open doorway.

I went closer. The entire room was dense with glittering midges. I saw Charleze unconscious on the bed, and beside her, Alyssa. The midges crawled all over the girl, like flies on roadkill. All my instincts told me to scare them off. Alyssa seemed suddenly to be floating, or held aloft by a veil of midges. Their humming intensified, as did their heat. I saw only flashes of what was happening.

They were peeling Alyssa's arm apart. I cried out and tried to come closer, to stop them. A wall of midges pushed me back firmly. And then I could barely see her anymore, just a glimpse of her face covered in midges, forming a terrible mask without nose or mouth holes.

I cursed and cried and tried to push through, to do *something*, but the midges held me back until, suddenly, they were streaming past me into the family room. I whirled as they poured up through the chimney, through gaps around the windows. When I turned back to the bedroom, Alyssa was sleeping comfortably. Her face was as it used to be, the skin smooth and beautiful. Her arm no longer sprang crookedly from her elbow. The puncture wounds had also disappeared.

I felt a strange tingling around my wrist. When I glanced down, a few stray midges were flitting off my arm, leaving behind a shredded loop of gauze bandage. My skin was free of angry bite marks. There weren't even scars.

Patt barked in the hallway, awake now. Charleze opened her eyes at the same moment as Alyssa, and both looked at me in confusion, as if I'd appeared from nowhere. Then Charleze turned to her daughter and cried out in joy. Behind me I heard Mackenzie coming downstairs saying, "Zay, why're you here?" and then Riley burst into the house, looking confused and fearful, but only until he saw Alyssa.

"What happened?" the Jacksons kept saying, over and over, through their tears. "Zay, did you see what happened?"

28

When they came for dinner that night, it was hard to stop staring at Alyssa. It was a beautiful evening, still warm enough to sit outside without a sweater. We'd set the table on the deck. On the grass nearby, Alyssa was running around with Noah, laughing, like she'd already forgotten what had happened—like *nothing* had happened. Not a single mark on her face or arm.

The glow from Nia's beeswax candles amplified the happiness around the table. We toasted Alyssa's health, Noah toasted her again, and then Riley raised a glass to me for being a crack shot. After that I toasted Mackenzie for being so brave at the pond and fighting them off. It was so good to see her smile at me. She touched my leg under the table, and I felt forgiven.

After the meal, when it got darker, Charleze told Noah and Alyssa to go inside to play. We were assuming we'd killed all the coyotes, but no one wanted to take any chances. There was no objection from the kids, because Mackenzie had lugged over Alyssa's entire princess castle and a bulging backpack of her favorite things.

"I'll get them some dessert," I said, and Mackenzie followed me inside.

From the bedroom came the happy sounds of princesses, farm animals, and a mutant Barbie rampaging around the castle. Mackenzie and I stood in the hallway and held each other. Being separated from her these past few days, I hadn't been able to sleep properly or think straight. I pressed my face into her hair and just breathed.

"I was worried you hated me," I said.

She looked astonished. "How could I?"

"I thought maybe you blamed me. I didn't know what you were thinking; you wouldn't really look at me or talk to me when I came over."

"I was just so sick about Alyssa." She put her hands gently on either side of my face. "You did everything right, Zay. You always do."

And she kissed me.

When we got back, the adults had finished off the wine and moved on to whiskey. Riley poured me a shot. Dad raised his eyebrows, then gave me a little nod.

"You've raised one hell of a boy," Riley said to my father. "He's earned that drink."

I took it back in a single swallow and it scorched all the way down. I felt like I'd survived a calamity and was temporarily immortal.

"And *that's* how you do it!" Riley said.

"To better times," my father added, downing his glass.

Before the Jacksons arrived for dinner, we'd all agreed not to talk about Alyssa, our captors, or the balloon. Riley's family had been through a terrible ordeal, and tonight was just going to be about having a meal together and feeling grateful.

All day, though, an uncomfortable question had been banging against my skull, like a fly against glass. Why had *they* waited so long to heal Alyssa? Was it to make a point, to make the Jacksons suffer so they'd reconsider their plans? And why had they done it right after we'd killed the coyotes? Like some kind of reward. But for what? Teamwork? Good shooting? I didn't have any answers. I didn't know the rules.

"Soon as I finish the harnesses," Riley was saying with a smile, "we're good to go."

For the first time, an awkward silence spread across the table. My gaze bounced between Dad and Nia. I knew they were hoping Riley would finally call it quits. After everything that had happened to his daughter—her injury and healing—surely he'd realize how dangerous it was to risk further punishment. He had to accept that his captors were not humans, but extraterrestrials with unfathomable powers.

"I know what you want to say, Caleb," Riley went on, "and I know how you want me to reply."

Dad stayed silent. This morning, right after the midges had healed Alyssa, I'd told the Jacksons what had happened. Maybe because they'd just woken up and were so overwhelmed, they hadn't taken much in.

Riley said, "What you saw, Xavier—and I trust you—it still doesn't change my mind."

"What I saw couldn't have been human," I replied. "The midges fixed her in *seconds*. They were *levitating* her."

"I believe you, I do."

"And sometimes they weren't even touching her, but"—I lowered my voice—"her arm was sliced open and her bones were moving and veins and things were growing. Then all her skin was suddenly back on."

"Nanodrones," Riley said. "Repurposed with surgical capabilities."

My breath leaked out of me. Could he be right? Maybe. What seemed like the tiniest possibility to me was total fact to Riley. His certainty was like an acid, and I didn't want it eating away at my own. I wondered if there was anything that could convince him we were in outer space. This guy could probably shrug off a close encounter with an alien facehugger.

"We're worried what they might do next," Nia said bluntly.

"Us too," said Charleze.

It was scary thinking how they would top the coyotes. A velociraptor? Or maybe they'd go smaller and send a virus so we could have a little pandemic of our very own.

"That's why we aren't waiting around to see," Riley said. "Now's the time."

I could tell Nia was about to say something angry, but luckily Dad got in first.

"I don't know anything about ballooning," he said, "but I understand it's quite a science."

It was the right move, and he and Riley talked amicably about adverse winds, how to steer the balloon toward the opening. It would be like threading a needle. And would it even fit through the hatch?

"I appreciate your concern, Caleb. But I'm pretty sure I can handle it."

I caught Mackenzie's eye...and she didn't look one hundred percent convinced.

"What d'you think it's going to be like, once you're through the hatch?" I asked.

Riley chuckled. "Well, it won't involve aliens."

When he'd first started the balloon, Dad and Nia hadn't even thought it would get built. Now it was finished, and everyone was thinking about the actual flight. I knew Nia had decided the launch was doomed. But had anyone thought about what *might* be waiting on the other side of the sky?

"Okay," I said. "No aliens. But there's bound to be guards up there, right? They'll probably see you coming."

"Ah," said Riley, amused, "are you running a scenario for me?"

"Yes."

I glanced at Dad, wondering if he'd try to shut me down. But he said nothing, maybe hoping that I'd succeed where he'd failed. Even if Riley truly was in some evil government base, how did he think he was going to get out? He'd be outnumbered and outgunned.

"This kid can think a thing through," Riley said. "Let's do it. Shoot."

"Your balloon floats toward the hatch. Just before it gets there, the midges come swarming out."

"We open fire with our sawed-off shotguns."

"That knocks out some of them, but they release a gas that puts everyone to sleep. When you wake up, you're back on the ground."

"Not so. I have a couple tear gas masks."

"Really?"

"In the storeroom. Care of the Department of Corrections."

"Wow. Okay, let's say that works. So. Before you get to the hatch, they puncture your balloon and you start sinking back to earth."

"Patch it up, try again."

"They do it again."

"Patch it up, try again."

I could see this was a dead end. I fast-forwarded. "Okay. You actually make it through the hatch into some kind of loading bay. There are four armed guards waiting for you."

"Now you're talking. I will tell you exactly what I'll do." As he launched into it, it became obvious he'd thought about this a lot. He predicted where the guards would be positioned, their weaponry, their tactics. With chilling detail, he laid out how he would use the propane tank as a bomb to create a distraction, how he would wound one guard, seize his weapons, and use him as a human shield.

"I will do whatever's necessary," he said, "to stay alive and protect my family and friends."

Everyone was quiet for a couple seconds. I wasn't going to push anymore, but Nia did.

"Things might not turn out that way," she said.

"That's true. But I've got to try it, or what kind of man am I?"

"So what happens if you get out?" she asked. She didn't say *when* we get out, but Riley didn't seem to notice. "Say deep government did put you here. Aren't you worried they'll catch you and put you right back?"

"They'll try, sure. But it's our duty to expose what they're doing with these camps. The mainstream media won't help us. They're all in on it. We need to go underground, go grassroots, spread the word however we can. Our friends will take us in and shelter us. We'll be hiding out for some time, no question."

Mackenzie now looked queasy. So much for being vice president of the school council. So much for NYU. So much for a *life*. I got the sense she hadn't imagined her return to Earth would be as a fugitive.

"But if we work together," her father was saying, "eventually we'll win. And at least my girls will be safe."

His eyes were suddenly wet. Charleze put her arm around him, and Mackenzie called him "Daddy" and hugged him.

"It's been an awful lot," Charleze said to us.

Even Nia looked abashed.

I got up to take Kimmy for his walk, and Mackenzie said she'd come, too. On our way out the door, my whole body felt electric at the prospect of being alone with her again. But outside, when she turned to me, my smile evaporated. Her face was cold and accusatory.

"Do you even *want* us to escape?"

"Yeah, of course, but—"

"At the pond, I just remembered this, you said you didn't want the balloon *ever to leave the ground*."

I cursed myself. I'd said it rashly in a moment of swelling love. "Okay, what I meant was—I was afraid if we ever did get out, I'd never see you again."

Her face softened. "Why'd you have to be so discouraging just now?"

"That wasn't discouraging. That was realistic. You can't *still* think we're on Earth."

"I don't know anymore." She was quiet for a second. "I trust you, Zay, about what you saw when they fixed Alyssa. It's not that. But I still can't wrap my head around us being in outer space. And whoever's up there, they're dangerous. Daddy's right: We've got to at least try to get out."

"It's going to fail."

"You don't know that. Not for sure."

"If they don't want us to leave, no way are we leaving."

I sounded like my father, I sounded like Nia, and hated myself for a second. But after everything I'd seen, I'd decided there was no scenario that ended well.

"I want a life, Zay!"

"You can have one here."

"You're joking. In a snow globe six miles across?"

"Before you came, I felt exactly the same."

"Zay—"

"I love you," I blurted.

Instantly I knew it was a mistake. I'd hoped that it would melt her, but she looked exasperated.

"I'm just the first girl you've seen in three years. We barely know each other!"

"I know you don't love me," I said. "It's pretty soon, I get that. But maybe you'll love me eventually. After a while. I want to spend the rest of my life with you."

She winced sadly. "We don't have a future like that, Zay."

"I'd be really good to you."

"I've already met my forever partner."

My chest felt like it was filling with wet concrete. "Lucas?"

"I know it in my heart."

I had to turn away. "Lucas. The guy you've been so angry at?"

"Doesn't stop me loving him. I can't just swipe him off the screen."

"The guy who treated you badly?"

"That's my business, Zay." She looked so angry right now. "You don't get to choose who I love. And I'm not responsible for how you feel either."

"Nope."

She took my hand. Her touch didn't feel electric like it usually did. "I know I might've been sending mixed signals. With all the messing around we did."

Messing around. It sounded trivial. Like what a little kid did with finger paints.

I pulled my hand free. "I thought it was more than messing around." Even if it was ordinary to her, it was a big deal to me.

"Zay. You are handsome, funny, and kind, and you are going to meet so many girls who will be dying to go out with you."

I looked right and left. "I'm not seeing them."

"Once we get out of here!"

I said nothing.

"You're not coming with us on the balloon, are you?"

I shook my head. "And you shouldn't go either."

"When'd you decide this?"

I sighed. "After I saw alien technology heal your sister like magic."

"So you thought I'd just stick around and pair off with you because you're the only available male in the galaxy?"

"You seemed to like me all right."

"I was just brought up here to be your breeding partner? That's super romantic."

"Hey, none of this was my idea!"

"And I guess Noah and Alyssa are also meant to end up together one day, right?"

"This is what we got dumped into. It's what we have. It's what's *possible*."

"Oh my God. I am not being part of some zoo mating program!"

I waited for Kimmy to have his pee—partly on my shoe because I wasn't paying attention I was so upset—and then we headed back to the deck.

"Acceptance?" Charleze was saying when we got there. "That's the gospel you're preaching, Caleb? They put us in jail, they maim my child, and you want us to *accept* it?"

"They healed Alyssa," Nia gently reminded her.

"After letting her suffer three days. Whatever's motivating them, it is *not* mercy."

"I'm just asking you to consider another possibility," said Dad. "Another choice."

Riley swallowed some whiskey. "No. This is what they do. They take *away* your choices and make you accept theirs. The only choice I'm interested in is freedom."

Nia smacked the table. "Your kind of freedom is going to get us killed!"

"Listen to that," said Riley sadly. "You just admitted it. I didn't think you were so far gone, Nia. But you've let them beat you."

"You are not on Earth, Riley."

"Unproven."

"You are somewhere very far away, and whoever's keeping us here doesn't give a damn about your freedom. They want to keep us here. Nothing we can do about it."

"Watch me."

The mood of celebration, the toasts, the gratitude—all that was now a sour memory.

"Riley, Charleze, I agree with you," my father said. "There is nothing fair, nothing just, about this situation. But we haven't lost all our freedoms. Liberty of movement, yes. And that is huge. But you still have freedom of speech, freedom of assembly, freedom of religion . . ."

"See how long that lasts," said Charleze darkly.

"Right to bear arms," Nia added cheekily. "They gave you back your ammunition."

Riley gave a bitter chuckle that worried me.

"We're still free to live with dignity," my father said, and I felt like he was really pulling out all the stops now. This was Boardroom Dad. "Life here is more than good. We have plenty of food. There's no disease, not so much as the flu. Certainly no pandemics. No heat domes or climate catastrophe. Perfect medical care." I thought this one was a little risky, given what had just happened to Alyssa. "And you have your family with you, and they are healthy and happy and safe."

I gave a little shudder as Riley started clapping. Big loud sarcastic claps, while he shook his head with a pitying smile.

"Caleb, that is a stirring oration. You're living up to your biblical namesake."

"Riley," said Charleze in dismay.

"Caleb the spy. Except you're not spying for the right team."

"I'm not a spy," my father said.

"Riley doesn't mean it," Charleze told us.

"They've been taking very good care of the Oaks." Riley tapped his glass lightly against the table. "Both our little ones were at the pond that day."

He didn't need to say, *But it was only mine who got mauled.*

"Riley, that is unkind," said Charleze. "The Oaks have nothing to do with the actions of these evil people."

"I don't think they're evil," Nia said. "But if you keep trying to escape, they'll keep throwing stuff at us."

"And even if, somehow, you get the balloon through that opening," my father said, "you will not be one bit closer to home. If you even survive the ride."

"If we don't escape, we're dying here anyway," Riley said.

"After a full life," Nia told him. "Think of your kids. They could have a future here."

"Nia," I said, cringing. After the rage I just got from Mackenzie, I didn't want this.

She went on. "Even after we're gone, our kids wouldn't have to be alone. They could start their own families."

Mackenzie was glaring at me. Why did Nia have to bring that up, now of all times?

"Well, I can see you've given this a lot of thought," said Riley. It was darker now, and the light from the candles no longer imparted a benevolent glow to our faces. It hollowed us out, socketed our eyes, made us all sinister. And something else had happened to Riley's face that couldn't be explained by the shadow play. It looked like he was fighting to control a facial spasm.

"I think my children deserve more choice who they marry," he said.

"I can't marry Noah!" cried Alyssa from below the deck.

Her piping voice was so unexpected I broke out in goose bumps. I went to the railing and looked down. Alyssa and Noah sat cross-legged on the grass, listening—for how long, who knew? They must've gone out the front door for a little adventure.

"Get up here!" Riley shouted. "When it's dark, you stay inside. You want the coyotes to get you again?"

She stomped up the steps, frowning. "I like Noah but I can't marry him, because of the Surge."

"Shush now!" Charleze said severely.

Everyone was already well and truly shushed. I didn't know what Alyssa was talking about, but Nia's face was rigid with anger. She turned to Riley.

"I didn't know the Great Surge Theory was part of your conspiracy list."

"What is that?" I asked, looking at Dad, who was breathing through his mouth, like he was trying to slow an angry pulse.

"Go on, Riley," said Nia. "Explain it to Zay."

"I don't need to explain myself."

In bewilderment I looked at Mackenzie. She wouldn't meet my eye.

"Some people," Nia said, "believe that deep government is planning a Great Surge where people of color pour into countries to make white folks extinct."

I remembered my flashlight beam lighting up the book on Riley's night table. *Extinction*. I'd thought it was about the climate emergency, maybe species extinction.

"No. It's not racial," Riley said. "Nothing to do with the color of your skin. It's about bloodlines. Some white folks have the reptilian bloodline, too."

If ever there was a phrase to stop conversation, it was *reptilian bloodline*. It sounded dimly familiar. An internet meme, a joke in the school hallways. Another conspiracy theory.

"Riley, this is not the time." Charleze looked mortified. I wasn't sure if it was because she thought her husband was full of crap, or because she didn't want their secrets splashing out on the deck.

Mackenzie stared hard at the table. Why wasn't she saying anything? She'd called out her father before, about climate change, and this was way worse.

"I thought you didn't believe in aliens, Riley," Dad said.

"These aren't aliens. They evolved alongside us. Didn't you guys study evolution? *Homo sapiens* wasn't the only game in town. Way back there was *Homo habilis*, *Homo erectus*, *Homo neanderthalensis*—and *Homo reptiliansis*. A hybrid mammalian reptile. Unlike the others, they did not die out."

"Holy shit, Riley," said Nia. "That is not true."

"It's in the fossil record. I've seen pictures."

Numbly I wondered if he thought I had a reptilian bloodline, too—if our whole family did.

"Jesus," said my father. "You can't be serious."

"It's nothing racist," Charleze hurried in, like she didn't want any hurt feelings. "It's just about preservation, keeping everything as it should be."

I saw Noah standing by himself in the corner, looking confused and miserable. I motioned him over and wrapped my arms around him.

"We are so awfully fond of your whole family," Charleze said, looking pained.

"And we want to get you out of here, too," Riley said.

"We're not going anywhere with you," said Nia.

Hearing her say it aloud, I felt something tear inside me. Despite my decision, and all my doubts, despite the crap I'd just heard, the idea of that balloon was still powerful. It carried the hope of escape, the chance of being back in the real world with Sam and Mom.

"I'd like you to leave now," Nia said, standing.

"Maybe we should let things simmer down a bit," said Charleze, and I could see her pat her husband's leg.

"We should be getting back anyway," said Riley. "Thank you for the dinner. If I could get my other rifle, I'd appreciate it."

We'd left it in the barn, with the boxes of ammo on the highest shelf. I was standing to go get it when Nia said:

"We'll hold on to it. In case another coyote shows up."

I studied her face, trying to figure out if she was sincere—and was pretty sure she wasn't. She'd never talked about this. She hated having the gun around. My eyes slid worriedly over to Riley.

"Wouldn't mind having it for the walk home," he said, "in the dark."

"You have the one you brought," said Nia. "You'll be fine."

"We'll get your rifle," my father told him.

"No!" Nia said, giving Dad a look of hostility I'd never witnessed before. "I feel safer having some protection of my own."

"I'm sorry you feel so threatened," Riley remarked.

"Damn right I do." Her entire body was vibrating.

"Nia—" my father said

"No, no, it's all right," Riley said, standing. "You hold on to it, Nia. Not like this is the first time you've tried to disarm me."

Nia didn't even bother widening her eyes in pretend ignorance.

"But I did want to thank you, for bringing my ammo back," said Riley. "I knew it didn't come from the people upstairs." He gave me a little nod. "I'm grateful. But the fact is, I can't trust you folks anymore."

"Riley, stop," said Charleze. "Let's not talk like this."

"I think it's best," said Riley, "if our families steer clear of each other."

29

"Keeping that gun's only going to antagonize him," Dad told Nia after the Jacksons had left.

"Too bad. You can't expect people with reptilian bloodlines to be reasonable."

It was too insane to comprehend. I'd grown up in a school with people of all different skin colors and it was normal to me. The idea of wanting to be surrounded only by white people was so bizarre I could barely take it seriously. And the image of people slithering around with reptile blood, trying to take over the world, was from a bad movie.

"Okay," said Dad. "But people with guns are far more likely to get shot than people without, especially women."

"You don't need to tell me statistics," she snapped. "Can you just be outraged, Caleb, for once? Take off those velvet gloves and fight alongside me. Go ahead, just for me. Be angry!"

"I don't want to replace anyone," said Noah.

We'd been so swept up in the conversation, we'd forgotten he was here. We all turned to him now. Nia's face furrowed with sorrow, and she took him in her arms.

"You haven't done anything wrong," she said. "Some people believe silly, silly things."

While she tucked Noah in and read to him, Dad and I washed up. The evening had started with such hope, and now it was like clearing up after a funeral. I scrubbed Mackenzie's plate and glass. She'd said nothing. All that crap her father had spewed and she'd stayed silent. It could only mean she believed it.

"You don't think he's actually dangerous, do you?" I said. I wanted some reassurance. I almost told him about Riley's PTSD and the whole prison business. It would've been so good to dump the weight of that secret, but I stopped myself. I was too ashamed now, too worried of what my dad would think of me, holding back something like that.

"I don't think so," Dad said. "But us having a gun—he might see that as a threat."

"I could take it back."

"Let's think about it," he said, which meant he and Nia would decide. He looked at me severely. "You are not to take it back, Zay."

One day passed, then four. I milked goats and harvested crops and stacked shelves with preserves. We let Herk breed with two of the does to keep up our milk supply. I did all the things I'd been doing for the three years before the Jacksons came.

They'd changed everything, the entire stage set of our domed lives. *Enter Jacksons, stage left! Act I. They introduce a new hope of escape! Act II. Look, there's Mackenzie and Xavier kissing! Act III. There they are, backlit by the sunset, living happily ever after—but wait! Mackenzie believes in human-reptile hybrids intent on taking over the planet!*

She was right about one thing, though: I was an idiot to fall for her. I was like a caveman, cryogenically frozen at age thirteen, then thawed out knowing nothing about girls. Too stupid to see that she'd been stringing me along, rewarding me with kisses and hand jobs so I'd keep her secrets. I'd loved her and been a good little servant, and it turned out she was delusional like her father. I was disgusted by her, and disgusted at myself.

None of this stopped me from dreaming about her. We were on Mount Royal, the whole city spread below us, and she spoke lovingly to me and I woke up with such an ache in my heart. Over the years I'd had to give up on the idea of ever having a partner, someone to love and be loved by, someone with whom I could talk and laugh and share my life. But when Mackenzie came, it suddenly seemed possible, and I automatically assumed she would be that person.

Nia wasn't sleeping much. She wanted us to take turns keeping watch. She worried Riley would break into the house in the middle of the night, looking for his gun. She worried we'd be shot.

We stumbled on with our lives. We stayed away from the Jacksons, and they did the same. We didn't see any signs of more coyotes, which was good news. Still, we were waiting to see what might come next. We didn't talk about it around Noah, and not even much among ourselves, but we were all anxious. By now Riley had to be in the final stages of rigging the balloon, getting ready to launch. Would there be more punishments? Every night, I wondered what I'd wake up to. How far would *they* go to discourage Riley's escape?

I played more with Noah. I made a very simple D&D campaign for him, and it was more fun than I'd thought. It took my mind off things, and he got such a kick out of battling orcs and opening his first treasure chest. He reminded me of myself, playing for the first time with Sam. And it made me realize I hadn't been the greatest big brother. Probably I'd blamed Noah, not for anything he'd done, but just because he wasn't Sam.

"Alyssa was fun to play with," Noah said all of a sudden.

"I know. It sucks."

"It's okay if she doesn't want to marry me. I just liked playing with her."

My heart crumpled up a bit, the way he looked at me so seriously, like he could solve everyone's problems if only he agreed that Alyssa didn't have to marry him.

"Come on," I said. "You're being attacked by a gelatinous cube. What do you do?"

My forever partner, Mackenzie had said about Lucas.

How nice for you, Mackenzie, I thought. *I hope you two will be very happy together, living in an underground bunker after your escape.*

But would there be an escape? Of course not. The balloon wouldn't launch or something would go wrong in flight. Then the question would be, would they live through it? Would Riley launch a second flight? Or would he hatch some other plan—keeping us all punished until none of us survived?

Three days later, just after I'd started morning chores, I heard Mackenzie call my name. My reaction was instantaneous. I dropped everything and ran toward her voice. My heart and body couldn't betray my mind fast enough. She called out again, and when we saw each other, she ran, too—the way I'd always craved. She was crying. She threw her arms around me, and I held her and asked her if she was okay.

I didn't think about how she'd said we had no future and were just messing around. I didn't think about Lucas. I didn't think about reptilian bloodlines. None of that mattered now that I was holding her.

Dad and Nia had been working outside, and headed toward us. I didn't think they'd ever seen us like this, embracing, and there was a strange look on Dad's face, a mournful look. Like maybe he was sorry, finally, for everything I'd been missing and stood to lose again.

"Mackenzie, what's happened?" Nia asked.

I was disappointed when Mackenzie gently pulled back. Swiping away tears, she said, "I wanted to apologize for the things my parents said. I should've said something, because I don't think like that."

At those words, I felt such an updraft of joy. "Come and sit down," I said, and we headed for the deck.

I went inside to get her a glass of water. Noah wanted to come out and ask about Alyssa, maybe vow never to marry her, but I told him to wait inside for just a bit and play with Kimmy. He scowled and stomped back to our room.

"Thanks," said Mackenzie when I brought the water out to her.

She seemed so upset, I didn't think she'd come just to apologize, but I didn't want to rush her. When Dad asked how things had been going, she said her father had been working round the clock, preparing for the launch. Riley had figured out how to heat the balloon with the stove, and he'd started chopping trees for fuel at the launch site. They'd been feeding and watering the animals, but not doing much else on the farm. Mostly they'd been eating their canned meat and some harvested vegetables.

"They had a big fight last night," she said. "Mama was saying maybe there should be a test flight before we all went up. And Daddy said there wasn't time, or enough propane in the tank. We'd only have one shot. They kept at it, and Daddy got pretty mad, and said why didn't she trust him. And she said if there's danger up there, people shooting, someone was bound to get injured. He said she was starting to talk like the Oaks. And then he said..." Her lips trembled and she closed her eyes, but tears still squeezed out. "Daddy said he was starting to think she'd been 3D printed, just like the house, and maybe she wasn't his real wife at all. Because his real wife would've supported him one hundred percent. But maybe she was back on Earth, along with his real children."

Gooseflesh flared icily along my arms. It was such a terrifying notion, and even more terrifying that someone might actually believe it.

"I don't think he meant it," she hurried on, like she was trying to console herself. "He'd been drinking. I think he was just saying it because he was angry."

"Has he ever gotten like this before?" my father asked.

"Well, he gets worked up sometimes, but usually it doesn't last quite so long. Mama stayed real calm, but when she asked if he'd taken his pills, he really blew up."

"What pills?" Nia asked, each word a chisel blow.

Mackenzie's eyes flicked guiltily my way.

"Mackenzie, what kind of pills was he taking?" Nia persisted.

"Mood stabilizers."

"Why was he on mood stabilizers?"

It all came out: the incident at the prison, the investigation, the PTSD.

Nia turned to me. I didn't know if she was too stunned, or too enraged, to speak.

"You knew about this?" Dad asked me.

I nodded.

"You knew he killed someone—and you gave him back his ammo?" Nia said. It was not a question but an accusation. "You didn't think about the risk? To all of us?"

"I thought the coyotes were more of a risk."

"My father's not a psychopath!" Mackenzie said. "He'd never shoot anyone."

"Just an inmate," said Nia.

"It was a Taser," I said.

My father held up a hand to shut us both up, then turned to Mackenzie. "Has he been taking his medication?"

She shook her head miserably. "No. He said he'd flushed it all down the toilet."

"Holy shit," exhaled Nia.

No more medicine for Riley. No refill at the nearest galactic pharmacy.

Our silence seemed to scare Mackenzie because she blurted, "It might not be so bad. The whole time we've been here, I'd say he skipped them mostly. And he's been pretty okay."

Nia sniffed, as if to say, *Debatable.*

"Mama got him to take some Valium and a sleeping pill. He was still out when I left."

Nia said, "Mackenzie, go home, right now."

Mackenzie's eyes widened—maybe at Nia's abrupt tone, or fear at the idea of going home.

"What if she doesn't want to?" I said, glaring.

"If your father knows you've been here, it's going to create even more tension. He'll think you've taken sides, or that we're trying to brainwash you."

Mackenzie blew out a long, helpless breath.

"Did he hit you?" I asked.

"No!"

Nia said, "If I were you, I'd hide his ammunition."

Indignantly, Mackenzie replied, "You're talking about him like he's a maniac."

"Why'd you come here if you're not scared?" Nia snapped.

"Because I *am* scared of going up in that balloon!"

"And you thought we could help?" Nia asked.

"I don't know... Maybe you could talk to him."

"We've been trying for weeks," my father reminded her. "I don't think he wants to hear any more from us."

"Go home, Mackenzie," said Nia wearily. "I'm sorry you're scared, but you coming here was very selfish."

"Geez, Nia," I said.

I looked at Dad to back me up, but saw that he agreed with her.

"I'm sorry," Mackenzie said, standing. "I'll go."

"I'll walk you back," I said.

"Bad idea," said Nia.

"Let him," said Dad.

"I don't need permission," I retorted over my shoulder.

As I walked away, I heard my father say, "Best if you don't let anyone see you, Zay."

"Can you just not go? In the balloon?" I asked her after we'd walked in silence for a couple minutes.

"And let the rest of my family go?"

"Doesn't sound like your mom wants to go either."

"No."

"What would he do if you told him?"

"It seems cowardly, to let him go by himself."

Let him go ahead and fail, I'd told Nia and my father earlier, so rashly. The idea of a failed Riley now seemed pretty terrible. A bitter, unstable, armed Riley.

"It's not cowardly," I said.

"I'm sorry I got mean that other night," she said. "I hadn't thought much about what the balloon ride would be like. And you *made* me start thinking about it, with all your doubts. It's not your fault—it was smart. I should've thought about it way sooner."

She took my hand. As our fingers interlaced I was perfectly content. We continued along the path she and I had helped create. Our hands parted only briefly so we could jump the stones across the creek.

"So, all that Great Surge stuff?" I said, needing to be sure.

"I used to believe it."

I looked over at her sharply.

"Everyone we knew did. When I was little, they'd be over at the house and I'd hear them talking, and you just assume it's true because they're your parents and they know everything, so of course you trust them. Wouldn't you?"

Reluctantly I nodded. Probably I would've been exactly the same.

"But then I went to school, and Ms. Taylor got through to me. After that it was terrible in a different way, when you know your parents are dead wrong, but you still love them."

"Does Lucas believe that crap?"

She was quiet a moment. "We don't talk about it."

We were getting close to the farm, and I knew I should turn back, but I wanted to spend every second I could with her. We came out of the trees and I could see their lodge. The porch was empty. I stopped her.

"Don't go up in that balloon," I said.

She kissed me. "If I was shipwrecked on a desert island," she said, "you'd be the best person to wash up with."

I smiled because it sounded like a promise: If she truly was stuck here, we had a future together. She didn't love me now, but she might someday.

Her father's voice made us step apart.

"Figured you two might be having a visit," Riley said, walking out from the corn with a basket of eggs and vegetables. "Morning, Xavier."

I stood rigid, trying to read his mood. His parting words had been to keep away from his family, but he seemed so calm and gentle now I didn't feel frightened of him.

"Hey, sweetheart," he said to Mackenzie with an apologetic smile. She went to him without hesitation, and he kissed the top of her head and said how sorry he was. He looked over at me. "I disgraced myself last night. Frightened my family."

I didn't know what to say, so kept my mouth shut. Talking to an adult could be tricky at the best of times, especially to one who'd told his family they were 3D printed.

"I didn't flush my pills," he said to Mackenzie. He put down the basket and pulled a vial from his pocket. Gave it a rattle. "And I'll be taking them."

She looked at him severely. "Promise."

"I promise. I can't tell you how sorry I am, scaring you all like that."

She hugged him, and he said, "Come have some breakfast with us, Xavier."

"I should probably head back."

"Just a quick visit. Charleze'll be sad to miss you."

Mackenzie gave me a beseeching look, so I walked with them toward the lodge.

"I owe you an apology, too, Xavier," he said. "I owe one to your whole family, for the things I got into that night."

Did that mean he didn't believe in the Great Surge and reptilian bloodlines? Or just that he was sorry he'd brought them up? I wasn't about to ask right now.

Charleze came out onto the porch and embraced Mackenzie. "You should've told me you were going out. I worried." Then she opened her right arm to wave me in. "Oh, Xavier, we have missed you!"

Her eyes were puffy from lack of sleep and shining with tears, and I felt a little emotional myself. They were our only neighbors. Our racist, conspiracy-theorist neighbors, but they were all we had.

Alyssa came out and shouted my name happily, then asked if Noah was here. When I said no, she lost interest and retreated inside the house.

"Have you had breakfast?" Charleze asked me, and I said I had. "Let me get you a drink at least." At the door she looked back at her husband and said, "Have you told her?"

"What?" Mackenzie asked nervously.

Riley sat down in the creaky rocking chair. "I've decided to go up alone. I'm not putting any of you at risk."

It seemed like a lot had changed in a few hours. Relief started to pull my mouth into a smile, but I caught it, in case it seemed callous.

"You sure you want to do it at all?" I asked.

"It's gotta be done."

I heard the steel of his conviction, and didn't want to push things.

Charleze returned with a glass of water for me.

"When d'you think you'll be ready to launch?" I asked.

"Three days."

I had to swallow twice to make the water go down. I hadn't thought he was quite so close.

"I'll deal with whatever's up there myself," he said, "and figure out how to open this cage for good. I'll come back for the rest of you."

It seems cowardly to let him go by himself, Mackenzie had said. I felt the same pang now. Shouldn't I be offering to go with him? Shouldn't my father? But I had the sense to keep quiet.

"I do have one thing to ask," Riley said.

The muscles around my neck and shoulders bunched up.

"Your family's already done so much for us. I haven't been properly grateful.

You're good people, I know that. If anything, God forbid, happens to me up there..."

"Daddy, stop!" said Mackenzie.

"I want you folks to look over my family."

I felt like someone had just handed me his beating heart for safekeeping.

I nodded. "Yes. Of course. But, Mr. Jackson, maybe you just want a breather to think about this a little more."

"I've thought about it every which way. I've got to do this. To *try*."

I felt terrible, seeing Mackenzie cry again. So much of this was my fault. Launching the idea of that stupid hot-air balloon. When it was just a distant, shiny thing it had seemed so exciting. As a D&D idea it was clever, ingenious even. If you crash-landed, maybe you'd lose some hit points; worst-case scenario, you died. There was usually a resurrection spell you could lay your hands on, then try all over again. In the real world, you had one try and no coming back from the dead.

30

When I returned to our farm, I told them how Riley had decided to make a solo flight. How much calmer he'd seemed. How he'd promised to take his pills.

"Even if he does," said Nia, "he's going to run out eventually. And then what?"

She was assuming, sooner or later, he would hurt himself or his family. Or us.

"He might get better," I said.

"But will he 'get better' from thinking Noah and I are part of the Great Surge? He might've always been delusional."

It was hard to balance Riley's unhinged conspiracy theories with the humble man I'd just seen, asking us to look after his family if he died.

"He might be delusional," said my father, "or maybe he was force-fed garbage all his life. All we know is what we grow up with, what's put into us. By our parents, friends, teachers, what we read and watch. But people can change. If he stayed here with us, he'd eventually have a change of heart."

I looked at my father, encouraged by his optimism. It was a relief to hear a hopeful thing right now, after Nia's usual oil spill of negativity and anger.

"And I think that's the most likely scenario," Dad said. "That he'll end up here. Launching that balloon will be tougher than he thinks."

I'd watched a video once. They laid the balloon flat along the ground and held the skirt open while they blasted cold air inside with a huge fan. When it was partially inflated, they used the burner to jet flame inside. It looked pretty complicated and took a lot of people. And that was just the prep.

"So he's going to heat it up over the woodstove," I said, my mind vaulting ahead. "Say that gets him off the ground. How long before he needs to start using the propane?"

Dad shook his head. "No idea. He might use it all up, just getting to the top."

"And if he can't get through the hatch?" The ascent was one thing; the descent was something else. "Would he come down slow, or too fast?"

"I don't know, Zay."

I imagined the balloon slamming into the earth, until a more comforting image came to me.

"Maybe the balloon acts like a big parachute, though?"

Dad winced. "Not sure it has the same surface area as a parachute, to slow it. That's why it's best it never gets off the ground."

Nia chewed thoughtfully on her lower lip. "We should help him. Make sure that balloon goes up."

I looked at her warily. "You want to *help* him now?"

"He has a chance. You said it yourself, Zay. A tiny, infinitesimal chance that he gets out and frees us all. Why not help him?"

I shook my head. "You just want him to go up and die."

"Riley wants to take that risk." She turned to my father. "Whatever the outcome, don't you think it would be best for all of us?"

"Jesus, Nia. That's pretty brutal," I said.

"Nia, if you offer to help him right now," Dad said, "he'll be suspicious. He'll think you're trying to sabotage him."

She considered this. "Okay, but he won't be suspicious of Zay."

I might've helped Riley with the launch, but now it felt tainted. Like I'd be doing something dirty and awful. Helping someone to their possible death.

"I don't want Zay helping," Dad told her sharply. I could tell from the angle of his eyebrows that he was worried about me. "Riley's too volatile right now. I don't want you close to him, Zay. I won't have you getting hurt."

It took me by surprise when he hugged me and kissed the top of my head. I felt like these past weeks, he'd always been at least a little angry with me—and probably a *lot* angry when he found out about Riley's history.

"Okay," I said.

"Riley can decide his own fate," said Dad.

Something occurred to me for the first time. "You think they'd *let* him die?"

I could tell Dad and Nia hadn't considered this either.

"Even if things go wrong up there," I went on, "they'd save him, right? Like they've saved everyone else."

"Well," Nia said, "we'd better hope our keepers have our best interests at heart."

A couple days later, end of the afternoon, Mackenzie came over to tell us that the launch was tomorrow.

"First thing," she said. "When the wind's lightest."

We all sat on the deck, drinking pear juice.

"We wish him all the best," my father said.

"Every success," Nia added, which I knew was a bald-faced lie.

"Is Alyssa going back to Erf, too?" Noah asked, stroking Kimmy on his lap.

"No, she's staying here with us for a bit," said Mackenzie.

"Oh good," said Noah. "Can she come over soon? I miss her."

"She misses you something awful," Mackenzie told him. "Oh, and she wanted me to give you this."

She pulled Alyssa's favorite princess from her jeans pocket and handed it to Noah.

"Really?" he said in amazement, like he'd just been handed the Orb of Power.

"Okay, I need to get something." He dashed inside, Kimmy chasing after him, toenails clicking on the hardwood.

"How's your father doing?" Dad asked Mackenzie, which I knew meant: *Has Riley been taking his meds and is he stable?*

"Pretty good, yeah. Very focused."

Noah came pelting back out. "This is for Alyssa." He handed over Rumpety, then said, slightly anxiously, "We can still trade, next time we're playing."

"We'll arrange something soon," Nia promised.

And then Mackenzie and I had some time alone, just the two of us. We went for a walk around the farm, and ended up in the barn loft. We lay down and kissed and touched each other for a long time. She asked me to come to the launch tomorrow.

"I want to," I said, "but I promised my dad I wouldn't."

She looked crestfallen. "I'm worried."

I wanted to tell her that Riley would be fine, but I couldn't lie, so I said, "I'd be worried, too. But he's a very capable guy. If anyone can pull it off, it's your dad."

"No. I'm worried he'll . . . It's stupid maybe, but I'm worried he's been lying to us."

"How?"

"About going alone. I'm worried he'll force Mama and me and Alyssa to go with him."

I sat up a little. "Has he said anything?"

"No, but . . ."

"You said he was okay, that he's taking his pills."

She exhaled. "Those pills he showed me, I'm not sure they're the real pills."

I remembered the bottle he'd rattled for us that morning.

"Are you serious?"

"I think they might just be vitamins."

"We should tell my father and Nia."

"No, no," she said, putting her hand on my face. "I'm not one hundred percent sure. I'm probably just imagining this. I just really want you there with me tomorrow."

It made my guts twist, the image of Mackenzie being hooked onto that balloon, terrified, soaring up into a doomed sky.

"Yeah, I'll come," I said. "Absolutely, I'll be there."

31

I got up just before sunrise, dressed, and slipped out the bedroom window without waking Noah.

The morning was cool and still, the grass wet. I tied my shoelaces tight, and pulled a hoodie over my T-shirt. The fake sky was just starting to turn the palest blue, and before long the fake sun would clear the fake horizon. And yet, all of it was still beautiful.

I was cutting across the orchard when I heard footsteps behind me and whirled to see Noah trying to scurry behind a tree.

"What're you doing?" I hissed.

"I want to see the balloon!"

"You idiot, go back right now!"

"No! And if you try to make me, I'll scream."

I glared at him, trying to figure out if he'd actually do it. The little blackmailer looked pretty sure of himself. He'd never done anything like this before, and I suddenly had no idea what he was capable of.

"You're going to see it! I want to see it!" Noah insisted. His face was flushed, and he started taking deep breaths like he was priming his lungs.

A single good shout would bring Dad and Nia running. There'd be a huge scene and they'd try to force me to stay. I couldn't miss the launch. Even if Riley was true to his word and went alone, I wanted to be there with

Mackenzie. And if anything did go wrong, I absolutely *needed* to be there.

"Yes! Okay."

Noah's face froze between complaint and disbelief. "Really?"

"Yes, really. Come on. But you stay close to me. And do what I tell you."

He fell into rapid step beside me, and took my hand. Nia was going to have my head on a platter with vegan trimmings.

Eventually we came out onto the launch field. At the far end, a big section of grass had been trampled, or maybe scythed down, and the bright patchwork balloon was spread flat for sixty feet or so, rippling slightly. Mackenzie, Charleze, and Riley were holding the balloon's skirt open with tent poles, directly over the woodstove. Deep orange fire danced behind the stove's glass door. I saw heat shimmering off the iron surface, rippling up from the stubby stovepipe into the envelope. Riley stood dangerously near the stove, making sure the fabric didn't sag against it and get melted.

"Look!" said Noah in wonder.

On the grass the long spread of fabric began to swell. Riley stepped back from the skirt, prodding more of the balloon fabric higher, helping it fill more easily. Before long, he didn't need to help.

Seeing that balloon fill, my heart swelled with it. It was magnificent, a blaze of color, towering above the field like a monument to the human spirit. I felt suddenly hopeful. *Jesus. This might work. This thing might fly.*

"Come on. I see Alyssa!" said Noah, pointing. She was sitting on the grass with Patt, watching mesmerized as the balloon inflated.

We hurried closer.

"What do you think?" Riley shouted when he saw us. "Look at her!"

"It's amazing!"

Charleze and Mackenzie turned to me, their damp faces bright with hope. I felt the heat from the stove; it must have been almost unbearable to be closer. The balloon was fully off the ground now, tethered to two spikes, and you could see up inside its billowy interior.

Riley said, "Seems pretty airtight so far!"

All his gear was nearby, a backpack, a rifle, and a crossbow. The pockets of his cargo pants bulged. From his belt dangled a gas mask. He already wore his harness. Lines hung from the metal frame ready to hook on to him. The only thing that wasn't yet in place was the propane tank, which I spotted farther away. Obviously, he didn't want it sitting close to all that heat from the stove.

As the balloon continued to fill, I saw the tether lines tauten.

"We're close!" Riley said.

He was talking in exclamation marks, and seemed to have boundless energy. He leaped about, checking the tethers, various parts of the frame.

"Come wish your daddy good luck!" Charleze called out to Alyssa, and she came running with Patt at her side.

Riley scooped her off the ground and held her tight. "See you soon, darling."

I almost couldn't bear looking at the little girl's face, because it was so oblivious to the danger her father was sailing toward. She gave her dad a loud kiss on the cheek. When he put her down, Charleze and Mackenzie gave him hugs.

"No tears, sweetheart!" he told his daughter, beaming. "Everything's all right."

She nodded, trying to smile, but I don't think she trusted herself to speak without sobbing. She came and stood beside me, lacing her fingers through mine and squeezing tight.

"I'll be back before you know it! Let's roll this out of the way now."

I hadn't realized the stove rested on a wheeled platform. He'd planned for everything. I grabbed one of the ropes and helped Riley haul the stove to one side. After that he fitted the propane tank into its cradle—the cradle we'd worked so hard to make in the forge. He attached the hose to the burner. Charleze helped him on with his backpack and he ducked his head so she could put his binoculars around his neck. He slung the crossbow and rifle over opposite shoulders.

When he dropped some grass to test the wind, it fell straight.

"Smooth sailing," he said. He licked his dry lips, peered up into the sky, as if trying to measure the unknowable distance between himself and the hatch. Something changed in his face and for just a second his resolve seemed to falter. My stomach felt liquidy even thinking about going up in that balloon.

"You're like an astronaut!" Noah said to Riley admiringly.

Riley made a sound that wasn't quite a chuckle. "Think so? Well, how about you come along for the ride?"

"To Erf?"

"Yep. Come on, let's hook you up."

Noah's forehead creased. "I don't want to go!"

Nervously I said, "Mr. Jackson's not going to take you, Noah."

"Sure I am," he said, and when I looked over, his rifle was aimed at us.

"Riley!" Charleze shouted. "You're scaring them!"

Patt circled around us, making a low growl, triggered by his master.

"Noah's good luck," Riley said. "He's their favorite. They've been watching out for that boy since day one. Probably putting experimental drugs in his food and water to make him so smart and grow so fast. They're not gonna hurt me if he comes along."

I didn't recognize the crackle of my own voice as I said, "Come on, Mr. Jackson!"

"Daddy! Put down that gun," cried Mackenzie.

"It's very clear to me," said Riley, "that this trip could go sideways, and I want a little insurance, is all. No one's going to get hurt. Charleze, get me the harness I made for Alyssa, just over there."

"Don't talk nonsense, Riley," said Charleze.

"Mr. Jackson," I pleaded, "don't do this!"

"Real quick now. I don't want the air cooling."

"Daddy, stop!" shouted Mackenzie.

"Everyone just settle down!" Riley shouted. "A man can hardly think. Charleze, get me that harness!"

Noah was clinging to my legs, trying to disappear behind them. I thought about picking him up and running. Would Riley shoot us in the back? I'd never seen his eyes this way. He looked like a man who'd woken up, terrified, in a different life.

"Take me," I blurted. "I can help." My voice trembled and I tried to clamp it down. "Noah's not gonna be any good to you up there. He can't shoot a rifle. I'm a good shot. You said."

Riley looked at me, as though startled by the sound of my voice. Then he nodded like we'd just entered into a friendly agreement. "All right, Xavier, I'm gonna take you up on that."

His rifle was lowered now, almost lazily. I thought again of scooping up Noah and making a run for it. Patt was facing us, ears pointy and alert. We wouldn't get halfway across the field before that dog had his jaws into us.

"Noah should go home," I said.

"He might like to watch," Riley said. "He should stay and watch."

Noah was staring up at me, terrified, his hand gripping mine.

"It's all right," I told him. "I'll be right back."

"Charleze, we'll need the bigger harness, let's be quick about this, goddamn it!" The gun had lifted again, this time at his own wife.

"Riley—" she began.

I flinched when he fired a shot over her head. Noah began bawling.

"Do as I tell you!" Riley said, looking miserable. "I'm sorry, darling, but this needs doing. Help him into it."

Charleze brought the harness over to me, her face streaked with the last of her makeup. "I'm so sorry," she kept saying. "I'm so sorry, Xavier." She showed me how to get into the harness, and helped me with the clasps.

Noah threw his arms around me. "Don't go, Zay."

I bent to hug him tight. I didn't want to let go. I promised myself I'd be so much better to him if I came back. "Everything's gonna be okay," I said, making sure my voice didn't shake. "Now you go over there with Mrs. Jackson and Alyssa, all right?"

"Your big brother'll be just fine," Charleze said, taking Noah by the hand.

"Mackenzie, hook us both up," Riley said. "Way I showed you."

I watched her as she took the lines dangling from the metal frame and clipped them on to various points on our harnesses. When she finally let her eyes meet mine, I saw the regret, but was surprised by their eerie calm. She must've been in shock. Like me. Then she kissed me on the mouth and clenched her fists in my hair and whispered, "I'm sorry."

"Launch us now!" Riley barked.

Mackenzie went to one of the spikes, and Charleze to the other. At the same time, they unhooked the lines. For a moment nothing happened. My feet still touched the ground. Riley still stood.

We were too heavy.

After all this, the balloon simply wasn't big enough. It didn't have enough lift. Not for two people anyway. Maybe not even for one.

Then Riley pulled a chain, and flame leaped from the burner over our heads. One, two, three seconds, and I was no longer standing. I dangled, gripping my harness lines as the ground fell away. It was slow at first, and I thought of that first time I'd been on a roller coaster, that lull of security during the unhurried climb to the peak.

"Be ready!" he shouted down to his family. "I'm coming back for you. I'm busting this whole place apart!"

I didn't know what he imagined. Shattering the dome like a snow globe; finding some hidden doorway at the base that we'd all flee through.

Another blast from the burner, and we picked up speed. It got so fast I wanted to close my eyes. I felt like I was held by a thread, yanked into the sky by an uncaring hand.

"Open your eyes!" Riley shouted at me.

Wind, noisy against my ears. Was it wind, or just our velocity? I could barely hear Riley, even though he dangled just a few feet away. I heard a tortured creak and looked at the metal frame, the one I'd helped bend in our makeshift forge, and hoped we hadn't bungled the job too badly.

Riley gave another long blast of the burner.

"Save some for the way back!" I hollered.

He said something I couldn't make out.

"What?" I yelled.

"One-way trip," he bellowed. He passed me the rifle. "Five rounds in there! In this together now. No point shooting me!"

Hadn't even occurred to me. Maybe it should've. Even if I shot Riley—and I knew I couldn't—I wasn't sure how the balloon worked to land it. Not that he did.

I clutched the gun, afraid I'd drop it. We went through a layer of cloud. For a few seconds I couldn't see anything, shivering uncontrollably. We came out the top, drenched with dew, into the sun that wasn't a real sun, but was still warm, and I was grateful.

Below us was scattered cloud. It was a view from an airplane window. I saw our entire little world encircled. There was our cottage and red barn, and not far away the Jacksons' place. How small it seemed. But I longed for it, this place that might have been big enough for a lifetime, if only we hadn't been so stupid.

Another long blast of the burner. A problem I'd never thought about—maybe Riley had—was that we were flying blind. The swelling balloon completely blocked our view directly overhead. How were we supposed to aim for the hatch? Not that we could really aim this thing.

Riley was looking through his binoculars, shouting and pointing—and I could only assume he'd sighted the hatch. It seemed a long way off to the side.

"We're off course!" I said. "We can't get over there. Take us down!"

"Wind might change," Riley said. "We're close."

I thought: *My idea was insane.*

I thought: *He's insane.*

I knew: *We are going to die.*

On the ground, we'd had so much, everything we needed, and now I was in the sky, and when we ran out of fuel, we'd plummet. I hoped the end would come fast so I wouldn't feel anything.

Somehow, as if Riley's conviction altered the laws of physics, we were drifting toward the hatch. Maybe it was wind, maybe it was suction.

"Here we go!" he cried, peering through his binoculars.

Now that we were closer, the hatch did not look like a simple hole. More like the mouth of a huge barnacle. From inside, spindly hooked tentacles slowly protruded, waving in the air, reaching for us. Animal or machine, I couldn't tell, but I had a terrible feeling we were about to be swallowed.

"Take us down!" I screamed.

"No stopping us now!"

I couldn't see the hatch anymore, because we were right underneath. There was a bump, a moment where we seemed to hang motionless. Then, with a faint gurgling, like the sound someone with a snotty nose makes, the balloon was moving again.

I looked up into the fabric and saw the darkness descending toward us as we were lifted inside.

32

I readied my rifle. Riley loaded his crossbow. My hands were shaking so hard I kept my finger away from the trigger in case I fired by accident. I glanced at my harness clasps, and for a second thought of releasing them. Falling to my death might be better than what was about to happen to us.

It got dark. I had a flash memory of going through a car wash, those big robot arms blasting the windows with colored fluid and shammies and air. Engulfed by the noise of it. There was no muscle, no tendon in my body that wasn't ready to explode or snap. I could see nothing, not even Riley a few feet away. I waited for something to touch me, some barbed tongue to snare me. My ears popped. Suddenly it went very quiet.

The balloon was shunted roughly to the side and my harness cables went slack. I was standing on a floor that emanated pale light. The balloon had dipped lower so we were actually inside it now, the fabric undulating around us and high overhead.

Swiftly, Riley unclipped his harness, then mine, and forced me down into a crouch beside him. He held my eye and slowly shook his head: *Don't move, don't speak.* I wasn't capable of either. I expected to be crushed into paste by some terrible set of jaws. I tried to listen, but the only sound was inside my head: my ricocheting heart, the gale of my own breath.

It took me a moment to realize that the floor was transparent. Through it I saw sky, clouds, and, with a weird magnified clarity, forests and fields. Was that the clearing where we'd launched? Those tiny dots, could those be Charleze and Mackenzie, Alyssa and Noah?

Riley pushed his mouth against my ear and whispered:

"The balloon gives us good cover. Stick close."

He uncoupled the hose from the propane tank and hefted it out of its cradle. He rolled it ahead of him as he commando crawled toward the balloon's skirt, now puddled on the floor. From one of his many pockets he produced a hunting knife and slit the fabric. He parted it so we could both peek through.

My first glimpse was so overwhelming I involuntarily ducked my head and gripped the floor. Afraid I'd go spinning off into the universe. Above us, stars blazed in darkness. There were two distant suns of vastly different sizes, one orange-red, the other a superheated blue. Closer, a moon hung above a planet that was absolutely not Erf.

The sight was so vivid, it seemed there was nothing between it and me. But I soon realized I was looking through the transparent ceiling of some vast chamber. It stretched out in all directions without any walls or doors. A short distance away was the hatch we'd come through, a kind of mesh membrane in the floor, with barbed arms retracted around its periphery. Nowhere did I see any signs of activity, not even the flicker of tiny midges.

"Where the hell is everyone?" Riley muttered. "The guards?"

"Riley! We're in fucking outer space!"

"This?" He jerked his head at the cosmic view. "Just another screen. I've seen movies with better special effects. They knew we were coming, decided to put on a show."

I studied his face for some frayed corner in his conviction, something I could peel back to reveal uncertainty. It was pointless. Nothing would change his mind.

He quickly loaded his crossbow and fired at the sky. The arrow buried itself deep in the ceiling, or whatever substance was between us and the bright universe.

"Ceiling's not more than sixty feet up," Riley said. "Let's move."

He made the slit bigger, pushed the propane tank through, and we crawled out and crouched beside the deflating balloon. No way could we ever refill it with what was left in the tank. There'd be no descent.

Cautiously we stood and turned in a slow circle, trying to decide which way to go. In all directions the floor seemed to slope gently downward; it could only mean we were in some kind of narrow layer between the top of our dome and the cosmos.

"There's something that way," Riley said decisively, and hefted the propane tank. I remembered him saying he'd use it as a bomb, but surely there couldn't be much propane left. I fell into step beside him.

The view overhead was mesmerizing. Two suns. That planet. And now I could see an archipelago of tiny, faraway planets, each with a promising swirl of blue and white and green. Hundreds of them. Each seemed to have a distinct hue and texture. On one I thought I could make out the wrinkle of mountains; on another, the dark rippled surface of ocean.

We walked on. I looked back over my shoulder and was surprised I couldn't see the wreck of our balloon anymore. It had disappeared over the horizon. The floor was definitely curving, just like our domed sky, but somehow, we weren't falling as the angle increased. Some weird gravity kept us on the floor.

Outside in space, a small bright slit opened in the darkness. Suddenly a ship was there—or what I assumed must be a ship because it was moving. It was teardrop shaped, and within its transparent belly, I made out four sleeping elephants. This ship was *close*. My sense of distance got even more dizzyingly readjusted when the ship nudged against one of the tiny blue-and-white planets. Not distant planets. More like globes. It was like watching microscopic footage of one cell fusing to another: the membrane between ship and globe dissolved. The elephants drifted down inside the globe—were they being ferried by the midges?—until I lost sight of them.

"Holy shit! Did you see that?" I asked Riley.

"What?"

"That ship. There! It had elephants in it!"

He glanced up and grunted.

"They just put *elephants* into one of those globes. See all those little things? I thought they were planets. They're globes! Like this one!"

Dismissively he said, "Yeah, alien zoo, right."

I looked at all the nearby spheres and imagined what they might hold.

"Maybe it's not a zoo," I said. "Maybe more like a preserve."

For decades on Earth we'd had warnings of climate change, then climate emergency, then climate disaster, and done nowhere near enough. We'd just kicked the problem down the road for someone else to figure out, and now our habitat was at risk. Maybe worse than that: doomed. For the first time since we'd arrived, it occurred to me that what *they* had done to us might not be imprisonment, but an act of kindness. They'd given us sanctuary.

"Maybe they're moving us. Everything. Like a Noah's Ark situation." I thought that one might get his attention, being biblical, but all he said was:

"Something up ahead."

In the distance was a tall shadow. It took us a while to reach it, a square column, fifteen feet thick, that rose from floor to ceiling.

Riley grinned. "This look like an access shaft to you?" I could see how dry his lips were. His cheeks were gaunt. We walked all the way around it without finding any doorway. Riley put the propane tank against the column and hunched over, taking things from his pockets, doing something with the valve.

"You making some kind of bomb?"

"Yep."

I didn't know why he thought this would work when every kind of wall we'd encountered in the dome had been impregnable. No digging, drilling, or chainsawing had gotten us through. With a barbecue lighter, Riley sparked a piece of rope fiber.

"Run!" he shouted.

We raced around to the far side of the column. The floor shook, but the explosion was almost soundless, the noise absorbed within the vast space. When we walked back, the ground was littered with debris. Smoke uncurled in the air. A large hole had been blasted in the side of the column.

"Look at that!" Riley crowed. "You look in there and tell me what you see!"

Through the hole was a staircase, familiar from any office building or grubby parking garage, down to the scuffed walls and chipped treads.

"Call me crazy," said Riley, "but this does not look like the work of an advanced alien culture."

I felt the fault line in my beliefs give a little tremor. I didn't want it to build to a full-blown quake, but I couldn't quell my excitement. A set of very human stairs leading up. Up and out. To Sam. To Mom. To the whole world of people and things and possibilities.

"How come there's no guards?" I asked.

"They don't need guards. Look at you. You're still half convinced you're in space. They don't need guards to keep people like you here."

I looked up at the vault of the universe. Real, or a marvelous fake?

"You coming?" Riley asked.

He readied his crossbow, clipped extra arrows onto a strap around his chest. He asked me where my ammo was, and I patted my pockets. When he ducked through the hole, I followed him.

Up the stairs we went, taking a careful turn at every landing, following the square outline of the column.

"Up top," Riley said quietly. "That's where we'll get resistance if there's any coming. You see someone with any kind of weapon, you do not hesitate to pull that trigger. We clear?"

I said nothing. I wasn't sure I could do that.

"These people will not be friendly. They do not have your best interests at heart."

After the last turn, the stairs dead-ended at a fire escape with a metal push bar. There was a small wire-reinforced window, through which I could see a drab hallway with fluorescent lights.

"Like I thought," said Riley. "We've been underground this whole time. This is some kind of emergency evacuation tunnel. Come on."

I shook my head. "Riley. Wait. What if, you know, that door opens right into outer space?"

"It's a hallway!"

He looked at me in incomprehension. I couldn't explain it. I wanted to push open that door so badly I felt like throwing up. But I was also terrified of opening it.

I took a step back.

"They have well and truly broken you. Gimme my gun."

I handed it over.

"I'll come back for all of you."

"Don't open it, Riley," I pleaded.

He placed his hand on the bar and pushed. His hand disappeared into the door. When he tried to pull it out, he stumbled forward as though something had tugged him. His arm was yanked in up to its elbow.

"Riley!"

With his free arm he fired shot after shot into the door. The bullets disappeared in tiny craters that rippled, then disappeared. I grabbed him around his waist and pulled. The door was stronger. Riley's chest and face got dragged into it. I should have pulled harder, but I let go. I was afraid of getting sucked in with him. Riley's legs thrashed . . . and he was gone.

Instantly the door became translucent, and I saw Riley's silhouette struggling within it, looking like someone trying to do karate in slow motion. Any second it would spit him back out, like it had my father. He was being tumbled this way and that in a grotesque dance choreography, still gripping his rifle.

Then the translucent wall changed again, and became fully transparent.

Before me was the bright universe.

And there was Riley, slowly falling backward into it. His eyes and mouth were wide. The fingers of one hand were splayed like he was waving goodbye. His rifle and crossbow rotated near his frozen, ruptured body.

"Riley!" I screamed. He was so close, but there was nothing I could do for him.

I couldn't look anymore, and started staggering down the stairs, gulping air. Above me came an insistent hum and I saw a swarm of midges eating the stairwell. They were disassembling it, just as easily as they must have made it, maybe just for us, or just for Riley, to give him what he finally wanted.

Escape.

Freedom.

I hurried down. Seconds after I reached the ground, the midges devoured the last of the column and the stairs. They hovered around me as I sat on the floor and cried.

When I woke up, Dad was shaking me gently, and Noah was saying my name over and over, and Mackenzie and Nia were looking down at me, and I was back on the field.

SIX MONTHS LATER

33

In the Jacksons' orchard, we waited at the grave until Charleze was ready.

Mackenzie had her arm around her mother as she cried, and Nia placed a hand consolingly on her shoulder. Charleze put her own hand over Nia's and gave a thankful squeeze. Noah kept giving Alyssa little pats on her back, then offered her her favorite princess to hold. She accepted. I shared a sad smile with Dad. Kimmy, leashed to a nearby tree, yipped impatiently because he wanted to sniff and eat everything. Then Charleze gave a quick nod, dabbed her eyes, and said hoarsely, "Come on back to the lodge. I made some refreshments."

It had been six months since it happened. The midges had carried my unconscious body down through the sky and left me on the field. Everyone had seen it, including Dad and Nia, who'd come looking for me and Noah the moment they woke up and realized we were missing.

Over the next few days, I'd told the story many times. Even though I tried really hard to keep all the facts and details the same, I felt like everyone heard them differently. Like they all had particular things they wanted, or hoped, to hear. They all had different questions. But one question everyone asked was:

"Did you see *them*?"

"You must've seen something."

"Are you sure you didn't see *them*?"

And I could only say no, I'd just seen midges, I hadn't seen *them*.

I wish I had. I would've liked to know who they were and what they looked like. Did they resemble us, or were they like latex rejects from a B movie? Were they huge as dinosaurs, or smaller than ants? Maybe they'd always remain a mystery. Probably Charleze still hoped that *they* were human, but I knew they weren't.

Life without Riley was a lot different: sadder for his family, but less stressful and much more harmonious. No more coyotes or starlings, no more plagues and punishments. We'd gotten through the winter fine, sharing what we had, and we'd just done our first spring seedings on both farms. The Jacksons seemed to have accepted that this was their new home, and that there likely—maybe probably, maybe even *certainly*—wouldn't be another.

I'd had lots of time to think about what had happened up there.

What I thought was this:

The Earth was doomed. We had been rescued. The same way that humans took endangered species out of dangerous habitats and put them into sanctuaries, *they* had done the same for us. Maybe they'd been watching us for decades and decided we couldn't take care of ourselves. Which was true. And when you couldn't take care of yourself, sometimes you had to let other people do it for you.

As we walked back to the lodge, Noah asked me for a piggyback. I wasn't sure if piggybacks were allowed at funerals, but then Alyssa piped up that she wanted one, too, and her mother smiled and said she didn't see why not. Mackenzie knelt so Alyssa could clamber aboard, and I hoisted Noah onto my shoulders. Nia gave me a very kind look. Things were better between us now. When she'd first heard how Riley wanted to take Noah in the balloon, but I'd gone instead, she burst into tears and hugged me and said, "Thank you," over and over again.

I held my little brother's legs tight as he swayed and giggled. I liked the way he grabbed hold of my head, the bundled heat and joy of him. I thought of Sam and Mom, how I'd never see them again. Never was a hard thing to accept. I hoped one day I could, or at least that it wouldn't hurt so much. Most of all I hoped that they were safe, that they weren't too chewed up inside, worrying about what had become of us.

"You're wiggling too much!" Mackenzie laughed, and lowered Alyssa to the ground.

Noah wanted to go down, too, and I plonked him beside his friend.

Mackenzie leaned against me and I put my arm around her waist. There had been a question kicking around my head the past six months, but I hadn't asked her, because it made me feel grubby and guilty just to think it. And in the end, did it even matter?

When you asked me, up in the barn, to come to the balloon launch, did you know what would happen? Did your father tell you to invite me so I could go up with him?

You could waste a lot of time wishing things were otherwise. And that had definitely been part of the problem from the outset. Striving for things that were impossible.

I didn't know what was to come. Maybe one day, another house would get built before my eyes and a new family would arrive. Maybe one day those other snow globe worlds I'd glimpsed would be joined up, and we'd be reintroduced to other Erf things, or a new world entirely. Or maybe it would stay just us.

The only possible world for us was this one, right now, and that's what made it the best of all worlds.

ACKNOWLEDGMENTS

Many thanks to Chris Torbay for that hot-air balloon idea, which became such a double-edged sword in this story. I'd also like to thank Kevin White, Arun Maini, Stuart Law, and Bill Macgregor for generously imagining how they'd feel about waking up on a farm. As always, great thanks to my early readers, Philippa Sheppard, Nathaniel Oppel, and Steven Malk, whose thoughts about this story were fascinatingly varied. Most of all, thank you to my editors Lynne Missen, David Levithan, and Bella Pearson for so wholeheartedly embracing this book.

ABOUT THE AUTHOR

KENNETH OPPEL is the bestselling author of the Silverwing trilogy, which has sold over a million copies around the world, and *Airborn*, winner of a Michael L. Printz Honor and Canada's Governor General's Literary Award. His most recent novels include the Bloom trilogy and *Ghostlight*. He lives with his family in Toronto.